FRACTURED HEALER

FRACTURED HEALER

Chris Norris

Copyright © 2025 Chris Norris

The moral right of the author has been asserted.

Apart from any fair dealing for the purposes of research or private study, or criticism or review, as permitted under the Copyright, Designs and Patents Act 1988, this publication may only be reproduced, stored or transmitted, in any form or by any means, with the prior permission in writing of the publishers, or in the case of reprographic reproduction in accordance with the terms of licences issued by the Copyright Licensing Agency. Enquiries concerning reproduction outside those terms should be sent to the publishers.

The manufacturer's authorised representative in the EU for product safety is Authorised Rep Compliance Ltd, 71 Lower Baggot Street, Dublin D02 P593 Ireland
(www.arccompliance.com)

This is a work of fiction. Names, characters, businesses, places, events and incidents are either the products of the author's imagination or used in a fictitious manner. Any resemblance to actual persons, living or dead, or actual events is purely coincidental.

Troubador Publishing Ltd
Unit E2 Airfield Business Park,
Harrison Road, Market Harborough,
Leicestershire. LE16 7UL
Tel: 0116 2792299
Email: books@troubador.co.uk
Web: www.troubador.co.uk

ISBN 978 1836283 416

British Library Cataloguing in Publication Data.
A catalogue record for this book is available from the British Library.

Printed and bound in Great Britain by 4edge Limited
Typeset in 11pt Minion Pro by Troubador Publishing Ltd, Leicester, UK

For Hildi and Sophie - my girls

1

2010

Top of her profession

Liz dominated the vast stage of the lecture theatre. She was picked out by a single spotlight on her head and shoulders giving her an ethereal appearance. The modern oak lectern she stood behind was warmed by a shaded light glowing across its surface. Vast sponsor adverts were backlit either side of the stage, promoting arthritis cream on one side and a surgical instrument on the other. Liz was a tall, statuesque figure in a perfectly fitted designer suit, crisp white blouse, and expensive flat black shoes. Her lithe physique had been toned in the gym and on the road, but her unshakeable confidence was forged in the tense heat of the operating theatre. All eyes were fixed on her. She turned away from the screen and looked down at the ground, savouring the moment. Feeling the wooden platform beneath her feet, and the slightly raised crack where the two pieces of stage came together, she was grounded, and ready. The spotlight warmed her shoulders, and she sensed the contrast between its heat and the cool air of the stage on her legs. She was aware of the crowd immersed in darkness out of the corner of her eye and felt its energy seeping into her. She silently pressed the slide changer held in her left hand and felt a subtle give as the button depressed. With a distant mechanical clunk, the final slide appeared, flooding the screen with intense, vivid blue. A picture of an old man sitting with his head bowed, shoulders hunched in defeat, and a female doctor with her hand on his shoulder giving reassurance. Liz looked up from the floor and fixed her eyes on the audience, searching the faces one by one in silence. Dozens of moon shapes shrouded in shadow, like expectant ghosts waiting for her next words.

"Always remember, it is a privilege that the patient has invited us into their lives and entrusted us with the care of their health."

She paused for a second, building anticipation, and then said in a firm, accusative voice "Do… not… willingly… fail… them. Thank you!"

After a two-second hesitation, the room erupted like an earthquake. The clapping was thunderous. Those at the front of the hall were on their feet, some with tears in their eyes. Students at the back stamped their feet. Those at the edge of the rows were in the aisles clapping with their hands held high. Cheers, whistles, and shouts of "hear, hear" cut the air. Anyone who entered the hall now would be in no doubt Dr Liz McClennan was a god within the medical profession. She published papers in leading scientific journals, authored textbooks which all students read, and even had a surgical procedure named after her. She exuded confidence and majesty from every pore. She lived in a secure development of flats protected by their own concierge, drove a brand-new white, whisper-quiet Mercedes, and exercised in an exclusive members-only health club. She had truly made it and then some.

As she left the stage the crowd was still in rapture, and she was guided to a side door by a friendly hand. Walking down the corridor outside the lecture hall, she could still hear the wall of noise, and she tried to maintain a friendly but neutral facial expression, walking with slow, measured steps. The air of the corridor felt cool and fresh in contrast to the pressure cooker of the lecture theatre. The dimmed lighting was welcome after the darkness of the crowd. She passed through the fire doors into the trade show, and the bright lights made her squint. People broke off their conversations and turned towards her as she arrived. Moving forwards, she shook hands with several members of the great and the good, smiling and making small talk as she did so. Sales reps who had not heard the lecture but were aware of the noise whispered to each other and looked in her direction as word went around that something memorable had occurred. Gradually, a few brave students came up to her and asked questions, and eventually she was surrounded by a small throng of admirers wanting to bathe in her glory. She chatted, answered questions, and posed for several selfies with them.

"I loved your paper on the fallacy of scans," said a voice.

"Thank you," she replied to the group in general.

"Would you sign my book, Ms McClennan?"

"Of course. Who should I address the message to?" She smiled at a young male.

"Your paper on subjective and objective examination got me through my finals!"

"Good to hear, thank you."

Fifteen minutes later, walking from the trade show to the reception hall, she was greeted by an enthusiastic Dr Kerry, the conference organiser.

"Your keynote went down really well; people are still talking about it!"

"Thanks, they were a great audience which always helps."

This was a line which Liz had used many times before and was always amazed that it had an effect. Conference organisers liked to view keynote speakers as rock stars, imagining the audience to be as enthusiastic as Glastonbury. The fact was that the speaker stood on stage behind a lectern picked out by a spotlight, and the audience was seated below in dimmed house lighting and looking up. The effect was a sea of unrecognisable faces, with any individual reaction impossible to see.

"Have a sherry!" Dr Kerry looked at Liz and smiled while he held out the glass.

A smiling male holding out a drink and the smell of alcohol punched the breath from her chest and made her feel giddy. She had to widen her feet to steady herself and make an effort to consciously retain her smile. She had always hated the smell and taste of alcohol. She was brought up in a virtually teetotal house – sherry for the few guests they ever had, with her dad having half a lager if he went out for a drink with workmates at Christmas. Her first taste of alcohol as an experimental teenager resulted in her throwing up after trying vodka from a bottle one of the girls had smuggled into the Friday night school disco. But there was more to it than that, much more. The smell, taste, and very thought of alcohol knotted her stomach and turned her legs to jelly. It took her back over twenty years to a party in Leeds at university that had changed her life. Ever since that day, a fear had haunted her. When her mind wandered, it would creep in as though someone was just there, just out of sight, watching her. She would sometimes wake in a cold sweat in the middle of the night, fearing that someone was standing over her. Dreams would involve music, a bedroom, and the clawing sickly smell of alcohol. She would wake scratching at her face, trying to get it away, but it never really left. Relationships with men failed each time, casual but never long term. Normal relationships are between two people, but they did not work for her because in her mind there was always another person there, watching, judging, sneering. As she touched the glass, the contrast between the high energy of her lecture and the utter failure of the personal life struck her like cold stone. Yes, she was successful but not with men. It was as though she had two parts since university. One had grown, gained numerous qualifications, and become a leading practitioner. The other had not changed since that bedroom. It was stuck never to move on. Something tethered her to that night and would not let go.

Liz knew a few things about bones, and she recognised

a fracture when she saw one. She had been fractured in an upstairs room at a uni party in her first year, and she now knew beyond any doubt that she had not healed. The fragments inside her mind had not mended and the sore was still festering after all these years. It underscored everything she did, every relationship she tried. Wounds that are not clean do not heal; they needed drastic action. Cut into the patient, wrench the tissue layers apart, and scrape out the infection. Build a scaffold around the pieces, with wire, plate, or pins. Pierce, screw, hammer, twist. Nothing subtle, nothing mild. It took confidence and courage, and that is what she must display now. It came to her as an almost divine flash. She spread her feet slightly to firm her stance and reached out to grip the sherry glass offered to her. She fixed Dr Kerry's eyes in a cold hard stare and a look of shock flicked across his face as though he had been slapped.

"Thank you," she said and turned away. The first step had been taken.

2

1978

Schooldays

Liz sat in the second to front row between Rachel on the right and Tommy on the left. Liz and Rachel often shared coloured pens, and both had the same set from the stationery shop in the high street. They had three shades of green, but four of blue, which Liz preferred. Liz's pencil case was very neat because each evening she would remove any pieces of fluff which became trapped in the zipper. She pulled it all out, dropped it on the floor and hid it under the bed. Tommy often forgot his pen and Liz would have to lend him one. She always gave him an old one because he was a boy, and anyway he would chew the top off it if the teacher asked him a question, leaving it with teeth marks. She could always recognise a pencil that Tommy had chewed because it had two small indentations on one side and one on the other. Liz got on with the boys better than the girls really, as she found the boys played better games and the girls often just talked about TV shows or clothes.

Her dad said she was becoming a tomboy, but she didn't mind. Rachel and the other girls went to ballet classes, but Liz went to Brownies. She had once tried ballet, but they had to wear a green leotard which she thought looked silly. Liz's and Rachel's mums would often get together after school and the girls would play upstairs in Rachel's house. Liz thought the house smelt of flowers, and it had a bottle in the kitchen with a melted candle in the top. Rachel had two dolls which Liz thought were boring, so she would go into Rachel's brother's room and play with his Lego bricks. She once built a tower up to the ceiling, but Rachel had come in and pushed it over.

When it came to sports at school, she didn't really like netball, and hockey was always cold outside because you just hung around until someone passed to you, which, in Liz's case, they rarely did. They had once had to run around the school field, which the games mistress told them was called cross-country. All the girls had complained and kept stopping and starting, but Liz just ran and ran, feeling the wind in her hair and smelling the newly mowed grass beneath her feet. She could hear the birds singing and thought it was fantastic being outside in the middle of a school day. When she got to the end of the two laps, the teacher said, "Well done," and she realised that the next girl had been miles behind. She told her dad when she got home, and he said she was obviously a natural runner.

From then on, Liz ran through life. She was chosen for the house team because they knew she would do well, and she ran the cross-country in the winter months, getting lots of points for her schoolhouse.

***

When she went to secondary school, Liz was in the top sets and got a reputation for being a bit of a bookworm. As an only child, she would spend most of her time studying in her bedroom. She loved the smell and feel of books. The shiny paper and crisp flick of the pages, the reassuring weight in her hand. She would cover the pages with adhesive page markers and write pencil notes in the margins. She had a white metal bookshelf over her desk, with the books arranged in height order and held in place at one end by a pottery bookend shaped like a rabbit. Matching posters from a zoo trip when she was thirteen lined one wall, each in assorted colours arranged in a perfect row on her wall. On her ceiling she had luminous stars arranged in a circle above her head which glowed reassuringly at night. Her dad had put them up one summer when she was young, and she always remembered him doing it when she looked at them. As Liz got older and bigger, her bedroom seemed so much smaller, but it still felt homely. At night after her mum and dad had said goodnight, she would lie awake looking at the stars until the next thing she knew it was time to get up and go downstairs for breakfast. One summer when she went back to university, she took a solitary star with her and put it on the ceiling over the bed in her shared student house. A reminder of home and an anchor to her roots.

At school in the sixth form, Liz got top grades in her mock exams and she was encouraged to apply to leading universities and go into a profession. The careers advisor talked about medicine and law. She thought law would be boring and always inside sitting at a desk. She was interested in the body, and her best subject was biology, but she did not like blood and thought she wouldn't cope with injuries and ill people. She thought about being a PE teacher but did not think she would like teaching at a school. One day in the library, she was reading a university prospectus and came across sports science. She had never heard of this subject but thought it would be really interesting because it dealt with the body but without sick people. Also, in the pictures they had a runner on a treadmill wearing a mask with a tube connected to a computer. As a runner herself, she thought this was really interesting, and much better than doing PE, having to play hockey and netball which she wasn't any good at. The careers teacher said she was undervaluing herself, but Liz was determined. She wanted to play with Lego, not dolls. She thought green leotards were stupid, and she liked running but not sports. She would go to university to study sports science, not medicine, and that was that.

After the exams, her parents took Liz to the cinema, and they had a pizza afterwards. Normally, Liz sat in the back of the car, with her mum in the front. Today they swapped around with Liz in the front, as her dad said it would be good for her to watch him changing gears and get to know about clutch control when pulling off from junctions. She was going to have driving lessons for her seventeenth birthday, as had some of her friends. Aimee had only taken ten lessons to pass, but Liz thought she might need more. In the cinema they all had popcorn, the salty one, not the sweet one, as her mum said it was better for her teeth. In the restaurant after the film, she and her dad ordered pizza and her mum had a salad with low-fat dressing.

"Can I have a shandy?"

"No, because you're not eighteen and it contains alcohol," her mum replied.

"But Rachel had alcohol at her party, and I can't even have a shandy!"

"Go on, let her have a shandy," said her dad.

Liz and her dad looked at each other, and there was a twinkle in his eye.

"She can wind you around her little finger! It's been the same since she was five!"

"What can I say – dads and daughters. Sometimes you just have to take a risk!"

They all laughed, and Liz felt warm and cosy. Here with her parents, in the town where she grew up. The pizza restaurant with its dimmed lights and flock wallpaper, on the street where she caught the bus to go swimming with her friends in the summer holidays. Across the road from the stationery shop where she bought all her pens and pencils since her days at infants' school. She remembered when the light-up bollards at the end of the road had been replaced by ones on big springs, and when someone from the street parallel to theirs had been knocked off her bike at the T-junction. This was her entire world, and it had nurtured her and kept her safe. A baby bird secure in its down-filled nest. But soon Liz would leave as the baby had outgrown its nest, and she felt a little flutter in her stomach at the thought.

***

The sixth-form chemistry lab always made Mark uncomfortable. He would get butterflies in his stomach as he walked up the stairs and into the short corridor leading to it. With his mates he was always slightly over chatty as he approached it, a nervous tick he had since starting secondary school. He often got overexcited in situations and would lose control. Queuing outside today, he was in the middle of the group. Ahead were the three girls who always got top grades in their homework, and were known amongst his friends as the Supremes, after the American pop group. He had once stood in front of them doing a little jig and singing 'A Woman Needs a Good Man'. He had gone bright red when Donna, one of the three, had pointed out that the song was by The Three Degrees and not the Supremes. Next were two boys he hardly knew, as they were in a different schoolhouse. Mark and his friends were in Oak, and they were in Birch, so any sports teams were different. He sometimes played in the Oak rugby team because he was big. However, he regularly dropped the ball so nobody passed to him, and he would just run up and down until there was a scrum when he was one of the props. He would just push and elbow people out of the way if the scrum collapsed. As they went into the sixth form and rugby became more skilled and less of a free-for-all, he was often left out of the team and would be picked only if Oak struggled for numbers.

Lab 2B was a place where his experiments always went wrong or failed completely. Chemistry lessons left him floundering as he did not understand the basics and as the class moved on, he was left behind. He tried to cover this up by joking and being disruptive. He would distract Stewart sitting next to him by writing messages in the margins of his file, and kick Belinda's chair from behind until she turned around and scowled at him. He always sat on the back bench, trying to avoid the teacher's gaze and would look down, avoiding eye contact whenever a question was asked. He had read all the initials and words carved into the ageing wooden surface and all the rhyming lines inked over and usually misspelled. He hated the pairs of gas taps because they brought back memories of the first time he lit his Bunsen burner and the flame went too high, making everyone laugh. The walls were covered with reminders of his inadequacy. The periodic table of elements he knew so little about, safety notices for procedures he could not do, examples of top-grade work which were never his. The fume cupboard was the only thing remotely acceptable to him because it was an ancient wooden contraption with a very stiff vertical sliding door which some of the girls could not lift, so he was asked to help. He liked being able to use his strength to show up the puny boys and help the girls, and he associated the acrid smell of generations of chemicals with a small reprieve from academia.

As they had moved into the sixth form and many had Saturday jobs in shops in the town, conversation turned to things they wanted but could rarely afford. They had taken to speaking in pseudo-posh accents they had heard on the TV.

"I can buy a pro camera, my old sport, even a 35mm SLR!"

"Yeah, well, I'm good for Ace trousers and shirts. So, who pulls now, hey?"

Mark and Pete both had jobs in small independent stores. Mark's was working at ISO400, a small camera shop in Swindon, and Pete was in Henry James, a younger-men's fashion store. Both were able to get staff discount, so spent all of their money on stuff from the stores. Mark was buying a second-hand Hanimex 110 camera and Pete had his eye on a bomber jacket he had seen worn on *Top of the Pops*.

"Why do you want a 110 camera, anyway, thought you said the Zenit B was the one you would go for?"

"Yeah, well, the Zenit has a better lens and the 35mm negative gives a top-quality picture, but the Hanimex is smaller so you can take pictures without anyone knowing."

"Sneaky, so a bit of a James Bond, are you?"

"Something like that, sport. If it works, you'll be well impressed, believe me."

Over the holidays Mark had worked two weeks in ISO400, and some days trade was very slow. He would end up playing with the cameras when the manager went round the back of the shop for a cigarette. Mark had discovered he could press the shutter of a camera without anyone nearby hearing it if the camera was held close to the ground. He had tried this several times without any film in the camera while showing products to customers. It was better to hold the camera with his fingers and fire the shutter with his thumb. That way, he could point the lens forwards or even upwards. After practising a few times with some out-of-date film, he was ready to impress.

Stuart from his chemistry group was always bringing in pictures he had cut out from his brother's *Men Only* magazines. In one, Mark had seen an upskirt photo and thought this was incredible. It was a real girl, not a glamour model, and apparently taken on the underground by a bloke standing behind the girl on an escalator. He had never been on an escalator, but at lesson change the boys often deliberately lagged behind so they could follow the girls upstairs. They would stay two steps below and bend down pretending to tie a shoelace, challenging each other to see what colour knickers a particular girl was wearing. Stuart had won last time, saying that Gayle Duncan was wearing pale blue, but then someone had said his sister always wore pale blue anyway because that's what his mum bought her. His mum had said if she bought white, they went pale blue eventually because one of the boy's navy socks always found its way into the wash, so what was the point.

The plan was for the boys to follow the girls up the stairs as they went from maths1 to physics. Mark had brought his camera in and would take the picture while Pete was look out, making sure none of the girls looked around. They chose Gayle Duncan's group because she always walked around with Susan Pritchard and Clare Smith. Mark thought Gayle was nice, but Pete was keener on Susan, as she always left the top button of her blouse undone after PE and he was sure she was teasing him.

On the day, they gathered outside the maths room as the bell went. Mark showed them the camera, demonstrating his holding technique and how the shutter fired. Pete wanted to have a go, but Mark wouldn't let him. He only had twenty-four frames on the film cassette and had already taken fourteen, so might need all ten left. They followed the girls up the corridor, about three steps behind. As the girls climbed the stairs, Mark pointed the camera up and bent down to touch his shoe, firing the shutter at the same time. He dropped the camera, sending it clattering down the three stairs to spin on the floor at the bottom. He ran down to retrieve it, only to find Duncan Hoodie's group on top of him.

"What's that, Smith? You mum's best camera?" and he kicked it, sending it spinning towards the skirting board of the corridor. It struck the skirting and bounced off.

"If you've broken that!"

"You'll what, Smith? Tell your mum?"

The whole group laughed. Mark felt his face go hot. The girls were going through the physics room door on the top corridor now as the bell rang. Mark had to pick up the camera and race up the stairs two at a time after his friends not to be late.

3

1981

Off to uni

Liz drove down to university with her mum and dad and a car full of belongings. After her results, she worked in the local supermarket over the summer. She had felt free. For the first time in her life, she was not thinking about schoolwork or exams. In the summer she had talked to her mum a couple of times about the practicalities of leaving home, which clothes to bring and what to take. But her mum had never been to university, so it was her dad she learnt most from. He had actually lived the experience of university, so understood what she was going through.

As she sat in silence in the back of the car, she looked up and saw her dad's eyes looking back at her in the driving mirror. He smiled gently and briefly raised his eyebrows, and she knew he was in her corner, as he always had been. As they drove on, her mind wandered back to the period when she had looked at universities. She had mainly visited her various choices with her mum. It was good, but her mum pointed out all the logical stuff, which was good, but… When she travelled with her dad, it had been fun. She felt a twinge of guilt feeling this, because she spent hours just sitting and talking to her mum, but with her dad, it was different. She was in Trentfield Hall at Leeds, and they had been shown around. She remembered her initial shock at the old building, with long corridors, a green carpet with hideous, spiral pattern and the paint was flaking off the walls. They had been shown inside a room, and her face dropped. It had drawing-pin holes in the wall, the mirror was cracked, and the carpet threadbare. It had a slightly musty smell reminiscent of the storeroom in the art block at school. In the car on the way back home, her dad had said that when he was at university, he taped plastic sheeting over the window in his room as it was unheated and freezing in the winter. Also, he had had to share with another boy who had very smelly feet because he only changed his socks once a week. This had made her feel her situation wasn't so bad, and they laughed so much about it on the way home that Liz had tears streaming down her face.

As they turned off the main road and into the drive up to Trentfield, she felt butterflies in her stomach and thought she was going to be sick. This was her first time away from home and it felt like jumping off something and being in mid-air. She couldn't cling on to the security of the home she had known as a child but had not yet reached firm ground. She felt alone and afraid. As they swung into the car park, it was like arriving at a fair and her mood instantly changed. There were five or six cars with boots open and bags on the floor. People her age milled around, hugging younger siblings and parents, and carrying bags and boxes in and out of the building. As she approached the door, she noticed a big banner saying, 'Welcome class of 1981', and as she walked through the door, she noticed out of the corner of her eye her dad put his arm around her mum's shoulder and slowed down. Briefly she wondered why he had done this and then an explosion hit her. A wall of sound greeted her with whistles, football rattles, and party horns. There were balloons hung everywhere in a blaze of colour and people clapped and cheered each student as they came it. They were all like her, young, smiling faces with life in front of them. She was excited, embarrassed, relieved, and happy all at the same time.

Liz and her parents made several trips from their car to her room. She got the key to her room and a goody bag, and they went upstairs and put the key in the lock. She had a brief pause as she thought, whatever is on the other side will stay with me for at least a year, but then she turned the key, and they were in. It was the same musty smell she had noticed when she visited earlier in the year with her dad, but it had an opening window and overlooked some parkland with trees which she liked. During the road trip, she had felt trepidation, and then elation during the welcome downstairs. Now she felt satisfaction that she was actually here. She had clothes, trainers, running kit, pots and pans, her old music player, and a much loved stuffed bear called Heston. She put Heston on her pillow, squidging his black nose as she did so. She remembered washing him when she was about seven, and her mum mending one of his seams. He was a bit worn now, but, still, he was family. Liz's mum had said she could always come home for a weekend to pick anything up that she had forgotten. At the time this made her feel secure, but now all she wanted was to stay and fit in. As they were unpacking her case and boxes, someone knocked the door, and she looked at her mum, who just waited. It was the first time it dawned on Liz that she was the one in charge in her world now. When she opened the door, a girl was standing in the corridor in jeans, trainers, and a blue sweatshirt. She had dyed green hair with a bright red pointed paper hat on top. She smelt faintly of strawberries and was carrying a shiny toy wand.

"Hi, I'm Judith. I'm your wizard."

Liz stared at her blankly.

"Did they not explain? All new students get a second year to show them around and introduce stuff. We are called wizards because we're supposed to be able to make things happen for you!"

"That's brilliant! That's what I get for not reading all the bumf they sent through. Nice to meet you."

"I can see you have your folks with you, so I'll leave you alone. I'm in room 224 if you need me. See you tonight at the welcome party."

When they finished unpacking – clothes in the wardrobe, books on the shelf, and multiple pairs of trainers under the bed – it was another hour before the welcome speech, and Liz had left her door open to see people coming and going. She was just going to suggest tea when a girl put her head round the door.

"Hi, I'm Suzanne. I'm next door. Are you going to the welcome thingy at four?"

"Yes, I think so."

"Can I come with you, as my folks had to go."

"Yes, sure."

Liz's mum and dad looked at each other for a second.

"Actually, I think we'll make tracks and leave you guys to explore," her dad said.

"OK, that's fine. We'll go over together, and I'll phone you later in the week."

Liz hugged her mum first and felt a lump in her throat as she did so. When she hugged her dad, he looked at her and smiled with a twinkle in his eye. "Go for it, girl," he said.

As they left the room, Liz and Suzanne were already chatting excitedly.

Liz and Suzanne had rooms next to each other and quickly became friends. They were from similar backgrounds. Liz was brought up in the West Country, while Suzanne was from London. Liz was aware that she had been a bit of a bookworm at school and hadn't really been sociable. Suzanne was more of a party girl and had a wider circle of friends. Liz felt she could learn from Suzanne, and for her part, Suzanne liked the idea of a younger (by six months) protégé who she could guide, a bit like the younger sister she had always wanted.

Fairly quickly, Liz and Suzanne had rooms which just about matched. Colourful quilts, dried pampas grasses in an old wine bottle and posters on the wall. Suzanne had Dire Straits, while Liz had a picture of a sunrise over a forest saying 'I took the path less travelled, and it has made all the difference', which she bought from Athena in Leeds in the first month of uni. The rooms even smelt the same, the result of a large pack of incense sticks Liz had bought in an alternative clothes shop when she was buying a pair of Thai pants to do her tai chi class in. The shop had been called Positive Healing, and the incense was honey and bergamot, although Suzanne thought it smelt a bit like the cannabis she had tried in Morocco.

Suzanne's room became a bit of a hub for the corridor, with evenings spent drinking tea and eating toast, crumpets, or teacakes – whichever had been reduced in the local supermarket at the end of the day. They would all sit around telling stories from school or life in general. Usually, there were three or four girls, but occasionally a random man would appear. A friend or acquaintance from one of the halls, or a potential boyfriend someone had brought along. It always amazed Liz that even though they had lived through the same years in the same country, their experiences were so different. Even the language was different. Suzanne had an East End twang which was exaggerated when she got excited or was talking about something involving drinking and parties. Jo, a girl from the corridor below, was from Glasgow and often used words which nobody else had heard of.

"I'm off to the cludgie, back in a mo."

"What the hell's a cludgie?"

"Have you never heard of a cludgie? Toilet, lav, loo, bog."

"Got it."

From then on, they all adopted the word and the toilet on the corridor below was always referred to as the cludgie until they moved out of Trentfield Hall.

Sometimes the sessions in Suzanne's room would go on past midnight until someone got heavy eyelids. Liz would occasionally leave early to go and do some uni work in the library or to read up on a subject before an upcoming lecture, but normally she just liked to bathe in the variety of the experiences which were on show.

When she was back in her room, Liz would lie in bed listening to the sounds of the hall as stereos stopped, taps ran, and lights switched off. She missed home but liked uni in equal measure. She liked quiet times, early in the morning when she went for a run, or late at night when everyone was in bed. Around other girls, she enjoyed company and having a laugh, but she was comfortable in her own space. Her room was as familiar now as her bedroom had been at home. Each item had a memory attached, and when she got in and closed her door, it felt like being hugged by her parents as a small child.

***

In the second week of term, Suzanne heard of a party in a house outside uni. Some second years were sharing a house and Suzanne had an invite through a contact she made in the student union bar. She asked Liz if she wanted to come.

"You'll be able to meet loads of people from other faculties and years, it will be fun."

"Not sure. I never really went to parties at school. I'm more a cinema and pizza kind of girl."

"Time to branch out, girly. Life is for living and all that. We can catch the bus from the end of the road and then it's two streets' walk. Leafy suburb. You should like that!"

"Well, OK. I suppose it can be part of the new me."

"Exactly. It'll be Liz the re-launch edition. Music, food, drink, and men. But not necessarily in that order."

"Are we going jeans and trainers, or summer dress?"

"I think I'll go summer dress to show off my tanned legs from the back garden."

"OK, me too. Although my legs are not as tanned, as I was in the superstore."

"No, but you're a runner. Hence the great legs."

"Legs up to her oxsters, my dad would say, but then he was part Scottish."

They arrived at the house after a walk in the warm autumn evening, an Indian summer Suzanne had said. As they left the bus stop, their walk into the leafy suburb had taken them into progressively nicer housing, and the pavement had changed from patched tarmac to old wobbly paving stones with tufts of grass growing through the cracks. They both had set out with coats on, but Suzanne was now carrying hers in her hand and Liz had hers open and was feeling a bit warm. Liz carried a bottle of supermarket wine and Suzanne had a four pack of lager cans. They could hear the party before they saw the house. The dull bass thud carrying over the sound of traffic. As they approached the house, they saw flashing lights behind the drawn curtains and a stocky male ran out of the front door with a feather hat on his head, a girl chasing him shouting, "Give it back, you loser!"

"I think we've arrived," said Suzanne.

"Looks that way, you take me to all the best places."

"Stick with me, kid, and you'll be Miss Popular."

Liz smiled and stayed silent. She admired Suzanne's confidence and street-smart attitude and hoped some of it would rub off. She had always been slightly withdrawn; down, she thought, to her overcautious mother. She loved her parents and the area where she had grown up, but having now been exposed to girls with other backgrounds, a whole new world was opening up before her eyes. She had worked in a superstore over the summer to earn some money, as had many other girls, but some who were from better-off families had spent time abroad, one on her parents' yacht! When they were all gathered on Suzanne's floor one night, Debbie, a girl from the corridor below, had come in still wearing her Tesco uniform and another girl had assumed she was someones sister who worked in the local supermarket. It had taken some time before Liz and Suzanne were able to explain that Debbie was a university student, and she needed to work to help support herself.

When they got in the house, they headed for the kitchen to put their drink on the table. As they passed two lads, one of them said, "Hi Suz. Love the dress, can I take it off for you later?"

"In your dreams, Mikey."

"Who's your friend? She looks like my type."

"This is Liz, and she's intelligent so might be a bit too much for you."

As they entered the kitchen, they left behind cheers and catcalls.

"Mikey and his mate are both rugby players. Loud but harmless."

Liz laughed. "I've met a few like that at school. I can generally outrun them!"

They both started chatting to a group of girls and Liz found that she knew two from her course and another girl who had a room on the corridor above her at Trentfield Hall. She decided now was the time to open up a bit and enjoy herself. Goodbye, Miss Bookworm, and hello, new life. One of the boys was handing out glühwein which he said was his own special recipe and packed quite a punch. All the girls were taking glasses, so Liz did as well. It was hot, smelt of cinnamon and tasted quite fruity. She liked it, it reminded her of Christmas. She chatted to a couple of girls in the kitchen and ate a few crisps; there was only cheese and onion, how boring, she thought.

Suzanne was dancing with a group of girls in the living room, so Liz went to join them. As she walked out of the kitchen, she noticed her face felt hot and she was a bit wobbly, so she steadied herself on the doorframe as she walked through. She felt really good and was enjoying herself. What had she been missing all this time!

The party got more and more crowded, with several groups of people arriving. Some Suzanne had seen before, but most were unfamiliar faces. Liz overheard people saying that there was a group of medics over from Sheffield and some students from Huddersfield who were sleeping on someone's floor. Two of the Huddersfield girls were wearing the same top and they were all laughing about it, asking who copied who. There were a few local lads who had been invited to keep the neighbours happy and a few general hangers-on, it seemed. Liz had never been to a party with so many people.

As the night wore on, Suzanne left Liz dancing and went to the kitchen to get a drink of water. When she came back, she noticed more people dancing and some of the lads had joined in. Liz was gradually getting wilder with her dancing, and a couple of the lads were watching her. She thought she had better take her outside for a bit of fresh air as the glühwein had obviously been mixed with vodka or some other spirit the boys had dug up. Just as she was about to move, someone tapped her arm and said, "Hi, Suz!" It was Rachel from further down their corridor at Trentfield. They chatted about freshers' week and the upcoming quiz night at the union bar, deciding who they should have on their team. By the time Suzanne remembered what she had intended to do, Liz was nowhere to be seen.

She went into the kitchen, where a few boys were finishing the crisps and sausage rolls someone had brought, but she wasn't there. Suzanne assumed Liz had gone to the toilet, as there was a long queue on the landing. She moved through the party chatting to people and had a couple of dances with Rachel and another girl, but Liz did not reappear. She looked in the garden where some people were smoking but no joy. Surely, she couldn't have gone home without telling me, she thought. She kept asking around.

"Have you guys seen Liz, tall girl with auburn hair wearing a blue summer dress and Nike trainers?"

"Not seen her."

"Do you know what happened to the tall girl who was dancing?"

Nobody knew anything, and then one of the girls from Huddersfield said, "She had a few dances with a guy and then they went upstairs, I think."

Suzanne wasn't sure what to do. If she had gone upstairs with a boy, she would definitely not want to be disturbed, but Liz didn't strike her as the type who would do this. Then again, she had only known Liz for two weeks, so did she really know her, or had she just assumed she was quiet and reserved when actually she was a bit frisky when she let her hair down. It's always the quiet ones, she thought.

When it went past midnight Suzanne was starting to panic, as things just didn't feel right. She asked Rachel what she thought, and although she did not know Liz well, she too thought it was unusual behaviour for her. They both went upstairs and knocked on the door of one of the bedrooms. An aggressive male voice shouted from inside, "Sod off!" closely followed by a panting female voice saying, "Just a minute."

Liz and Rachel looked at each other and collapsed into hysterical laughter, before moving on to the second bedroom door across the landing. They knocked. No reply. They knocked again without success, and then Rachel tried the door handle. The door swung open. The smiles on their faces dropped like stone. There was Liz, passed out on the bed. For Suzanne, time stood still. She took in the smell of alcohol, sweat, and vomit. The flowery quilt cover on the bed, the pillow on the floor and coats thrown over the chair. She gazed at Liz, and she struggled to breathe, a cold sweat broke out over her whole body, and the hairs on her bare arms stood on edge. Liz's dress was pulled up and her pants abandoned on the floor. Her head was turned into the bed and pressed flat on one side. Mascara had run down her cheeks in tears, and a line of yellow dribble stretched from the side of her mouth onto the bed. A patch of thin vomit had soaked into the quilt close to her. As they entered the room, Suzanne hissed, "Liz, Liz, oh God, Liz!" choking on her words as she tried to get them out. Rachel touched Liz's shoulder, initiating a groan. They both shook her, and she started to come round.

"Liz, Liz, wake up!"

"What, what," she mumbled, her eyes barely opening.

"We've got to get her home and to bed," Rachel said.

"Mikey's got a car, I'll see if he can give us a lift," Suzanne replied.

She rushed out of the room, pushing past several people as she thundered down the stairs. Mikey was at the door with a group of friends in the process of leaving.

"Mikey! It's Liz, I think she's been... attacked."

One look at Suzanne's face sobered him up instantly.

"Where is she?" he barked, shock and panic written all over his face.

"Upstairs with Rachel. Can you give us a lift to Trentfield?"

"Yeah, no problem, I'll fetch the car," and he ran down

the front drive, elbowing two boys out of the way as he did, and went out onto the street. Suzanne rushed upstairs, taking two stairs at a time, and back to the bedroom. Rachel had got Liz dressed and wiped her face with a tissue. Liz was staring at Rachel with a glazed expression.

"Is it time to go? I feel dizzy and sick."

Suzanne and Rachel supported her, and they walked out onto the landing. Heads turned as they pushed past, and they overhead snippets of comments.

"What's happened to her, too much to drink?" said a girl.

"Silly cow can't hold her drink," said a boy on the stairs. The girl with him said, "Don't be stupid, Miles."

"What? What did I do?"

Rachel fetched their coats as Suzanne supported Liz at the front door. She had her arm around her shoulder as though she were a child. Why had she left her friend, and why had she not checked on her when she first noticed she was gone? Her grandmother had a framed embroidery on her wall which a friend had bought her in the war. It read 'To have a friend is to be one', and Grandma had always said how it was true and that she had lived by that saying. I've failed my friend, and I've failed you, Grandma, she thought.

When they were covered up, they walked out into the night air, stopping once when Suzanne thought Liz was going to throw up – she didn't. In the back of Mikey's car, Liz rested her head against Suzanne's shoulder, making occasional groaning noises and sniffing back her running nose.

Once at Trentfield they thanked Mikey and took Liz up to her room. They found her keys in her bag and let her into the room, undressing her and putting her to bed. Throughout all this activity, Liz moaned and groaned in a semi-conscious state. They put her light out and closed her door.

"Do you think one of us should stay with her?" Suzanne asked.

"I think she'll just sleep it off. She's obviously not used to drinking, and the hot glühwein combined with not eating much probably got to her."

"What do you think happened with the boy? She never mentioned having had sex before, but I've only known her a couple of weeks so don't know what she is normally like."

"From what I've heard of her, there's no way she would have had sex if she was sober. I think whoever he was took advantage of her."

"Rape, you mean."

"Looks like that."

"She should go to the police tomorrow, then," Suzanne said.

As she left the room, Suzanne turned and looked at Liz asleep in her bed, curled up like a hurt child. She felt her face hot and tears prickling behind her eyes. She had let her friend down and she felt ashamed.

4

1981

Outcomes

Mark knew the envelope would come today and woke up early, having tossed and turned the whole night. He held on to the fact that at present nothing had changed, but he knew that after the envelope came, everything would be different. He had applied to several universities and been offered a place at two, but knew he had to get the grades. Even to get into a polytechnic or college, he needed to pass at least two A levels, and his chemistry was hopeless. His stomach tightened and twisted as he remembered his theory paper, where he only really answered two of the four questions. In the other two he had been close to tears as he just waffled and made stuff up. In the practical he had had no idea what he was really doing, and so had never finished. Part of him thought he might get lucky and scrape through, but he knew deep down that there was no chance. But at the moment, until the envelope came, he was the same as all of his mates.

Everyone was looking forward to leaving school, and, for most, leaving their hometown and going on to other, more exciting things. He had worked at the camera shop in the period after the exams and occasionally gone out with his mates. When they all went to the local outdoor pool and sunbathed, he constantly felt a weight hanging over him. A gnawing feeling of impending doom, like a big hand pressing down and suffocating him. His mates would pass their A levels and go forwards; he would fail and get stuck. Left behind floundering as the boat sailed off.

He heard the letterbox slam shut and letters land on the carpet with a fluttering thud. A flailing bird which had been knocked down and would never fly again. He could hardly breathe. His mum normally fetched the mail, but today she stayed in the kitchen humming to herself, and he knew she was waiting for him to come downstairs. He could almost touch her anticipation. He had to be brave, he knew that. But he did not feel brave, he felt helpless. Time was ticking on, and the letter was on the mat. His breath became short, and he could feel his heartbeat pounding in his chest. Fear, panic, and finally rage gripped him, and he opened his bedroom door and ran downstairs. A magazine, a bill, and a plain brown envelope addressed to Mark Smith.

His hand was trembling, and he thought he might pass out as he reached down and picked it up. He put his forefinger under the corner of the flap and slid it along, tearing the paper jaggedly. It seemed appropriate that his execution should be rough and ready rather than neat and controlled. In his mind's eye, he could see Donna James opening her letter with a neat cut from a letter opener, and Stephan Wyatt smiling as his mum put her arm around his shoulder and his dad shook his hand and playfully punched his shoulder. He looked at the paper. Slim and oblong, with just a few lines of print. Biology C, Pass. Chemistry F, Fail. It was over. There was no hope now of going to even the most basic technical college, never mind university. To study for a degree, he needed two passes, and he had one. He now stood out amongst his peer group in the raw, blazing light of failure. He could no longer disguise himself with jokes and playful banter. He imagined himself nude, standing on a stage in a single spotlight while the audience mocked him. His mum came from the kitchen and looked at him with a weak, sympathetic smile. She put her arm around his shoulder, and he cried as he had done when he was ten and fell off his roller skates, skinning his knees. As he had done when he was twelve and three boys from the technical college threw his bike into a ditch.

"I'm sorry, Mum."

"I know, it will be OK."

But it wouldn't. She could not change this. She couldn't pick him up and brush him down, giving him a cooling pine-smelling cream to rub in, and his dad couldn't hose down his bike and polish the chrome with an oily rag from the garage. He was on his own. Throughout his life, his family had supported him. They had been a team, travelling through life together. Eating the same meals, watching the same TV programmes. In winter they had stayed inside together. His dad always said, when it was windy and raining, "Let's batten down the hatches," and the family had gathered in front of the TV with him drinking hot milk. Now he had failed them, not just himself. He had been asked to step up to the challenge and been found wanting.

The school offered a results counselling session, which he went to. No longer with his friends in the top set, they were all bundled together now. The misfits from across all the year. Boys and girls he hardly recognised. His world had been those taking sciences, and a smattering of younger pupils in Oak House. But now there were faces he did not know who had taken subjects he had hardly heard of. For years, any conversations he heard in the background were about biology, chemistry, maths, or physics. This had been his side of school, the science group. But now, conversations on each side of him used unfamiliar terms. He heard parents talking about technical drawing, design, and apprenticeships. Teachers gave out leaflets about employment opportunities and local company schemes. This was not his world! Then he felt a weight in the pit of his stomach as it dawned on him that it was his world now. He was no longer a potential college boy, he had to think of jobs and training, not academia. He felt slightly nauseous, but above all, helpless. He was a piece of flotsam pushed along with the flow of a river. His destination was unknown and out of his control.

Mark took a job in a big department store in his hometown. His idea was to work full-time for a year and at the same time take some evening classes to get the results he needed for university. He thought this was OK, because some of his schoolmates had taken a year out travelling before going up to university, so he viewed his year as something similar. OK, he was still living at home, but he was earning money which his mates were not, and he was also getting life experience which would look good on his CV.

Now he had some money, he started to buy a few clothes and joined a local bodybuilding gym to build himself up before going to uni. He would spend his year working on himself to become better read, more muscular and get a girlfriend. At school he had only had one girlfriend and was conscious that he was still a virgin when most of his mates at school had claimed not to be.

"Lost my cherry at the weekend" had been a typical phrase filtering through the boys in the sixth-form common room, followed by an extended description of exactly what had happened and where. This usually involved a house when parents were out or the back seat of a car if someone had learnt to drive. Everyone knew most of these descriptions were either exaggerated or simply made up, but Mark still thought he was a bit of a sexual outsider. He had met Joanne early in his upper sixth when she was in the lower. They had been out on a couple of dates, once to the cinema and once to a local cafe. Most of his mates thought she was pretty, and some even implied she was sexy when they saw her in her hockey skirt because she had slightly darker skin from her Italian dad. Although his mates at the time had required a blow-by-blow account of exactly what was happening between him and Joanne, he had just liked her to talk to. She was interesting (she was good at art and could draw cartoons) and she would talk about things no one else did. She had once shown him a fox run in the fields at the back of her garden, and she had a dog called Mutch which they used to walk. At the end of the year, she had changed schools and so they had lost touch. He was quite sad but had told his mates that she was frigid and far too young for him. He said he had been upstairs and downstairs, a phrase they had picked up from the TV which meant you had touched the skin under a girl's bra and knickers. He had done neither and had not tried because he was embarrassed to do so but had bragged to gain approval. He often did this and would feel guilty afterwards. He wondered if Joanne would go on to uni and where she was now.

"This is my mate, Mark; he works in the electrical department. Colin's in menswear and Neil is a chef in the restaurant."

Mark had joined his friend Gareth from work in a local pub after work. The plan was to have a couple of beers and some food and then head off to the local disco in town for 8pm, as it was cheaper to get in during the week. Mark had seen Colin before in the staff canteen at work, but not Neil. Ever since starting to work out in the gym, Mark had compared other men's physiques to his own. Colin was tall and spindly, with a slightly stooped appearance, and Mark thought he would be about the same weight as he was. Neil was shorter and thickset, his head looked slightly too small for his neck, and he had sinewy forearms with tattoos. Mark judged that he was probably a bit heavier and more muscular than he was and made a mental note to work harder on his arms in the gym. Apparently, Neil worked on the hotplate in the restaurant, preparing basic meals. He lived in a hostel on the other side of town and seemed to know lots of people. As more beer was drunk, the stories began. Colin and Neil had a profitable sideline going in clothing. Colin would steal items of clothing from the storeroom before they went on the shop display and pass them to Neil. He would take them out of the store and sell them on to people he knew, splitting the profits. This seemed to work because Colin had to go past the security lodge when leaving the building, as he worked on the shop floor, whereas Neil came and went via a side entrance to the restaurant where the deliveries were made.

"Anything you can get from electrics, Mark?"

"I don't know really, it's all pretty big stuff."

"What about cassettes?" asked Neil. "They can be a good seller."

"Yeah, I could probably get a few of those."

"Great stuff. You get half of what I sell them for."

Mark had never really stolen anything. He remembered when he was eight, coming home with a toy car he had been playing with which belonged to a boy called David. It had been blue with a rounded bonnet and boot, and he had stroked his fingers across them, feeling their smooth, gentle curve. They had been pushing the car across the playground to each other, and when the bell went, Mark had put it in his pocket to give to David when they were in the classroom. He had forgotten because the teacher had started talking straight away. When he went to get his things, David had already left and was meeting his big sister, who picked him up from school. When Mark got home, he had been playing with the car when his mum asked him where he had got it. When he said it was David's, and he had just brought it home, his mum had been furious and said it was stealing. Mark had felt ashamed and started crying. His mum had walked with him around to David's house to apologise and return the car. He had never forgotten the horror in his mum's voice, and the feeling of shame that he had disappointed her. Even now he could imagine the curved, chunky feeling of the toy car and his guilt of his mum being disappointed in him. But he wanted to fit in. He wanted to be one of the gang, the popular crowd. He had always been just on the edge of groups at school, but now he had a chance in the big time. He would be a thief and get rich, like Raffles the gentleman thief he had seen in a film on TV recently.

Mark started taking cassettes from the department storeroom. He was cautious to take just one or two and to space out when he took them. Some days it would be a morning, other times an afternoon, and he would only take them on some weeks and not others. He figured that this amount of stock loss would be put down to shoplifters because the department store had a problem with them in general. He would put something in his pocket and slide the cassette in at the same time, or sometimes hide them in his lunchbox. It felt good to steal. It was a secret he knew about and those around him did not. Something just for him. He passed the cassettes on to Neil and would get money back in return. Neil had told him that he wouldn't get as much as Colin because he could steal fashionable shirts, and had once given him a pair of flared trousers and a Pepsi logo T-shirt which had gone down well. Mark didn't mind this because he just wanted to fit in and thought if the things he took were worth less, his stealing was not as serious as Colin's, so it was OK.

***

Neil said he was going to move out of the hostel and was renting a house with another guy on one of the new estates at the edge of town. It was a three-bedroomed house, and they needed a third person. Colin was still living at home but hoped to move in with his girlfriend, who had her name down for a council flat. Neil asked Mark if he wanted to take the third bedroom.

"It's the box room, so it's a bit small but it's OK. Got a new single bed and the house has good furniture as the owners are abroad."

"Where is the bus stop?"

"A two-minute walk to the main road and you're right there. All the buses stop because two routes merge and go straight into town. You can get the 110 or 135 and they come about every ten minutes. I use it all the time."

Mark thought about it. He was giving some money to his parents while living at home and earning enough from his full-time job. It would give him the chance to branch out on his own and move away from home as most of his schoolmates had done. Also, it would be good to bring girls back so his chances of picking someone up would be better. He was painfully aware that he was still a virgin and wanted to rectify this situation as soon as possible.

"OK, I'm in," he said.

"Great stuff. You can move in anytime and you start paying rent at the end of each month. We split gas, electric, and the phone bill three ways, and the rent includes everything else. Rates and house insurance are covered."

Mark moved in the next week. He put all his stuff in his dad's car, squeezing everything into the small boot, and drove round to the house. Neil was in but Ted, the other guy renting the house, was out. Mark had never met Ted, but Neil said he was OK. His dad helped him put all his stuff in his room and then left, leaving Mark suddenly alone. This was the first time he had been away from home permanently. He had been on a couple of school trips for a week to an outdoor pursuits centre, where they had all stayed in a dorm, boys in one and the girls in another. He lay on his bed, looking around his room. A wardrobe with a mirror on one door. The bed with a headboard which was much more modern than his at home. He had a chest of drawers and a small table with a lamp on. Neil knocked and came in.

"You all set? Need a few posters in here," he said, looking round the bare walls.

"Yeah, I'll go to the poster shop in my lunch break and get something."

"I've got that one of the tennis girl with the bare arse. Good to wank to!"

Mark didn't really know what to say, so he just smiled and cringed inside. On Tuesday evening Mark and Neil were eating at the kitchen table when Ted came in. Mark looked up from the table and felt his face flush slightly. Ted had a jagged scar down one cheek from his eye to the side of his mouth, and the tip of his right ear was missing. His eyes looked dead as he looked at Mark and grunted.

"Alright?"

Mark looked at him and opened his mouth, but no sound came out.

"Just getting some stuff and then meeting a couple of blokes at the Wheatsheaf. Got a bit of business going on."

"No problem," said Neil.

Ted left the kitchen and headed for his room.

"Ted is one on his own," said Neil. "Keeps to himself and is a bit of a headcase, to be honest. Good bloke to have on your side in a fight, though."

Mark had never been in a fight. He had once punched a boy in the stomach in the infants' school and had no effect. If there was ever a fight in school, everyone would crowd around chanting "fight, fight, fight" and a teacher would come and split the fighting boys up. They would have to shake hands and get a detention, which usually involved clearing up a classroom in silence for an hour after school on a Wednesday. Any other time, boys would push each other and say, "Come on, then," "Alright, I will," but it rarely came to anything. In Mark's world, fights had been baby birds ruffling their feathers and making a lot of noise to attract attention. He had seen football violence on TV and read about skinheads, but he had never encountered either. He wondered what his parents were doing now and what his mum had made for dinner.

Weeks went by without Ted ever appearing, and when he did, he would normally head off to the pub to do one of his business deals. Neil said Ted had links with a crime gang in the North of England somewhere but did not know where. Ted seemed to be the only person Neil was afraid of. He would get over-friendly and sycophantic when Ted came in and adapt an East End twang to his voice, calling him "mate" several times in one sentence.

One Friday evening Mark had gone out with some of the store staff after work to a leaving do of one of the longer-term employees. When he arrived home, he heard Neil and Ted talking in the living room and they had obviously been drinking.

"Slip something in her drink, mate, never fails. I've used vodka shots, or a new thing called roofies. Just pop one in her drink and you can do anything to her. I've used them a couple of times and got a result." It was Ted speaking.

Neil was laughing and saying, "Yeah, I'll have some of that!"

Mark had reached the top of the stairs, and the conversation became muffled. He went into his room and lay on the bed. His warm feeling from the party had evaporated and been replaced by a cold dread. He felt sweat on his forehead and palms, and panic rising in his chest. What had he heard, were they really talking about a date rape drug? Drugs were bad, he knew that. He cast his mind back to school and the embarrassment when he had tried and failed to take a photograph up a girl's skirt.

At work the next morning, he recounted the conversation he had overheard to Gareth.

"You need to get out of there, mate. A bit of shoplifting is one thing, but drugs are serious trouble. I read about that drug, in the paper. It's called Rohypnol. A girl had one put in her drink and died. I thought Neil was OK, but if he's thinking about that, he's bad news. Get rid, mate."

When he got home that evening, Neil was in the kitchen eating a pasty and chips.

"Colin's been caught by security at work with two T-shirts under his coat. He was called up to the manager's office. They think it's a one-off so have said they won't prosecute but he's been fired. Bloody close shave if you ask me. I'm going to move out and go live with my girlfriend. I need to get my head together and save some money."

"Oh, OK. I'll think I'll move back with my parents, then. I might start looking for another job as the store job's not going anywhere. Gareth was telling me about a new scheme his dad's work are involved with called the Youth Training Scheme."

5

1981

Leeds

Mark moved back with his parents in June. Summer was just beginning, and he quite enjoyed lying in the garden doing nothing much, while sunbathing and reading a book. He had decided to leave the department store mainly because of the stealing and what had happened to Colin but also because he thought the job was not going anywhere. He regretted the stealing. He wasn't the sort of person who stole things, he knew that. He had just got caught up in it and wanted to fit in and impress the others.

He had signed on at the job centre and saw a card promoting the Youth Training Scheme. He remembered Gareth from the store had mentioned this, but with the house move and signing on, he had forgotten all about it. He went to the desk and asked the girl for a leaflet, noticing that she was wearing a Black Sabbath sweatshirt and had a tattoo on her wrist which he thought was quite alternative.

"Think I might go for this, I fancy a bit of a challenge."

She looked through him and then reached across her desk for the leaflet, handing it to him with a blank stare.

"Right," she said.

He read it on the bus home, wondering if he should have made a comment about heavy metal music to the job centre girl. Perhaps he had missed a chance.

His dad said he had seen an advert on TV about YTS and Mark felt encouraged that his dad knew about it. Perhaps this was something he could do. He applied and got accepted by an engineering firm two bus rides away. He would earn £27.50 a week plus travel expenses, and felt so relieved to have something to look forward to that he was determined to make a go of it.

The engineering company was called Moorfields and it made aluminium window frames. These were mostly double-glazed units for the new office buildings which seemed to be springing up everywhere. Since the motorway extension had been built, workers had been relocating from London. London overspill, they called it, and Moorfields was reaping the benefits. The company took on three YTS trainees for a year, and in addition to the factory training, they also studied one day a week at the local college. Mark had read in the leaflet that the idea was to provide work-based learning, focusing on vocational training rather than academic. Doing stuff, rather than writing essays, his dad had explained.

In the introductory morning at Moorfields, they had been introduced to Alan from the shop floor, who had been with the company for eight years since leaving the army, and Mr Watson from personnel, a rotund elderly gentleman in a suit, perfectly ironed white shirt, and bright red tie. The first talk was from Mr Watson, who gave a boring one-hour drone about the history and benefits of YTS. Mark had simply switched off and noticed one of the other trainees had actually closed his eyes. When the talk finished, Alan thanked Mr Watson, who then left the room. After the door had closed, Alan turned to the three trainees and said:

"Well, that was a load of old bollocks, now let's get to the real work. There are lots of different YTS schemes, hairdressing, shops, garden centres, whatever. You are in engineering. That is where you could be killed, so safety is our first concern, and from now on, it is yours too!"

Nobody closed their eyes when Alan spoke. He introduced the trainees to safety gear which he called personal protective equipment, or PPE. They were all issued with gloves, safety goggles, and protective boots and shown how to use them. To Mark, it was incredible to wear these. He felt like he was in the army or perhaps a spaceman, and he guarded his gear with his life. He carefully wrote his initials on each item with an indelible felt-tip pen, and regularly cleaned his safety goggles with paper roll.

The trainees were shown around the factory and given details of where they would each work. Mark went on a cutting machine and was shown how to measure to a 1-millimetre tolerance using a special gauge, and then how to tension the machine chain by releasing and retightening the securing bolt. He felt so responsible when doing this and thought the job really suited him. It was so far away from school and the department store, and he was told that after training, if he was to be taken on as a maintenance engineer, he would be responsible for machines worth many thousands of pounds upon which the whole production process depended. He felt his chest puff out when he heard this. He loved this job. The noise and shouting of the shop floor, the quiet focus of the drawing room, the computer clatter of the office, even the fresh air and sweeping of the yard. He got to learn how to drive a forklift truck lifting single, then double pallets. He paid close attention to everything that was said, asked questions and hung on Alan's every word. After they had been on the scheme for a month, they were told that they would now go to college one day each week and study towards a City and Guilds Certificate in Engineering. He went to the local technical college with the two others, and his mum was so proud that he was studying again that she gave him a big hug when he told her. He pretended to be embarrassed.

"Oh, Mum, don't!"

It felt warm and secure when she hugged him, as it always had, and he felt tears begin to prickle on the inside of his closed eyelids.

She said, "I knew you would get back on your feet. You just had a bit of a wobble, that's all, but now you're back on track."

His dad said, "Well done, son, engineering is a good career. It's what built this country and what keeps it great. From Brunel onwards we've always led the world in engineering and now you can take the baton."

Mark felt so proud, not just of his job but of pleasing his parents. He had thought he let them down with his school exam results and now he was making it up to them. He was determined to do well in his City and Guilds to show that when it came to the important stuff in life, he was no dunce.

He had his appraisal meeting after being on the scheme for six months. For each task, the trainees had been marked in a logbook, and in turn they sat in the office with Alan and a YTS official. Mark was asked how he found the job and which areas he liked best. He mentioned maintenance and Alan said that he had fitted in well with all the staff and made the transition from school to the work environment well. He said he was the only trainee who had never been pulled up for forgetting safety gear and this was important. For his college work, his report said he had top marks. He had A grades in each subject with only one at B.

"Why do you think you have done well at college, when you failed your A levels at school?" the YTS supervisor asked.

He had rehearsed answers to potential questions all week with his dad and was ready with his reply.

"If I'm honest, I messed around a bit a school, but here things are more serious and the emphasis on safety has matured me, I think. I've taken that experience from the shop floor to the classroom."

Alan sat up straight and looked proud of his trainee, and the YTS supervisor said, "Excellent, that's what the scheme is all about."

When he finished his engineering certificate, Mark was sent to Moorfields' parent company in Leeds to complete a HNC at the local technical college. He had been staying in a local B&B for the first three weeks when he arrived and had visited flat rental agencies and scoured through newspaper ads for flats or house shares. He had looked at several options, but they were all a bit bleak. Some were just a rented room in a house, and others were too expensive. He eventually saw a flat on the accommodation board at work, which a girl was moving out of at the end of the month. She was relocating to London and was giving up the flat. The personnel assistant who was dealing with his B&B had phoned him at work and told him about it as she was putting the notice up. The flat was owned by the Portside Trust, who had invested in housing for single people. He thought it was ideal and close enough to work that he could cycle, which would save on bus fares. He paid his one-month deposit on the flat with his parents acting as guarantors and signed the rental agreement. He couldn't believe it. He was now going to live in his own flat on the third floor of a modern red-brick development in a fashionable area of Leeds. He felt he had turned a page and was ready to begin writing the rest of his life.

Mark's parents helped him move into his flat. He had two keys and the entrance to the building had a push button lock and intercom. Visitors pressed the button and a telephone on the wall in his hall buzzed. He then pressed the entry button on his telephone and the outside door would open. The whole process, he had been told, was called buzzing a person in, a phrase his mother thought was very modern, and they had tried it several times like young kids.

"All mod cons here, lad," she said.

"Double glazing, smoke alarms, and solid kitchen work surfaces!"

Mark had taken immense pleasure in showing his parents all the flat's features.

"Even got trip switches instead of a fuse box. Ultra-modern that," his dad had said.

"Need to get yourself a cooker, of course. Mum and I have agreed to buy you a new one from the electricity shop, as a moving-in present. They will deliver and fit it, and it will have a good guarantee. Can't mess around with electrics, got to be done right."

They went to the electricity store and the salesman explained all the features, talking about cooking benefits to his mum and reliability to his dad. When speaking to Mark, he emphasised how simple everything was to operate. The flat was unfurnished, but his parents had brought a small folding table and two chairs from home. Mark had found two breeze blocks from a building site and put a wide piece of chipboard across them and painted it black to put his stereo on. They bought a bed and wardrobe flat packed from a big furniture store on the outskirts of town. His mum stayed in the flat cleaning things as Mark and his dad went to the store and put the flat packs into the back of his dad's car with the hatchback open but tied down with a piece of rope. It was only a short, and slow, journey from the shop to the store, but quite a climb up three flights of stairs, but they managed. Mark loved that he could share the experience with his dad without his mum there. Man's work, his mum had said and had gladly left them to it.

When all the unpacking and furniture making was complete, they sat and had a cup of tea made with Mark's new kettle and his new set of mugs. They ate chocolate digestive biscuits he had bought from the corner shop two streets away, and it occurred to him that this was the first time he had bought food for his parents. When it was time for them to go, Mark had mixed emotions. He wanted to be alone in his shiny new flat and to start the next chapter of his life, but it was always a bit poignant when his parents left him. A memory flashed into his mind of his mum leaving him in the infants' school playground when he was five. He had felt abandoned and had wondered what he had done to deserve it. This had only lasted for about ten seconds when a boy had run up to him holding a yellow ball and said do you want to play?

One night he was sitting at his table studying when his telephone rang. He assumed it was his mum with some news from home and casually got up, walked over to the phone, and picking it up, said, "Hi."

"Mark, me old mate, how it's going, bud!"

Puzzled, he was silent for a few seconds, wondering who was calling.

"Who's speaking, please," he said in his best professional voice.

"Bloody hell, mate, not forgotten me already, have you? Ha, Ha!"

Mark remained silent.

"It's Neil, your old buddy."

Mark sensed the blood slowly drain from his face and felt his stomach knotting tightly. "Oh, hello."

"You sound pleased to see me."

"Yeah, well, I've got a new life now, mate."

"No problem. Just need a bit of a favour, that's all."

"How did you get my number?"

"Your mum gave it to me. Remember, you gave their details for the electric bill. Their house is just down the road. I pass it regular, like." There was menace in this last comment, Mark sensed.

"What do you want?"

"As I say, bit of a favour. Girlfriend's thrown me out, the bitch, and I've got a new gaff starting end of the month. Thought I might come see my old mate for a couple of days. I've got the chance of some business in Leeds anyhow. I'll stay for two days max, mate. What do you say?"

"I haven't got a spare bed."

"No probs, mate, I'll bring me sleeping bag."

"When do you want to come?"

"How about tomorrow, I can catch the coach up."

"Alright, but I'll be working."

"Yeah, yeah, that's fine. I won't get in your hair. As I say, bit of business, I've got a bloke to meet. Should be a nice earner, actually."

Neil arrived the next evening, having walked from the bus station with a rucksack. He pressed the entrance buzzer and Mark answered.

"Mark, mate, it's Neil. Bloody hell, this is posh, ha ha!"

Mark buzzed him in and greeted him at his front door.

"Long time, mate," said Mark.

"Yeah, got to be a year or more."

Mark looked at Neil, who had once seemed like a tough, fashionable guy to be admired. He somehow looked smaller and less threatening. He looked at Mark with slightly pitiful eyes, and Mark was surprised at himself for feeling slightly sorry for him. As they went into the flat, Mark said, "So, what did you do to make your girlfriend throw you out?"

"Oh, it was nothing really, she was a bit of a case to be honest." Most of the people Neil knew would fall into this category, Mark thought.

"Have you eaten?" said Mark.

"No, bloody starving."

"There's a couple of takeouts close by if you fancy."

"Sounds good to me. Couldn't lend me a few quid, could you? I'm a bit short what with the coach fare and all that."

"Don't worry about it, I'm buying. Chinese or Indian?"

"I could kill a curry."

They set off to the Basmati Gold Indian takeaway two streets away and chatted as they walked. Mark talked about his YTS scheme and transferring to Leeds for his HNC and asked what Neil had been doing since they had shared a house. He was a bit evasive.

"Bit of this and that, you know me, always changing."

"Have you had any work then?"

"Plenty mate. Made a mint and then lost it. Bit of time abroad soaking up the sun and getting the girls. Great laugh."

Mark doubted that any of this was true but didn't say anything, allowing Neil to save face. They ordered their food and headed back to the flat, both carrying hot, heavy paper bags. They spread the dishes out on the table and ate straight from the tinfoil containers. From the speed with which Neil ate, Mark thought he probably hadn't eaten anything all day.

"So, what's this business you have in Leeds?" asked Mark.

"You remember Ted from the house. It's a couple of his mates who have some work." Mark's mind flashed back to Ted with his scarred face and his deals with people in the local pub.

"So dodgy, then."

"Well, you know, a boy's got to do what a boy's got to do."

When he was living with Mark and Ted, he would have accepted this in silence, keeping his thoughts to himself. Now he had moved on in life and gained confidence.

"Have you ever thought of going straight? You were a chef, weren't you, could you not get back into that?"

Neil looked sheepish and said, "Yeah, but it's not that easy."

"Why not?"

"Well, there's exams and written stuff."

Mark was quiet and realised that he had never seen Neil read or write anything. He went to bed, leaving Neil on the floor with his sleeping bag. In the morning Mark was up early and had a shower, breakfast, and was out while Neil stayed fast asleep in his sleeping bag. Before he left, he opened a window to let the smell of stale curry out of the flat.

Mark was in the factory all day, going through a maintenance programme on one of the machines. When he got back to the flat, Neil was sitting on the sofa drinking from a milk bottle.

"Helped myself to some food, hope you didn't mind." Looking at him blankly and receiving a slightly guilty look in return, Mark said, "How did it go with Ted's mates?"

"Couple of possibles," Neil replied, sounding enigmatic.

"Possible what – jobs? Legal or illegal?"

Neil smiled and said nothing. "Got us invited to a party if you're interested."

"A party, how?"

"One of the guys lives in a street where some students are having a party, so they invited the locals to keep 'em sweat."

"And they don't mind others just turning up?"

"Don't think they know who lives where, so if we turn up with a bottle, we'll be fine. Could be good. Lots of young girly students."

Mark noticed the leer on Neil's face and remembered the conversation he had overheard between Ted and Neil at the house. He was not sure Neil could be trusted around young female students, but then again, it would be good to widen his own social circle. What harm could it do, he thought. He had been thinking about getting to know some girls away from work and thought this might be an opportunity.

"OK, we can give it a go. Just try not to get shit-faced or hit anyone."

"Can't promise anything."

Mark grunted.

"Let's go via the off-licence and pick up some cans."

As they left the flat, Neil said, "Any chance of lending me a tenner. I'm good for it, you know I am."

Mark sighed and reached for his wallet.

Walking away from the flat, they came into leafy suburbs which had once been quite grandiose but had lost a bit of their polish. Many of the flagstones on the pavement were uneven, leaving sharp edges to trip on. Some had been lifted to repair pipes underneath, Mark guessed, and had obviously broken in the process and been repaired with a patchwork of tarmac. Some flags had large gaps between with grass and weeds growing through; this, combined with the odd dog turd and empty drinks can, made for interrupted walking. Faintly they heard music and saw a group of young people at the door of a house. They followed a couple of lads who had bottles of wine and overheard them speaking with public-school accents.

"Bloody hell," said Neil. "Posh totty inside, me thinks."

"Remember, I live just around the corner, so try not to make a complete arse of yourself when I'm in sight."

As they went into the house, there was a small queue of people lining up to put drinks on the kitchen table. They deposited their drink and Neil picked up a can. They went into the living room where the music was on. Everyone was standing around chatting and they kept to themselves to begin with, Mark's eye casting a glance over the girls.

A BMW pulled up outside and two boys got out accompanied by two girls. They all spoke in cut public-school accents, each of the boys carrying a bottle of spirits, and the girls, bottles of wine.

"Money," said Neil. "And lots of it. Those jeans are designer and cost a mint, believe me."

Mark just smiled, thinking that he had never seen girls in jeans that tight, and high heels would damage the bare plank floor.

As the night went on the volume of chatter built up in the kitchen and Mark heard that some of the boys had made glühwein. He had a glass but found it a bit sweet and suspected they had put spirits in it. He got talking to a couple of lads who, it turned out, were in their first year studying engineering. They compared what they had covered, and Mark was surprised that their course had little practical in it. They said it was mostly academic until the third year when they went out to industry. Mark had more glühwein, as he was getting buoyed up by feeling slightly superior to the uni students, and he thought, what the hell. He decided that failing his exams, although painful, was, oddly, probably one of the best things to happen to him.

11.30pm

As the evening wore on some of the girls had begun dancing in a group together. He was always amazed at their ability to dance and still try to chat, shouting at each other occasionally and then splitting apart. He hadn't seen Neil for a while but then noticed him in the kitchen pouring vodka. Typical Neil, he thought, cadges money and food, and then brings a can to a party and drinks shorts. He really was a leech, and Mark would be glad to see the back of him.

The girls who were dancing were getting a bit wild, and he and the two mechanical engineering students were standing by the wall being entertained.

"You can see right through that girl's dress when she turns sideways in front of the lights," said one.

"It's all to do with the position of the light source, relative to the subject and the viewer," said the other.

They all laughed, and Mark said, "That, and she's got a great arse."

"That's why you're getting a better engineering education in industry than at uni," said the first. "Down-to-earth practical skills. Wish we had that!" Yes, thought Mark. I've done the right thing. He was feeling energised now and more confident.

11.45pm

Neil emerged from the kitchen holding a can and started doing a shuffling dance by himself. It was the first time Mark had seen Neil dance, and although he wasn't particularly impressed, he had to admire his courage. Mark thought there was no way he would have danced with those girls, firstly because he would have made a complete arse of himself as he couldn't dance, and secondly because they were getting more and more drunk. One was getting a bit wild and banging into the others, causing fits of hysteria all round. He saw Neil shuffle over to the girl in the dress and start dancing with her and chatting. He offered her a drink from his can, and she took it. She was obviously thirsty from the dancing, Mark thought, because she gulped it down.

One of the uni students said something to Mark and he turned to listen, feeling a bit dizzy. That glühwein must have been strong, he thought. When he turned back, he saw that both Neil and the girl in the dress with the lighting effect had both gone. He turned back to the two lads and continued talking for a while. They were all laughing, shouting over the music and spilling drinks in their enthusiasm. He moved through to the kitchen as one of the boys wanted to introduce him to a second year who was looking for an industrial placement for his final year.

By midnight people started to drift off and Mark went in search of Neil, steadying himself on pieces of furniture as he walked. He wasn't in the living room or kitchen, so assumed he must have gone to the toilet. By half twelve he decided to look in the garden but other than a straggling group of smokers there was nobody remaining. He really was feeling drunk now, and decided to go upstairs to see if Neil was there.

12.15am

He climbed the stairs, steadying himself on the banister, his head burning hot. There were several people queuing for the toilet, including the girl in the dress, who had slid down the wall and was sitting on the floor. Mark looked at her and she looked back through bleary eyes.

"You, OK?" he said.

She just stared blankly, then reached for his leg and started to pull herself up to her feet, giggling. Mark looked at her. He had never seen such a beautiful girl. Even drunk, she looked fresh-faced, and he thought she was in a league above all the other girls he saw at work. She giggled and leant forwards, half falling and put her arms around him. She kissed him, and he thought, my luck could be in here.

12.45am

"Oh, there you are. I was looking all over. Are we going?" said Neil.

"Yeah, let's call it a night."

"You look terrible, mate, you OK?"

"That bloody glühwein was powerful," Mark replied. He felt guilty and annoyed with himself.

They left the house and walked through intermittent bunches of students straggled along the road in various states of disrepair. A group of three lads were singing and a girl was trying (and failing) to climb a lamp post. Snippets of conversation came through.

"She was completely out of it, I'm telling you. They had to get a car to take her home," they caught from a group of girls.

"Did you see the guy pouring vodka into that can. Skilled operator, big respect." They heard from a public-school voice.

Mark felt nausea flood over him.

As they got further away from the house the noise faded, leaving the occasional shout in the distance, a car engine revving, and the clatter of a can being thrown.

"What happened to you?" said Neil.

"Nothing really, got chatting to a few uni students," Mark replied dismissively.

Mark was silent for a while and then said, "You off tomorrow, then?"

"Yeah, bus at ten."

"I'm leaving for work before that, so make sure you close the door properly."

"No problem."

When Mark came home from work the next day, Neil had gone, leaving little evidence that he had been there. No money returned, no note. Some dirty dishes left on the floor, and an unflushed toilet in the bathroom. He never heard from him again, but four years later, when he had finished his course and was working in Germany, his mum sent him a cutting from the local paper at home. It said a male aged thirty-five had been arrested for breaking and entering. When searching his bedsit, the police had found a variety of drugs under the mattress, including amphetamines and cocaine, and two stolen wallets. In addition, a search of the man's lockup had revealed a large quantity of stolen goods including electrical items, cigarettes, and alcohol valued at eight thousand pounds. The man had been jailed for five years. His name was Neil Carter-Brown.

6

The morning after

Liz tried to open her eyes, but they were sticky. She could feel the pillow beneath her left cheek and something tight around her, gripping and pinning her down. For a moment she panicked. Who was holding her? Stop it, stop it! She woke and realised her quilt was wrapped around her legs and noticed the early-morning sun filtering through a crack between the curtains. Her mouth felt metallic and there was a smell. What was that smell? Was someone cooking? No, too early, and anyhow, she was normally the first one up in this part of the corridor. Then she realised it was her. Her breath stank. She cupped her hand and breathed out, smelling a stale-sweat smell like an old pub carpet. Her throat was sore. She threw the quilt off and sat up on the side of the bed. Her head swam and she steadied herself on the side of the bed. She blinked a few times and then realised she was nude. She never slept nude, normally in shorts and a T-shirt. Then she started to remember. The party and images slowly floated into her mind.

She had gone with Suzanne on the bus to the party, and remembered the house and the boy running out of the front door with the feathery hat on. When she went through the front door with Suzanne, one of the boys saying to Suzanne who's your mate, she looks like my type. She had liked that, and it acted as a bit of a final catalyst for the night. She had already decided to drop prudish Liz from school and become cool Liz at uni. She was ready to join the in-crowd. Every time at school, the girls went drinking before the cinema and she never did, because of her parents, so she felt left out. She actually hated the taste of alcohol, but she had thought she would go for it. She drank some of the glühwein the boys had made, which tasted quite fruity, and then felt a bit lightheaded. She went from the kitchen to the living room and started dancing and felt really happy and carefree. She was dancing in front of some flashing lights the boys had set up and one of the girls had whispered in her ear to move because everyone could see her knickers through her dress. She didn't care and didn't move. She could see some boys looking at her and she liked it. A boy she didn't recognise from university came across and started dancing in her little group. He was holding a can and offered it to her. Not wanting to look like a prig she had swigged it a few times and tried not to choke or have a coughing fit as she was laughing so much. The boy was saying something to her, but she could not hear, so he had to shout. She remembered saying she had to go to the loo but did not know if he had heard. As she left and started to go upstairs, she felt really dizzy and had to hold on to the banister. The toilet was occupied, so she had waited, but she felt herself sliding down the wall to sit on the floor. Then things were fuzzy, and she could remember nothing concrete. Flashes, that's all. A pop song playing somewhere, shapes, snippets of conversations. She remembered kissing a boy, he was quite nice. She had thought she was being daring. Dancing, drinking, kissing. She had never done those much before. Then she remembered being pushed through a bedroom door and wondering what was happening. The boy put his hand up her skirt and she pushed his hand down, saying, no I don't want to! She remembered falling and the colour of the ceiling. It was a child's bedroom with a paper lampshade like a hot-air balloon. She remembered feeling pain inside and being sick. The smell of stale sweat and a deodorant that wasn't her own. Then there was Suzanne and another girl. She thought they wanted to dance, but she could hardly stand. One of the girls was dressing her, but she had thought, I haven't had a shower, why is she doing that? Going downstairs with them and being in the back of a car, or had she imagined that? She wasn't sure what was real and what had been a dream.

She stood up, feeling a bit unsteady and put her dressing gown on. Picking up her towel and washbag, she walked slowly down the corridor to the washroom. She had a wee and just sat there afterwards looking at the green pattern on the floor tiles, for what seemed like ages. When she moved she felt really rough, and saliva built up in her mouth. One shower was free, and someone was just finishing in the other.

A girl stepped out with a towel wrapped around her. Liz recognised her but did not know her name.

"Hi," she said. "God, you look awful."

"Thanks, I feel it."

"You're as white as a sheet. Have a good night?"

"Not my best night, to be honest. Party and drank too much."

"Hot shower, girl, cures everything."

"Hope so."

She stepped into the shower, hanging her dressing gown on the hook beyond the curtain. Turning the hot water on, she just stood under the jet without moving. The water powered over her, striking her head and cascading over the shoulders and down her back. It was too hot really, but she didn't care. She just wanted to be clean, to wash away what had happened. After about two minutes she squeezed shower gel into the palm of the left hand, rubbed her hands together and began to wash. The smell of pine with the hot water and steam slowly revived her. As she washed, she felt shallow indentations on her stomach and buttocks and felt them sting. Looking down, she saw deep pale red finger marks she hadn't noticed before. As she touched herself, she felt slightly itchy, and she had an unfamiliar feeling in her groin, and was slightly bigger down there. She noticed a smear of dark blood, although she was not due. This was all new to her, and then it hit her. She had had sex. She was no longer a virgin but could not remember anything of the sex act itself. She hadn't wanted this. Not her first time. At school the girls had fantasised about the perfect first time. A Caribbean beach in the moonlight, one had said. Another had said in a horse stable with a man in riding breeches. They had all laughed at that. But not this. Drunk at a party with a boy she didn't know and unable to remember what had happened the next day. She couldn't tell her parents. They would be so disappointed in her, and she was so ashamed. Just once, she had wanted to be in the popular crowd, but it had all gone wrong. She felt the breath had been knocked out of her. She turned the shower off and dried quickly, rubbing the towel rapidly almost violently over herself. Punishing her stupidity. What had she done, what had she done! Her heart rate raced and her breathing became shallow. She couldn't catch her breath, and she wanted to burst into tears. She tried to calm herself and held on to the shower hook where her dressing gown hung. She struggled to slow her breathing and put her dressing gown on. Slowly, she recovered enough to start walking to her room. As she was about to put her key in her lock, Suzanne arrived.

"Just checking on you, we were all a bit worried."

As they were in the room, she turned and looked at Suzanne, tears in her eyes.

"Oh God, what's wrong?"

"I… I…"

"Sit down, Liz, it'll be OK. Tell me what's happened."

Between sobbing tears and short sniffing breaths, Liz told Suzanne what she remembered from the party and what she had felt in the shower.

Suzanne listened with the occasional expletive. "Oh, bloody hell... The bastard... No!"

After an exhausting hour, two cups of tea (one went cold) and half a packet of chocolate digestives, they both felt better. Liz had got stuff off her chest, and Suzanne felt guilt at first for letting her friend down, but now her behaviour morphed into that of guardian angel. Partly to make herself feel better and partly to put the world right, she suggested action.

"We should go to the police. Report what has happened."

"But I don't want uni or my parents to know."

"We can ask them not to tell them. You're over eighteen, so they have no reason to tell your parents, and it wasn't on university land, so that should cover it."

When they arrived at the police station, they both stood at the desk while the policeman behind wrote in a book. Someone sat on a bench to the side quietly muttering to themselves, holding a dirty bloodstained cloth over their eye.

"What can I do for you, girls?"

"I want to report a possible rape or sexual assault," Liz said in a slightly quiet voice.

"Really, and when did this happen, miss?" boomed the policeman.

"Yesterday evening at a party."

"Students, are you, girls?"

"Yes, at university," said Suzanne.

The policeman stared blankly at her.

"OK, take a seat and I will get someone to talk to you."

The policeman left his desk, and they heard a door open and close. There was a girl clattering a typewriter on a desk behind reception, and the moaning man continued to their right. They heard mumbled voices in another room close by.

"Couple of students from the university been out partying. Say they've been raped."

"What, both?"

"No, just one, I think."

"But I've got these bloody car thefts to deal with. Oh, OK, send them through and I'll go through the motions."

The policeman returned to the desk.

"Girls?"

Liz and Suzanne stood up from the seat they had selected as far away from the moaning man as possible.

"DC Stallard will be with you in a moment."

A plain-clothes man in shirtsleeves came through the door to the side of the desk.

"Ladies. I'm DC Stallard. Who is making the accusation?"

"That's me," said Liz.

Looking at DC Stallard, she thought he was probably about ten years older than her. He had slightly greasy hair, acne scarring and wet marks in the armpits of his crumpled shirt. His cracked plastic trouser belt was pulled tight against his expanding belly and his breath smelt of cheese and onion crisps.

"Come with me, please." Liz caught Suzanne's eye, and she slightly shrugged her shoulders.

"Need to take some details first, miss, if you would."

Liz filled in a form, giving her details and explaining roughly what had happened. DC Stallard read through the form, incredibly slowly, Liz thought, and then said, "So, you went to the party to drink and have a good time and went up to the bedroom with this boy."

"Yes, but not to have sex."

"Well, that's what you say, but perhaps you wanted to have sex and then simply regretted it afterwards. It does happen. Bit of drink and high spirits and you lose your inhibitions and then you know when you wake up – cold light of day and all that. I'm not saying I don't believe you, but you see my point."

"No, it didn't happen like that."

DC Stallard looked at Liz for a while and she could almost see the thoughts going through his head. She noticed he had a small unshaven area on his jawline where his razor had missed. He looked down at the desk and back up again, brushing the stubble on his chin.

"Tell you what I think, miss. Seems to me that you've only chosen to report this as your friend – Susan, is it? – encouraged you. Were it not for her, you would probably simply forget about it. We see this all the time."

Liz simply stared at him, not knowing what to say. She didn't know what she had really expected. As a child, her parents had always taught her to respect the police. When she was seven and had got lost in town, her mother said if she was in any trouble or couldn't find her parents, she should find a policeman. But looking at DC Stallard now, all she could feel was disappointment bordering on disgust.

"These cases are always difficult, you know, where alcohol is involved. Rape is problematic to prosecute. I'll certainly take your statement but making a formal complaint is time-consuming, and I have to tell you, as you don't know the boy's name and you're not sure what happened, it will be extremely difficult. Best to drop it, in my opinion."

Liz could feel her face burning and her anger rising. "But you're making me feel as though it's my fault!"

DC Stallard looked slightly shocked, and Liz noticed the tips of his ears went red.

"No, no, miss, I'm just laying things out for you. There could be lots of interviews and paperwork and it will probably not get anywhere."

Having filled in a report, Liz left, feeling a combination of exhaustion and frustration. As they were leaving the police station, they saw DC Stallard talking to the desk officer and overheard him say, "Statistically, they say 60 per cent of rapes cases are made up anyway. Bloody students, God save us."

On the bus home Liz filled Suzanne in on the details of the interview with DC Stallard and what he had said.

"I think I'll just leave it. I've been bloody stupid, and that's it."

Next morning Suzanne knocked on Liz's door but there was no answer. She didn't see her at breakfast but noticed her sitting by herself at lunch, pushing a yoghurt pot around the table with a spoon, an uninterested look on her face.

"What's up, kid?" she said.

Liz continued to look down at her yoghurt pot, squeezing the sides gently.

"I don't know. Not sure it's all worth it."

"What do you mean?"

She looked up at Suzanne with a drawn expression on her face.

"Uni, exams, studying. Not sure I can hack it."

Suzanne looked at her friend for a couple of seconds and took in her unwashed hair – normally it had a vibrant sheen – and a few acne spots around her mouth which she had never seen before.

"Get off, you're getting top marks, aren't you. What about that essay? You got an A+ and were singled out at the next lecture as an example of what to aim for."

She threw her spoon into her yoghurt pot and scrunched the whole thing up.

"Yeah, that made me popular. Little Miss Frump."

Suzanne placed her hand on Liz's forearm.

"You're just down because of what happened. I can understand that, but my mum always says if someone hurts you, and you dwell on it, you're just allowing them to keep hurting you."

After a brief silence, Liz said, "I suppose."

"I told her what happened."

Liz looked up, shock over her face.

"You didn't!"

"She's a nurse and deals with this stuff all the time. She said the police were notoriously hopeless with sex stuff which is why some hospitals have set up special centres for sexual assault. Apparently, someone she trained with works in one and said they are totally different to going to the police. They're called sexual assault referral centres, or SARCs for short. I think we should go. Forget what happened with the police and try again. What do you think?"

Liz thought for a while, looking down at her fingernails and scratching off a piece of hard skin.

"I don't know. I went to the room with him, so it's as much my fault as his."

"What? No, it isn't. He just had a good time and a bit of a laugh. You're living with this. The marks, the flashbacks, all that stuff."

Liz looked up and fixed her eyes on Suzanne's for a moment and then looked away into the distance. She took a long in-breath, sat straighter and looked back.

"No, you're right, I suppose. So, is there one of these centres close?"

"I've got the details here," Suzanne said, producing a piece of paper from her rucksack.

"You just phone up to make an appointment and it's a couple of bus rides again, but in a different direction than yesterday!"

Liz felt her friend was in her corner. At school she had not really had many friends. Being an only child, hers had been a close-knit family. There had been a few playmates and clubs which she had joined at various stages of her school life, but she had always been a bit of a loner. Now she felt she had a friend, and it felt good.

***

As Liz and Suzanne walked down the hospital corridor, they followed the sign for the SARC. Liz felt apprehensive, but also slightly excited as she felt she was doing something and taking control. She had once read a personal-growth book which one of the sixth-form girls had brought into school which said you can only control things in the present, you can't go back into the past and you don't know what the future will hold. I can only live in the present, she said to herself. She felt she was doing something positive now, and in so doing, she was starting to leave the night of the party behind.

They entered the centre reception and were met by a lady called Jean who wore a badge saying crisis worker. Liz read her badge and thought crisis was an appropriate word, but so was hurt, panic, pain, shame, and regret. Jean left Suzanne sitting in reception reading a magazine and took Liz into a room, which surprised her. She thought it would be like a doctor's clinic, but it had two soft chairs and a small tea- and coffee-making area and was painted in nice colours rather than standard hospital green.

Jean explained what the centre offered and said Liz was free to choose what she wanted. Liz didn't know what she wanted and had a moment of panic that she would be expected to know. Jean took some details from her and then brought her through to the doctor.

"You can ask the doctor to stop any time if you want a breather, and I'll stay with you," she said.

The doctor smiled at Liz and sat beside her.

"We're really looking at two things," she said. "Firstly, your health, dealing with any injuries which may have occurred. Secondly, there will be a forensic examination where I'll use a swab to collect DNA evidence from injured areas. It won't hurt – in fact, you'll hardly notice it at all. It's a new technique which only some police forces have started to use. The swabs will be kept on file if they are ever needed by the police as evidence."

The doctor looked at each of Liz's limbs for skin marks or damage and then around her stomach, buttocks, and groin. She was covered in a gown, and each time a limb was examined, it was taken out of the gown and then covered up again before the next limb was exposed. This small gesture made Liz feel secure. The feel of the cotton gently touching her skin brought back memories of her mother dressing her when she was young; it was intimate but caring. As well as this external examination, she also conducted an internal examination. At first Liz thought this would be embarrassing, but strangely she found it reassuringly thorough, as though by going through this procedure and sharing what had happened, she was cleansing herself. She imagined all the guilt and hurt as darkness leaving her body. Tears welled up in her eyes, and Jean quietly offered her a tissue from a box. Liz didn't say anything, but when she looked at Jean, she saw comforting eyes and a gentle, almost imperceptible nod of the head.

Throughout the examination Jean was there. She didn't say anything, but Liz found her presence reassuring. Someone in her corner, someone to share the experience. A problem shared is a problem halved, her mother always said. Although she had not told her mum what happened, in some way she felt thinking about her was being more honest. She didn't want to hide what had happened from her parents but felt so ashamed and so stupid that she had allowed it to happen. All through her life her parents had protected her, and the first time she was truly on her own it had gone so horribly wrong. More than the physical effects of stupid drunken behaviour, she felt she had let them down. That was what was really hurting now.

The doctor confirmed that she had had sex and said she would like to perform a blood test to measure levels of alcohol and drugs. Liz looked at Jean and she said it was normal in rape cases where the victim couldn't remember what had happened. Liz said OK, but thought it was a bit odd, but then again, the whole hospital experience was new. She didn't really drink until the party and had never seen any drugs at uni but had heard some boys talking about smoking pot. Her mind wandered and she thought perhaps they were smoking pot at the party, and she had inhaled some.

When the examination was finished, Liz got dressed and Jean made her a cup of tea and said she could see a councillor next to talk about her experience. But if she felt she had already done too much she could do this later.

"Does the council need to get involved?" asked Liz. "I don't want uni or my parents to find out."

Jean looked at Liz, the ends of her mouth lifting slightly and she said gently, "She is a different type of councillor."

Liz looked puzzled for a split second and then burst out laughing.

"Oh God, you mean like a therapist! I thought you meant a local government official… from the council!"

They both laughed and Liz found she suddenly had weepy eyes again. It was the first time she had smiled or laughed in three days. The laughter turned to real tears which ran in small rivulets down her face. Jean put her arm around her shoulder, and Liz cried. She cried about what had happened, about being away from home, and missing her parents. She cried for the loss of innocence and for the guilt. She cried for the uncertain future. As the tears rolled, she felt better. Jean smelt of fresh washing and deodorant and it took her back to junior school when she had come home crying because a girl had hit her in the face with a netball. Her mum had put her arm around Liz's shoulder and just held her close. Sometimes we don't need words, she thought, we have something deeper.

On her next SARC visit she had an appointment to see the councillor, but firstly the doctor came in. She said they had expected to find alcohol in Liz's blood after drinking the glühwein, but her levels were much higher than that. She suspected Liz's drink had been spiked.

"What does that mean?"

"It's when someone puts a strong alcohol, normally vodka as it's relatively tasteless, into a drink without you knowing it."

"Oh God, who would do that?"

"Unfortunately, it's becoming more common. You mentioned the boy you were with gave you a can to share?"

"Well, yes, he was drinking it."

"Obviously, I don't know because I wasn't there. But we have had cases where someone spikes a drink, normally a can or a bottle and then pretends to drink it and offers it to someone else. You think you are drinking something which is not particularly strong, a lager or cider for example, but in fact you are drinking something with vodka in, but the other drink is disguising it."

"If you had sex with someone who had spiked your drink, you have been raped."

Liz went silent and just looked at the doctor. That was it. The cold light of day. There was no more it might have been this, or it could have been that. She had been raped by someone who intended to do it. Planned it, pushed her into a bedroom and knew she couldn't fight him off.

The doctor put her hand on Liz's shoulder.

"I'll get the councillor for you."

The councillor was called Isabella and was Spanish. Liz always thought non-Brits dressed so well. She remembered at parents' evening in her fifth form, one of the boys' mums had been French and Liz thought she looked fantastic compared to her mum, who looked as though she had bought all her clothes from the same department store. Comfortable was the best description. When she was older, she would often say to her mum, "You look so English" and she would reply, "That's because I am." That was not an accusation anyone would make about Isabella. Her clothes were simple and stylish, her hair short and fashionable, and she wore simple jewellery. Just a nice watch and a single chain around her neck. She smiled at Liz in a friendly, welcoming way and said, "Hello, shall we have a chat?"

Liz felt as though she was sinking into a nice warm bath. Isabella explained that the counselling would be tailored to Liz's needs and would be conducted on a one-to-one basis weekly for six sessions initially. The sessions usually had two aspects to them. Firstly, it was an opportunity just to talk in a secure environment knowing that nobody was listening or judging her. Secondly, if Liz thought it would be useful, they could go over some coping strategies. These were things that Liz could do on her own if she ever felt anxious or just struggled with daily life. They talked generally about Liz's life. Her upbringing and her running and then about the party and what Liz thought had happened. About showering and what she had found, and the visit to the police station.

When Liz spoke about dancing at the party and drinking glühwein, she said, "I feel so stupid now. That isn't really me, I was just showing off," and Isabella said, "We've all been there, it's what makes us human."

When she began to talk about going upstairs, she said, "I just can't remember; I know I needed the loo, and I can remember heading for the stairs. The next thing I know I was waiting outside the toilet as there was a queue, and I was leaning up against the wall. It's so weird, the more I try to remember, the harder it is."

"That's actually quite normal, people often don't remember things after alcohol but sometimes things come back in flashes, usually when you are just daydreaming. The key is not to try too hard."

Liz wasn't really used to not trying hard. Her exams at school, her running, all the things she did, she tried hard and did well. Her parents had always told her to 'do her best'; she had equated this with trying hard. She thought she would have to work at not trying hard now.

Throughout their chat Isabella asked how Liz had felt in each situation and encouraged her to express her feelings. Liz thought she was doing well. Sometimes she would stop, and Isabella would just wait for Liz to fill the silence. When she was asked to describe what happened in the shower, she began to speak but her throat became constricted, and she dried up. She had no words for how she felt. The physical discovery and mental realisation of what had happened was too much. She broke down into silent tears. She couldn't even make a sound.

"I did this to myself," she said. "I spoiled everything. I let my parents down, I could have got pregnant. I've ruined my life. Just because I wanted to fit in."

Isabella just listened.

Liz sniffed up some tears and said, "I should never have gone to the party. My dad always told me to stand up for myself, not to be swayed by others and led to do things I didn't really want to do."

Isabella was looking down at her hands, just listening.

"Oh God, what have I done? I've been so stupid," Liz said in a whisper. "I just want to go home. I'll quit uni and go home."

Isabella looked up and fixed her eyes on Liz. Liz looked, not knowing whether she was expected to speak or not. She felt raw and exposed.

Isabella said in a calm voice while looking Liz straight in the eyes, "Why are you raping yourself?"

Liz went cold. All the blood drained from her face, and she felt the sweat evaporate from her forehead, and a bead of sweat ran down from her armpit.

She looked at Isabella and said, "I... but... I'm not."

"The physical act of rape does not exist outside that bedroom at the party. Everything which has happened since then you are doing to yourself. You are not guilty of anything, and you have not failed in any way. But you are responsible. You are in control, and you have to decide. Will you keep torturing yourself, or will you move on. Only you can make that decision. It will take strength and determination. Liz the runner doesn't give up, does she. She keeps going. Through the cold and the rain. Through the mud and up the hills. When your lungs are bursting and your chest feels like it will explode, you keep going. Take that strength, Liz, and use it now. Only you can do this."

7

Stuck

Liz was lying on the floor of her uni room. It was 10pm and she had been at the library for four hours, head down, laptop on, beavering away. She had placed a folded towel beneath her head and had her dressing gown draped over her to keep warm. She was practising a mindfulness technique which Isabella had taught her, and she had said if Liz practised it before bed, it might help her sleep. This was good because Liz was having trouble getting to sleep. Her mind would wander back to the party and would churn away, stubbornly refusing to switch off. What if she hadn't drunk from the can, how did she get from the landing to the bedroom, why couldn't she remember. She had the words of a pop song going through her head. Something about whispers in her head. Liz felt like that. Things she couldn't quite reach, voices she couldn't make out. She was using a technique called progressive relaxation. She liked the name as it reminded her of the boys at school who were into old progressive rock, listening to Hawkwind and Jethro Tull. She hadn't really liked it but used to find the boys funny when they danced at the school disco shaking their heads around. Starting with tightening muscles and then releasing them, she flexed her feet up to feel tension in her shins and then pointed her feet down to feel her calves. The aim was to tense the muscles hard and then let go so they felt warm and heavy. She went through her body: thighs, bum, tummy, shoulders, arms, neck, and face. Each time, tighten hard and release quickly, tighten and release. The idea was for the body to relax, so the mind would follow. That was the idea, but she kept fidgeting. She could feel rough bits in the carpet and her tailbone pressing against the hard floor. Eventually she got comfortable, only to begin noticing sounds around the student residence. A door closing, someone's stereo with a bass note booming away, two people outside shouting to each other, "See you tomorrow. I'm not in tomorrow but I'll catch you Thursday." She thought she recognised one of the male voices as a boy who often sat on a table opposite when she sometimes ate a sandwich for lunch in the coffee shop near the library.

Dropping the muscle-tightening method, she switched to another technique Isabella had shown her. She had been sitting in one of the comfy chairs at the SARC centre and Isabella got her to close her eyes and listen to sounds. Initially, she had heard only things close by. A door opening, a hospital trolley being pushed along a corridor, and a phone ringing. But the more she practised, the more she heard. A bus pulling up outside the hospital. A child crying, a dog barking. Isabella had said this technique drew her focus away from herself towards the outside world and would help her to break the cycle of self-focus and criticism. She had to admit that she no longer noticed her aches and pains, so perhaps it was doing something. After five minutes she decided to go to bed. Having washed her face and cleaned her teeth, she sank into bed and did feel more relaxed. She lay there listening to sounds around the hall of residence and drifted off.

She woke in the middle of the night after a dream. She was saying, no, no, no, to the boy on the table in the coffee shop who was trying to kiss her when she was eating her sandwich. He said, you're just boring, that's why nobody likes you, and the people in the coffee shop had all turned around and were laughing at her and shouting prude, prude, prude! As she opened her eyes and sat up, the hall was quiet and still. She liked the stillness and felt secure knowing that everyone was sleeping. She got up and had a drink of water and went back to bed, trying to get back to sleep. It was no good – she just lay there and eventually got up and switched her laptop on.

***

Liz found it difficult to socialise since the freshers' party. She would see people in lectures and tutorials, and whilst civil, she turned down any offers to socialise. She felt more comfortable by herself in the library or her room. She still attended sessions with Isabella, her councillor at the SARC centre, and was now learning techniques Isabella called coping strategies. She learnt relaxation techniques and mindfulness, and each week Isabella would get her to agree on some action to perform which would take her outside her comfort zone.

Whilst she would engage in these and thought she was making some progress, she still had setbacks. In the days following the rape it had all been physical. Tests in the hospital and outward signs on her body which she had still felt in the shower. As these faded, however, they had been replaced by inward trauma. She would wake in the middle of the night for no reason and just lie there staring into the darkness. She practised a body-scan technique she had learnt from Isabella where she became aware of different parts of her body. She would focus on the feeling of her quilt on her feet, or the difference between her legs if one was turned differently to the other. Moving up her body, she noticed the contrast in pressure between sides when she was turned and would tense and release her arm muscles and then wriggle each finger in turn, noticing the positions each rested in when she stopped.

Sometimes in lectures she would notice her mind wandering back to the party and would cringe at the thought of dancing or drinking. The smell of alcohol, even on someone's breath if they had been drinking the night before could make her mouth fill with saliva and her heart race. Once she was so affected that she got up and rushed out of a lecture, causing the tutor to send someone after her to make sure she was OK.

At the end of the first term Liz went home for the Christmas vacation, as most people did, and the university halls became a bit of a *Mary Celeste*. She was travelling back home by train, and everyone else was too, it seemed. When she arrived at Leeds Station, it was packed. There was a sea of students with cases and bags of every colour, shape, and size. There were even potted plants and the occasional cuddly toy poking its head out of a rucksack. When her train arrived, it was a bit of a struggle getting on and finding a seat, but she managed and was actually able to put her rucksack on an overhead rack, which was virtually unheard of. She took a window seat of a table for four facing the direction of travel which she preferred. Travelling backwards always made her feel a bit queasy. She sat next to a boy she had seen around uni; he was in his final year, she thought, studying something in the business school. The two girls opposite obviously knew each other but she had not seen them before. They both smiled and said hi, then one put her headphones on and the other started to read a textbook. Liz settled down to read her running magazine, assuming the boy would be a non-communicative male, which he was. She just prayed he didn't fall asleep and begin leaning on her.

After reading for a while, she looked out of the window, seeing a patchwork of green fields flashing by, and wondered what would have changed back home. It had only been a couple of months, but a lot had changed for her. As she looked out, her mind wandered back to the last summer at home.

She had worked in the local superstore and remembered feeling so free. She had her grades and didn't have to think about any more school exams. It had felt so liberating. On one occasion they had run a charity event. She had worn a squirrel costume and walked around the store with another girl dressed as a hazelnut, both of them carrying buckets for people to throw coins into. It seemed so distant and surreal now. She had started with three others and wondered what they were all doing; one had been going to Nottingham uni, and one to Bristol. The boy was going in the army, she thought, and she wondered if he was now an officer and a gentleman. What things would have happened in their lives in the intervening months. She knew what had happened in hers, and never in a million years would she have imagined it when she was working in that superstore. It had all been talk about holidays, what their uni accommodation would be like, and who they would meet. Nobody imagined a drunken girl at a party being raped, and why should they. In the world she had been brought up in, these things never happened. Her life up until that point had been covered in snowflakes and icing sugar. Well, not now. She had nightmares, day shivers, rapid breathing, and silent tears. She was trying, she really was. She used all the techniques that Isabella had given her and occasionally she forgot about the rape. Then it would come back. It was like a lead weight pulling her down, stopping her moving forwards. Its very presence haunted her every thought, taunting her. Stupid girl, loser, drunk, victim – these were the words which kept floating into her mind.

"Do you want a Jaffa cake?"

Liz looked up to see one of the girls opposite proffering the open end of a packet.

"Oh thanks. I can't resist chocolate."

"Yes, me too. Bit of a chocoholic."

"I'm Kate, by the way, and this is Marie-Anne. Are you at the poly?"

"No, uni for my sins. Studying sports science."

"I'm on an art and design HND and Marie-Anne is fashion."

All three of them chatted for a while and Liz couldn't help thinking how normal it all seemed. But, at the back of her mind, she felt she had a hidden secret, a lie which she was hiding from people. She wanted to stand on the table and shout "I was raped at a party" to get it out of her system.

The train called into Cheltenham Spa and the two girls got off, exchanging cheerful goodbyes with Liz and ignoring the boy next to her. She dosed for a while, coming round almost an hour later as the announcement for the next station came over the tannoy. As the train pulled into the station, she waited for the boy next to her to stand up and move into the aisle. As she reached up to the overhead rack for her bag, he said, "Do you want a lift with that?"

She was so surprised that he had spoken for the first time in four hours that initially she just looked at him in mild shock.

"Oh, yes, thanks," she said.

He lifted her bag down, placing it on the table, smiled, and walked away. She looked at his back as she went, noting that he had broad shoulders and nice hair and wondered about him. Who was he, someone's boyfriend, brother, or son, she thought. What was he studying and where would his life take him? Passing like ships in the night, her father would say, and she felt slightly guilty that neither she nor the other girls had taken the trouble to find out anything about him. She made a mental note to talk to everyone around her on the return trip back to uni.

She stood in the aisle as part of a pack of expectant students at the end of the carriage waiting for the door to open. As she shuffled forwards and through the open door, she saw her father standing on the platform and smiling. She wanted to burst into tears, and her mind flashed back to when he used to pick her up from Brownies. Always there with the other dads, her rock and her guide. She wanted to tell him everything but knew it would hurt him so much that she could not.

8

Student union bar

Liz hated the student bar. No, hated was perhaps too strong a word. She disliked it intensely. Its old wooden floor was always sticky as you walked over it, making an annoying sucking sound as it clung to your shoes. It was either the spilled beer in the evenings or floor cleaner in the mornings. You had to choose your seat carefully. Some chairs had wobbly legs, which would jerk you unexpectedly and make you spill your drink, while others had torn seats which caught on your clothing. Her new black tights (bought especially for the end-of-year prize-giving ceremony) had lasted all of ten minutes before being laddered. She had to keep pulling her skirt down, and when she stood for a while, she held her programme behind her with both hands, casually covering the damage. On busy days you had to fight to get to the bar for a drink which she often didn't want but felt she should be seen to be drinking. She normally had sparkling mineral water anyway, and resented paying for something she could simply get out of the tap. It always amazed her how dingy it could be compared to the toastie bar next door, which, while in the same building, managed to be bright and inviting. She thought the smell of herby bread and feta cheese vastly superior to the stale beer of the union bar. She helped out there and it was the only social gathering she was genuinely happy with.

Suzanne, on the other hand, thought of the student bar as her second home. To her, it was warm and full of friends. Chatty students, familiar tables, and comfy chairs exuding memories of good times. In freshers' week she had met Dawn and Ellie, and they had turned out to be the best drinking partners, laughing partners, and weepy-film partners. She had met Manni here, and he had turned out to be, well, the best so far anyway. They had been together for six months and had done a lot of mutual growing up before drifting apart. Yes, the student bar was the hub around which her life revolved. In the first year she had made many friends; at the start of the second year she had tried to lose some, and now she was in a smaller, more elite set, but each time the student bar had been the canvas upon which she had painted her life. She read all the notices on the board, came to quiz nights with a small crowd of mates and went to every group, solo artist, or stand-up they offered. She even served behind the bar occasionally if they needed cover, and she was now a dab hand at pulling pints and working an optic.

Liz and Suzanne had become great friends but respected their different interests. Suzanne was a party girl, but money limited her partying ability, so the cheaper student bar was a godsend to her. Liz hated alcohol. The taste, the smell, and above all, the effect. Ever since the infamous party in her first term, whenever possible she avoided any social activities based around drinking. She was a runner and had been since schooldays. Her social life revolved around the university Harriers club, and whilst some of the Harriers finished training by having a few pints, her group was full of what was generally described as health nuts. One of the girls, ably assisted by her slightly less-willing boyfriend, made flapjacks and protein balls which she sold at the club, and another would cook wholemeal bread at home and bring the loaves in for club members. Liz herself was quite a good cook. She had a well-thumbed vegetarian cookbook, and, together with Tracey, who had been on her corridor in first year, she would make veggie stews, curries, spaghetti bolognaise using soya mince, and tofu stir-fry. The two girls would double up on the cooking and generally make a meal which lasted for two days. Occasionally they would eat in the university canteen, but the veggie choice was a bit limited. You either had cauliflower cheese, veggie lasagne, or a veggie burger. The cauliflower was normally overcooked and paired with stringy cheese, the lasagne a bit cardboard-like. The burger had a slightly odd taste, but they never found out why. Originally, they thought it was the ingredients, frozen onions, or dodgy chickpeas, perhaps. Then they decided it was the preparation. Perhaps the burger press was either dirty or had been cleaned with a strong bleach, or was it the cooking? Generally, the veggie burger was only eaten in extremis – you had to be pretty hungry and have used up most of your student grant for a university veggie burger to be your choice. When mentioned away from the canteen, the words 'veggie burger' would be accompanied by crossed fingers held up to the person daring to say the words.

Liz, Suzanne, Tracey, and big Dave now shared a house in their second year. The three girls had all met in Trentfield Hall and big Dave had gravitated towards them on bonfire night of the first term. He was, as his nickname would suggest, huge. Weighing in at 17 stone, Dave liked his beer and required a considerable amount of food to soak it up. Looking at him, most boys in uni would avoid walking in his path. He exuded menace and had the weight to back it up. However, beneath his copious exterior, a timid pussycat was to be found. On the bonfire night in question, he had arrived with two lads, and they were all drinking home brew from a large plastic container. The girls got chatting to the boys and gradually it became obvious that big Dave was frightened of fireworks. This was noticed slowly as he held back slightly at the start of the display, and when the loud bangs and crackles occurred, he would take a sudden in-breath and utter a single expletive. Although the word used was different each time (he had an extensive vocabulary of swear words), the effect was the same. Liz and Suzanne looked at each other with a slight frown and one of the boys confirmed their suspicions.

"Dave's a bit of a wuss when it comes to fireworks. Something to do with a friend putting one in a pocket when he was nine and needing a skin graft."

"Yeah," said the other, "but he hates spiders as well."

"True, there is that."

Towards the end of the evening, big Dave was standing next to Liz (she appearing to be the most responsible and also the tallest) and the two boys were chatting to Suzanne and Tracey.

When it came to house sharing, they had invited big Dave partly because they thought he would be an asset if they ever had a break-in, but also because he was left on his own when the four-bed house the boys were going for was taken and they had to settle for a three-bed on a short street at the top of a hill. The general (but unspoken) opinion was that big Dave would not be able to make the walk after a good night out and they couldn't carry him home, even between the three of them. The girls felt sorry for him, and Liz thought he looked like a big teddy bear she had once seen in a toyshop window when she was thirteen.

***

Liz was heading back from her lecture but was going via the student union to drop her essay off for Suzanne. Although it was not a subject Suzanne studied, the essay format was similar, and Suzanne had asked if she could take a look to know what good science format was. The essay talked about the PICO format, which she had explained to Suzanne stands for problem, intervention, comparison, and outcome, and Liz was surprised that Suzanne's tutor hadn't mentioned this.

"No one has mentioned PICO to me, I'm sure," said Suzanne.

"Don't give me that, they must have done. Bet you were away with the fairies again!"

"We had a lecture in geology about hypothesis and writing a literature review, but I'm sure they didn't cover PICO."

"Oh, well. That's why sports scientists are a superior race, I suppose!"

"Get off! Do you want a drink while you're here?"

"Go on then, just a sparkling mineral water for me, as I've got an early training session in the morning."

Liz trained with a small group of Harriers who had a penchant for starting at 7am when the air was cleaner. She watched as Suzanne headed to the bar and diverted to chat to two girls she did not really know. Liz was always amazed at how easily Suzanne could talk to people. Since the party in her first term Liz had withdrawn a bit socially. She focused on her studies and mostly went to Harriers' training sessions and a few spin-offs from that. In the back of her mind there was always a thought, just out of reach. What if it happens again?

She studied the bar mat on her table, trying to avoid making eye contact with anyone who thought drinking at this hour was a sensible idea.

"Not seen you here before, don't you run with the uni Harriers?"

Liz looked up to see a very gangly male with limp hair and a slightly sideways smile wearing a *Star Trek* T-shirt.

"I'm Graham, by the way," and he offered his hand.

"I'm Liz," she said, feeling her face burning red.

She suddenly realised she was staring and rushed to shake his hand before it was too obvious. His hand was warm, as was his smile. Something began to awaken deep within her. A feeling which had been suppressed for over two years. That thing which had nearly died in a bedroom at a party in a small suburban house found in a leafy suburb a bus ride away.

As Suzanne headed to the bar to get the drinks, the thought ran through her head that anyone who would want to get up early in the morning to run must be slightly barmy. What was wrong with the girl. The pleasure of a morning snug bed was too tempting, especially if there was a male to wake up to. She saw Dawn and Ellie at a table on the left of the bar and remembered the last time she had seen Ellie she was standing in a fountain with a traffic cone on her head while Dawn and her friends took a polaroid photo. It was still up in Ellie's bedroom.

"Hi, cone head!"

"Oh, come on, it was just one time!"

"Yeah, the other time you were sitting on a guy's face," said Dawn.

All three girls burst out laughing and Suzanne went to the bar.

Her thoughts cycled round to Liz again. The good thing about Liz was that she was reliable, if a little dull. She would never call her that to her face, but she thought it was true, nonetheless. Suzanne had lots of friends she could go drinking with and a few she could even show her parents. But Liz was a worker and an achiever. She had few friends, but Suzanne quite liked her. Liz was into *Star Trek* and Suzanne often thought of her as a female Mr Spock. Serious and unconcerned about what people thought, she just wanted to get the best grades. Her essays were always in first, her notes were perfectly neat and filed, and her room in halls in the first year had been just on the brighter side of dull. A few posters and dried grasses like most, but somehow it just missed the mark. After the first-year party that Suzanne still felt guilty about, she never thought that anything had happened or would happen in Liz's room, but Liz gave Suzanne a bit of comforting stability in her life. Liz had mentioned PICO format for science essays which Suzanne remembered they had covered, but she had not noted down what it meant, so she simply told Liz they hadn't covered it and got her to explain. Liz had offered to show her an essay she had written using the format. There was a brief twang of conscience in her mind at using her like this, but she really left herself open to it. Law of the jungle, thought Suzanne, the stronger shall prevail.

As she returned, she noticed Liz chatting to a guy which surprised her. So, Miss Spock can go fishing, she thought. I must keep an eye on her, don't want to lose my prodigy.

***

"I think I've seen you at a couple of training sessions. You are always at the front while I am at the back! I can't make the Tuesday evening runs but get to the Sunday one if I can," Graham said.

"Yeah, I try to make both if I can but sometimes have to miss if I have too much work," Liz replied.

"I'm just running for fitness really, what about you?"

"I'm mainly cross-country in the winter and 10k in the summer," said Liz. "Do a bit of gym work too if I can."

"Is that at the uni sports centre or the council one in Broadmore Street?"

"No, the uni one, it's cheaper!"

"Tell me about it. On the plus side, Broadmore Street has a sauna and steam room. It's a bit shabby but good in the winter, especially."

"I have to confess I've never been in a sauna but do like to use weights occasionally."

"I'm never sure what to do to be honest," said Graham. "I went once and there were a load of bodybuilders and rugby players there lifting massive weights. As you can see, I'm not really built for that."

Graham stood back and struck a pose, flexing his arm. Liz noticed there was very little muscle, but she quite liked his forearms, which had fine hairs on them, and he had long fingers. She hated men who had short, stubby fingers and dirty nails.

"Are you going to the Harriers' training session on Sunday morning?" Graham asked. "If you are, I'll see you there."

Liz did a quick double take – was he asking if she was going, in which case he would see her (together with everyone else), or was he hoping she was going, as he would like to see her. She was never confident talking to men socially ever since the first term. At this thought, a cascade of mental images passed like the pages of a flipbook. Hospital, tests, guilt, and lots of crying. She had met plenty of boys in lectures and tutorials, but they were study buddies, not boyfriend material. Graham had potential, she thought. Suzanne arrived with her drink.

"Hi," she said to Graham.

Graham smiled and said, "Hello, I'm just chatting up your mate."

"Is that because she's gorgeous or do you two have lectures together?"

"Running club," he said.

"Ah, you're a Harrier jump jet as well, are you?"

Graham laughed, "No, I'm more an *Enterprise*," he said, puffing out his chest and showing his T-shirt.

"I've got to go," he said, finishing his drink. "Meeting a guy about a computer drive."

"See you Sunday," he said to Liz, "providing I can keep up!"

"Live long and prosper," said Liz.

He returned a Vulcan salute, raising his hand, palm forwards and parted between the middle and ring finger. There was silence for a short while as Suzanne gave Liz a prolonged look.

"What?" she said.

"Should I get you two a room?"

Liz smiled gently and said nothing, being aware that she was probably turning slightly pink. Perhaps the union bar wasn't so bad after all.

9

Moving on

Liz was working her shift in the toastie bar. When she returned from the holidays, she was able to look at things slightly differently. She went home and her bedroom seemed smaller somehow. Everything was just as she had left it, and all her childhood possessions were reassuring to her, but they seemed distant now. Things from a previous life, fond memories of something she could never get back. Although she had only been away from home for a few months, it seemed a lot longer, as her life had leapt forwards. She had gone on her favourite runs and met up with a few old friends. This, combined with the distance from uni, had diluted the effect of what had happened at the party. She had returned determined to move forwards and pull herself out of the rut of depression she had been in at the end of the last term.

She did not feel like socialising by going out, but equally did not want to stay in and be a recluse either.

She could hear her mother's voice, "Idle hands are the devil's workshop." This was normally a precursor for being given jobs around the house, but she recognised now that it had been a distraction to stop her worrying about her grades at GCSE. Distraction was what she had needed, and volunteering to serve on the toastie bar had been a saviour to her, and she had helped out there ever since. She stacked the panini bread, putting the focaccia separate to the ciabatta and baguettes. She loved the smell of the focaccia as little sprigs of rosemary fell off when she brushed the surface of the bread against the box they came in and the smell drifted up to her nostrils. The bread was displayed in an ancient glass-fronted cabinet which had to be cleaned until it sparkled, or Joan would "tut" at you. Joan was the only paid member of staff and had been manager to several generations of students. Liz closed the glass door with a satisfying thud as the heavy metal rim struck the perished and flaking rubber seal around the cabinet.

She then checked the fillings: cheese slices, ham, cream cheese, bacon bits, and sausage halves. The bacon and sausage were frozen and had to be defrosted in an old clockwork dial microwave at the beginning of shift. She loved the way it whirred and lit up as its clanking turntable struggled to revolve. If successful, it gave an old-time "ping" when finished, reminding her of the doorbell in the corner shop near her parents' home. The confectionary consisted largely of bars which were intended to be eaten separately but would often take leading roles in bizarre requests from students seeking to impress their mates.

Bacon and Mars bar, and cream cheese with smarties being two notable recent requests. As she called out the hot and ready panini, such recipes would be greeted with a cheer and raucous clapping and foot stamping as the person who had ordered bit into the delicacy. The resulting facial expression recorded for posterity on a polaroid.

It was quiet tonight, with two female students sitting in a corner working, files open on the table in front of them, drinking coffee. They shared a mozzarella and tomato toastie and were now wiping one of their files with a paper tissue, having dropped a soggy tomato slice on it which had splattered impressively.

"Hi, girlie, how's things?"

Liz looked up to see Suzanne smiling accompanied by Tracey.

"All OK here, pretty quiet. You eating or passing?"

"I think I'll spoil myself and have a coffee."

"Big spender then."

"Always."

"And for you, Tracey, can I tempt you to a bacon and Mars bar toastie – guaranteed to make you retch?"

"Do people really eat that?"

"They do, it's a boy's thing mostly. Bless them."

Tracey screwed up her face.

"No thanks, I'm on a coffee as well."

As Liz poured the two coffees, Suzanne said, "So, have you seen young Graham again yet?"

"No, running club on Sunday."

"Good to test him out then," said Suzanne.

"Bit of stamina is always a good thing."

Tracey and Suzanne smiled at each other.

"I shall ignore that," said Liz, who continued to clean the work surface, smiling inwardly to herself.

***

Liz was in the uni weights gym. She tried to get in twice a week if she could. It gave her an upper-body workout to balance her running which was predominantly lower body. Also, she found it quite nice to be exercising alone – it gave her time to think and sort things out in her head. She liked to start on the rowing machine as a whole-body warm-up, and then go on to the seated chest press followed by the seated row. The combination of pushing and pulling gave her the work on her arms, shoulders, and chest that she thought she needed. She then did some dumbbell lateral raises because she thought her shoulders were a little narrow, and finished off with some crunches, with a view to building something of a six-pack. Although her running kept her lean and her stomach flat, she had seen one of the girls in the changing room with well-defined abs and thought it was quite a good look.

The only problem with working out alone was you often got a rugby player who would try to mansplain something to you. Why men assumed they knew more about weight training than women was puzzling to her. They mostly focused on bodybuilding, ending up looking like a Michelin man with no general fitness. Not a good look, in her opinion. As she exercised, she thought how she was more comfortable around men now. She wasn't sure when this had happened, gradually she supposed, but it struck her now that a few months ago she would have felt nervous around men who came physically close to her, but not anymore.

The seated chest press had a wonky weight block which tipped to one side and rubbed, giving the machine a jerky action. It was fine pushing, but as you lowered the weight it would often stick, only to clatter down at the last moment. Normally, this would cause another gym user to look at you with an accusatory expression on their face. Liz wanted to scream, "It's the bloody machine, not me," but she stayed silent and looked at the floor or sometimes stared at the accuser with her well-practised game face on.

Another girl came in the gym and said hi to Liz. She started stretching and then went on one of the spin bikes. A lad came in next and started chatting to the girl. Boyfriend or mate, thought Liz. He started on the leg press, making the rookie error of putting the pin in too low, only to realise that he could not move the weights at all and so had to reposition the pin twice until he found the right weight. Lost your cred there, mate, thought Liz.

Being a runner, Liz had strong legs and liked to use the leg press to build some more strength. However, she knew that she could lift considerably more than the boy who was now getting off the machine to join his girlfriend, or mate, on the bike. Liz didn't want to go onto the machine and either show him up or appear to be showing off, but did not want to lose her chance to use the machine if someone else jumped on it. She decided to use it anyway and kept her eyes firmly on the machine as she lifted twice the weight the boy had. She wasn't sure if he was looking or not.

Finishing off with a few stretches, Liz left the gym and got a shower. She loved the showers in the sports centre. They were one of the best bits of the workout. Hot, powerful, and much better than the dribbly one they had in her shared house.

The girl from the gym came in as Liz was towelling herself dry. Liz had never had a problem with nudity and although she didn't walk around naked all the time, thought covering up in a changing room was a bit too much. The girl from the gym wrapped a towel around herself and then got undressed by pulling her clothes off below the towel with great difficulty. Liz never understood this fear of being seen naked. Odd, she thought.

As she walked home, Liz had a silent discussion with herself, as she often did:

I'm not really a virgin, well, I sort of am. I haven't been with a boy consciously. I was raped, so I'm not a virgin, but I didn't choose to sleep with someone, so I am. Is virginity mental or physical, she wondered. A bit of both, she supposed.

Graham seemed quite a nice bloke, better than the guys in the weights gym. I know Suzanne thinks tough and muscly is the way to go, but I quite like geeky. I find boys who are a bit geeky more interesting. They have stuff to say rather than just grunting and flexing their muscles.

Would I sleep with a boy? she wondered.

Probably yes, if he was nice and I got to know him. I think I'm over the rape thing now as best as I can be. It will always be there, but the counselling helped, and it's been some time. Things move on, Dad always says, and he is right.

Time is a great healer, I once read. I wonder how much time is needed, though. I mean does a little time heal a bit or is there a cut-off point. Too little time and you haven't reached the level where healing begins. And what about too much time, can you get past the time when healing is possible? If I waited years to sleep with a boy, would I be any further healed from the rape, or would I just end up sad and alone.

She saw a girl and guy arm in arm approaching her from the other direction. I want that, she thought.

"Hi," said the girl as they passed, and she smiled at Liz.

"Hi," Liz replied. She looks happy, she thought. It must be nice to have someone to put their arm around you. A warm, cosy, and protected sort of feeling.

10

Liz & Graham

On the Sunday Harriers run, two people were thinking of things other than running. Liz was thinking shall I slow down to be closer to Graham, but thought it was so against her nature to give even an inch during a run that this was unlikely. Graham was thinking should he make eye contact, and if he did, what should he say? Should it be hi, good to see you, or should he make a *Star Trek* comment, which he thought might be overdoing it. On the other hand, would this all be too much and should he just smile and raise his eyebrows?

When the run started, Liz was in her small group leading the bunch. From an early age, Liz had always run fast to begin (she called it kicking for the front) to avoid getting trapped behind slower runners. She had had to tone this down a bit on Harriers' training runs and remind herself that they were for fun and not competitive. Liz always found putting the words run and non-competitive together difficult. Since school, running had always been her way to have a win. She could run faster and further than anyone who bullied her, or her friends. Because she won things, normally house points at school or medals, she was popular in a limited way with the cool kids. They would congratulate her grudgingly if she got their schoolhouse points, but then ignore her the rest of the time. Running always held a special part of her soul. If someone said something nasty to her, she would ignore it and think to herself, yes, but I can outrun you. Since the rape at the freshers' party, running had been her constant companion. Even during her darkest days, she would go for a run and begin to feel better. In those first days she had run in the wind and rain, in the early-morning mist, and sometimes even before sunrise, when she would wear a head torch. She knew everyone in her hall thought she was mad, but it had helped. It was something deeply personal to her, almost spiritual. A way of centring herself and connecting to something magical.

Liz maintained her normal pace, matching her stride leg for leg with Martha, the only other person who could match her. Martha and Liz never saw or spoke to each other outside running. In fact, they rarely communicated with words during training sessions but would use facial expressions, single words, and occasional grunts to pair up when you required a partner for stretching or sprint drills and would often check that the other person was going when competitions came around. Outside training sessions, the only communication would be messages about kit, often written on scraps of paper and slipped under the other's door. If one found a local running shop with an offer on shoes, tights, socks, sports bras, headbands, the other would know later in the day. Years later, they found each other again on social media and revived this process, posting each other messages about the best kit offers found on running websites. Kit buddy, they called each other.

Graham began the run in his normal place at the back of the group. He was faster than a couple of others who had just joined, also those who were running to lose weight and just jogged along chatting. He tried a bit harder today, moving up the group by lengthening his stride but found it hard. He could feel his lungs burn, and towards the second half of the run, got a stitch. He kept going and when he finished, gasping to breathe, he kept looking down in case Liz saw him in this state. After a couple of minutes, people were chatting and he saw Liz in the distance to his left, talking to a couple of girls. For a moment he just looked at her. Tall, lean, and fit, with toned legs enclosed in black running tights. She had light sweat glistening on her bare arms and her hair was tied back. She looked brilliant, he thought, and wondered if she wasn't just too good for him. Digging deep to raise his courage, he gradually made his way through the group, saying hello and exchanging a few words as he went to make sure his movements were not too obvious.

Liz saw a tall, gangly male who looked exhausted moving towards her, and her heart missed a beat. He was here. She hadn't seen him, and so throughout the run had wondered if he had come. She hoped he had but wondered if she had misread the situation. Perhaps he was generally chatty and was simply being friendly in the union bar. After all, he had spoken to Suzanne as well. Was he moving towards her, or was he simply coming this way anyway? She wasn't sure whether to look at him or not. If she looked and he wasn't really interested she would feel stupid. No, she thought, he was definitely heading for her. He made eye contact, and she couldn't stop herself. She had no control, her body responded by itself, and she smiled, feeling a glow inside her. She went to a yoga class once where the instructor had talked about igniting the female energy. She felt a flame flicker inside, and a warmth spread outward. Everything was tingling. He reached her, smiled, and said, "Hi, I found that run a bit tough."

She felt an odd wobble coming over her, but pulled herself out of it to say, "Yes, it can be, but you did it, that's what counts." She noticed his red face and a small tuft of unshaven hair on his chin.

"It was the fast group at the front who pushed the pace, I think."

He really was a nice guy, she thought!

"Yeah, we're natural leaders, you know."

"Fancy a drink or coffee or something?"

I do, but let's be cool. Don't look overenthusiastic, Liz told herself.

"Yes, OK. How about the coffee shop by the library?"

"Sounds great. They do good flapjacks. I need a flapjack." Liz knew there were two ways to a man's heart. She was happy that she had achieved the first but was dreading the second.

They set off together, at first part of a general bunch of sweaty runners, but as people peeled off in different directions, they were left as a pair. They took a corner table in the coffee shop, each with a drink and flapjack.

As they sat down and Graham bent forwards towards Liz, he caught an intoxicating mix of fresh female sweat, moisturiser, and washed skin, and thought it was the best smell he had ever known. If he was honest with himself, he hadn't done too well on the girlfriend front. He had come straight from school to university and was surprised to find he was quite innocent compared to some of the others. There were people from public school who had holidays in far-off places, a few who had lived abroad, and others who had taken a year off before uni to travel. Then there was the sporty crowd who were bigger than him and often sported designer stubble, when he only needed to shave about every three days. In his first year in hall, he was convinced he was the only one on his corridor who was still a virgin. This situation had been rectified by Paula in his first term. She had been six months older than him and considerably more experienced in every aspect of life. She knew which clubs to go to, drank drinks he had never heard of, and regularly played squash. She had initiated him in all things sexual, almost going through a tick list of techniques and positions. Eventually he realised that although the sex was quite good, he found her shallow, and they did not share any interests. Also, he found her a bit crude and embarrassing when she drank heavily, and she often did. She had gin and vodka in her room and would normally have shorts when he would stick to half pints. Eventually they drifted apart, and she went with a squash player who was in his third year studying medicine. Years later, he was to learn through social media that she had been prosecuted for drink-driving several times and had eventually died when she lost control of her soft-top sports car on the bend of a country road in heavy rain and hit a tree.

Liz always found personal stuff with men a bit difficult. She was fine with men in a non-personal situation. In lectures, or even out training. But since the party, a barrier always seemed to come up. When she had gone home for the Christmas holidays, she had met up with a girlfriend from school and in turn they had met some boys she had known since she was about twelve. This had been deliberate on her behalf because she knew she now found it difficult being relaxed around boys socially and had assumed that as these boys had been like brothers to her, it would be OK. She had hoped it would help to pull her out of herself. It hadn't worked. One of the boys had given her a hug when they met and she had frozen, going slightly dizzy, her heart rate racing. He had asked if she was OK, and she had brushed it off, saying she was recovering from a stomach bug.

"So, tell me all," Graham said, breaking her daydream. "Where are you from, how did you get into running, what are you studying and do you have a cat called Nigel."

"Bath, at school, sports science, and no cat. Don't tell me, you only like girls with cats."

"No, I can take or leave cats, to be honest. Now, if you have a big friendly dog, that would be a mark in your favour."

"I have a black Labrador called Felix, who I run with at home, if that counts."

"I love you already."

"Steady on, I haven't even started my flapjack!"

They both laughed which broke whatever ice was remaining, and Graham thought, this girl is perfect. Liz, for her part, was enjoying how easy she found it to talk to Graham. So far, she hadn't freaked out and her heart rate was normal. She kept staring at his long fingers as he played with his teaspoon, wondering why the fingernails on his right hand were longer than those on his left.

***

The next time they met it was in the gym of the university sports centre. This had been Liz's idea and Graham had agreed, wanting to appear keen but had his reservations. It had occurred to him that although it would be good to work out with Liz, especially if she was wearing shorts and displaying her bare long legs, she would also be able to compare his body to that of the inevitable rugby player or bodybuilder who would also be present. As it turned out, there were very few people in the gym. Two girls working out together but mostly doing stretches, and a lad who was shadow-boxing in the corner (lots of grunts).

Liz thought she would allow Graham to take the lead, as she was aware that men had delicate egos when it came to gyms. All men secretly wanted to be Arnie, and Graham most definitely was not. He chose the leg-press machine first and her heart sank. She knew she would probably be able to lift more than he could and had determined that she would always stick to a weight slightly below his. However, her plan was a damp squib as he went first and chose a weight she thought he wouldn't be able to lift. Sure enough, he couldn't move the weights at all and twice had to put the machine pin higher up in the weight stack to lighten the weights. She pretended not to notice but did not dare to lift her normal amount.

They continued their workout, chatting between sets, and Graham was happy to see that he could match or exceed the weights Liz lifted on the upper body exercises – it was only the legs where he lost out. Liz liked chatting when she was doing something, she always had. When she was young, she always felt awkward talking with someone face to face and would often reach for a toy to have in her hands. In the gym, she felt although they were both exercising, she had learnt a lot about Graham. She found out he played the classical guitar, explaining the disparity between the fingernail lengths of his hands, short for using on the fret and long for plucking the strings. She knew now that he had built his own computer after buying the components from a computer magazine and had even written a computer programme. He called this time-scribble, and it was a diary system for students which alerted the user when work was due in and gave a timetable of subjects in different colours showing the location of the lecture venue on a campus map. It also offered the ability to attach notes to each lecture and sort them using keywords which she thought was very clever. He had an older sister who had been into horse riding and broke her arm in a fall, and his father had worked abroad for two years coming home only for the Christmas holidays. After this workout, she could write an essay on the guy!

When they finished their workout, they showered and met in the sport centre coffee shop. Graham, being the first to be ready, had got the coffees. Liz had wet hair which she had put up on top of her head so she wouldn't keep him waiting for too long. Also, someone had once told her she had a nice long neck, so she hoped this was a good look. She noticed Graham's eyes flicking from hers to her neck, so thought she had achieved her aim. She noticed with approval that he had a clean T-shirt on. She had once been to the gym in a group and noticed a lad had showered and then put the same T-shirt he had been wearing to work out back on. When he had gone, Liz and the other girl she was with had both pretended to vomit.

They walked back towards university together, and then had to split up as they were heading in different directions. Liz had a lecture, and Graham was going to the library. Before they split up, Graham said, "There's a decent film on at the uni film society on Friday. Do you fancy going and grabbing a bite to eat after?"

"OK, great. We can go to that Thai place on Burnage Street which is supposed to be good. Short bus ride from uni."

"Yeah, I heard you get big portions of food there, so I'm in."

Liz smiled to herself as he walked away. What a typical male thing to say, she thought, and she loved it. Also, she had a pleasant, warm feeling inside herself, and her heart rate was still not racing. So far, so good.

***

Liz and Suzanne sat in Liz's room drinking coffee and sharing a KitKat which Suzanne had provided and was eating most of.

"So, tell me," said Suzanne, "what is it you like about Graham?"

"Well, he's got a nice personality, he's tall, intelligent, likes *Star Trek*, and makes me laugh."

"Seems reasonable, but is he good in bed?"

Liz burst out laughing and said, "Only you could have said that line, confirming that you are a disgusting brat." She dipped her finger in her tea and flicked it towards Suzanne.

"I have nothing to declare but my brat-ishness. Anyway, when are you seeing him next."

"We are going to the cinema and then having a bite to eat afterwards. What do you think I should wear?" Liz stood up and walked over to her hanging rack.

"I'm going for tight jeans and that black long sleeve T-shirt that shows off your boobs. Pair that with some nice trainers and your gold chain around your neck and you've got a sophisticated urban look which is not too intimidating but should do the job. With legs like yours, you need to either show them off in a short skirt or tight jeans, it's an unwritten law."

Liz smiled and said, "You are the best. I shall obey your law like a good girl."

"Just don't be too much of a good girl tonight," Suzanne said, putting her mug in the sink and heading for the door. "Have fun!"

Liz continued to smile after she had left, but as her smile faded, she began to wonder. It went well in the coffee shop after the run because there were lots of other people around, but how would she do one on one if things become closer. She didn't know, and in her first year she would have wanted to run and hide. But not now. Now time had gradually changed her. Isabella's techniques, which she was still using, trips home, and her work at the toasty bar had all added distance between her and the upstairs bedroom at that party. She was ready to move on, just very slowly.

***

Liz had noticed that Graham was not yet in the cinema foyer, so had slowed her pace to make sure she didn't arrive too early and have to stand around looking like a spare part. As she opened the door and was scanning the room, he arrived slightly out of breath.

"Sorry, missed my bus," he said.

She smiled. "You're forgiven."

"What's the film?"

"It's called *Cocoon*. It's sci-fi and gets great reviews."

"Sounds good, can't go wrong with a good sci fi," he said.

The cinema was quite small, and Liz recognised a few faces, while Graham had said hi to a girl in the foyer.

Before she sat down, she took her coat off and rolled it up to put behind her and pad the chair back.

"Personal cushion," she said.

She noticed Graham glance at her top as she bent down and silently thanked Suzanne for her advice. She was careful not to put her arm on the chair rest, as she didn't know yet how she would react to close male contact. The last thing she wanted was a bout of hyperventilation or to burst into tears, but so far, she felt nicely relaxed.

The film was good, and they chatted on their way to the Thai restaurant. Graham hadn't booked a table and suddenly had a bit of a panic that they would not get one. Liz remained silent, thinking typical, disorganised man. When they arrived, however, it was busy but there was only a five-minute wait, so they sat down in the small waiting area and ordered some drinks. Liz had a white wine and Graham a half pint of mild, the top of which he managed to slop on the tabletop. They both thought the idea of aliens being left on earth in the film was good and Liz liked the life-force theme. Graham thought there were probably as many things not known about the sea as there were in space, and Liz thought the whole life-force thing was similar to chi energy, which she had heard about from her yoga class. At that point, they were called to their table, and they took their drinks through. The waiter took their coats, and they sat down. As she took her coat off, Liz caught Graham's eye again flick over her top and glance at her gold chain. She noticed Graham had ironed his shirt, or at least most of it, because he had missed the bottom half of the right sleeve. She thought this was brilliant. He had made an effort, and she could imagine him carefully ironing his shirt in the kitchen of his shared house and being distracted by one of his mates. A perfectly imperfect male. Geeky, interested in running and nice. She so preferred him to the bodybuilders and rugby players she came across in the gym.

They both enjoyed the meal and shared dishes. Graham's choice was more cautious, but Liz encouraged him to try some of hers, which he quite liked. They had several dishes and set them up like a buffet, each dipping into each other's. When they finished Graham was particularly impressed with the steamed towels and mint chocolates. When the bill came, Graham said, "I'll get it."

"Not a chance," replied Liz. "Split it, I'm a modern girl."

On the bus home they both sat downstairs thinking that the upper deck was likely to be full of rowdies, and sure enough, they could hear a football chant going on. As they pulled into the third stop, a group of young lads got on who had obviously had too much to drink. The driver looked at them inquiringly and one of the lads said, "What?" in his face.

They paid their fares, and all remained standing at the front of the bus as it pulled out. Almost immediately they then began swearing generally, then started to single people out from the passengers to make fun of.

"Hey, slap head, how's it going!" they said to a middle-aged bald man sitting with his wife.

Loudly one of them said, "I'm glad I'm not that fat," and the other replied, "You mean like fatso at the back of the bus," looking at a young woman holding a sleeping child.

One of the boys looked round the bus and his eyes fell on Liz.

"Wow, what have we got here?" he said.

"She's a little darling!"

Another replied, "Love that long hair, imagine wrapping that around your member as she gives you head."

Graham stood up explosively, glowering at the boys and angling his body towards them. One of them said to his mates, "Oh, good, lads, we've got a hero, God save us."

Seeing the next scene playing out in her mind's eye, Liz said in a calm, loud voice, "It's OK, these lads have just got small penises, pimply skin, and smell like a toilet because they haven't changed their underwear in three weeks, and they miss their mums."

There was silence on the bus as the boys stared in disbelief at this crude tirade which issued from such an attractive, slim girl. The older man with a bald head said, "Hear, hear!"

Two ladies at the back started to clap and then everybody on the lower deck cheered. As the bus pulled into the next stop, the boys filed off looking like deflated seven-year-olds.

"Oh my God," said Graham. "Remind me never to pick a fight with you!"

"I learnt long ago if you don't have big hard fists, you need a very sharp tongue."

Liz felt her heart thumping so hard she thought it would burst out from her chest. The combination of alcohol, a nice man beside her and fear was making her high. Calm down, girl, she thought.

"Walk me home?" she asked.

Graham followed like a puppy as they walked towards her house. They stopped outside and Liz looked at Graham, seeing a gentle, wonderful man.

"Do you want to come in?" she asked, not knowing or caring where the evening would lead.

"Yes, alright," he said. Unfortunately, he said it far too quickly in a slightly squeaky high voice. Liz did not show she noticed but smiled inwardly. Of all the things he could have said and all the ways he could have said it, this was simply perfect.

11

Up to Liz's room

Liz punched her number code into the door lock. The code had been given to so many boyfriends and girlfriends that she wondered if it offered any security at all, but at least it was a lock. She let Graham in, and they climbed the stairs to her first-floor room. En route, they passed Tracey holding a mug of soup and a bread roll, and she said hi, giving Graham an appraising look. As they walked past, she said, "Nice!"

Liz smiled gently and Graham pretended not to notice.

Liz's room had a sign saying 'Lizzie Running' with a picture of a witch's hat mounted on running shoes. Graham frowned.

"It's from *Lizzie Dripping*, a TV show in the seventies about a young girl and a witch. Suzanne did it."

As Liz put her key in the bedroom door, she had a sudden thought. This is the first time I've been in a bedroom alone with a man since the party. She told herself, by knowing she was fully aware of what was happening, she was making a personal choice. This contrasted strongly with the last time where she was drunk, and as far as she remembered, she hadn't chosen to have sex at all. Whatever the evening was to hold from now on, she knew she was in charge. She had chosen this, it was her decision, and that gave her some control. She remembered Isabella's talk about guilt and responsibility. She hadn't been guilty of being raped but she could take responsibility for everything which happened subsequently. This put her in charge and gave her power. She turned the key in the lock, opened the door and walked in.

"Welcome to my world," she said.

Liz's room was pure Liz. Clean, neat, organised, and feminine without being girly. She had a row of running shoes lined up, just peaking out from underneath the bed, clothes on a rail, all ordered into item types, and a chest of drawers which, while being old, she had made fashionable using a piece of dark grey cloth and some red candlesticks. She noticed Graham looking around and taking everything in and wondered what his first impression would be.

"Coffee?" she said.

"Please. Actually, I don't suppose you have tea. I don't really like coffee."

"So, you mean you've been going to coffee shops and drinking cappuccino when you don't really like it?"

"Well, it's to be sociable. If it's milky, it's OK."

Liz looked at him with a surprised smile on her face and raised eyebrows. She slowly moved her head from side to side.

"Unbelievable! I have tea. I'll make it for us both. Black or green?"

"Oh God, you have green tea?"

"I do. It's Mao Feng whole leaf from China. I'll make it in the pot."

Liz reached into a drawer and produced a beautiful glass teapot with two matching handle-less teacups, as Graham's eyes followed her every move.

Having put the kettle on, she took great care unrolling a bamboo mat and placing the teapot and cups on it. She saw Graham looking on in awe, like a seven-year-old boy in a sweetshop.

"All from the Chinese supermarket next to the big Super Hong Kong restaurant in Chinatown in Manchester. Got it on a shopping trip last term and carried it back with great care on the train in a bag padded by my pullover."

"I'm impressed."

"I'm a girl of many talents." One of them is keeping my hands active to avoid my mind going into panic mode at having a boy in my room, she thought.

Graham smiled at Liz, looking directly into her eyes. For the first time, she noticed his eyes were green with little brown flecks. She matched his gaze, holding it for a few seconds and gently put her fingertip on the tip of his nose. The kettle boiled and she turned it off and poured water onto the tea leaves in the pot. Her heart was racing, and she was beginning to feel a bit light-headed.

"Now we just have to wait for a while so that things can brew," she said, and for me to get my bearings, she thought.

Liz turned round and began pouring the tea. She was quiet as she did this, taking care not to spill a drop. She was practically ceremonial in her actions and Graham responded with a respectful silence.

Liz noticed Graham's shirt, clean and ironed, with his sleeves folded halfway up his forearms and his top button undone. She thought, that is a good look, even if you are not muscly. He wore a nice pair of jeans. Probably from a department store, she thought, but they fitted well and contoured his nice bum. Slim and athletic would be the words she used. Somehow, his lack of confidence made her feel more relaxed. He was slightly shy and a little awkward in his actions, but an instinct told her he was a good person.

Inside, Liz was beginning to move into panic mode. Initially in the restaurant it had been OK, but when she brought him back to her room, she had felt a bit of a wobble. Ever since the rape in her first year, she had had problems with personal relationships, she knew that. Yes, there had been a few slow dances and the odd kiss but each time she drew back with images floating into her mind of the aftermath following that evening. She so liked Graham that she didn't want to spoil things by suddenly having a full-blown panic attack. From her meditation classes she knew to slow her breathing to calm herself, and she was now trying this as she poured the tea. Breathe in, pause, breathe out slowly. She was determined not to allow the experience of her first year to continue ruining her life. She had been raped, but she was no longer going to allow that monster to continue destroying her life. She made a promise to herself that now was the time to move forwards. In that moment, as Graham had looked into her eyes, something changed within her. A mental click, a turning of cogwheels, a primeval surge of life energy between two human animals. She could do this, she thought, and she turned and held a cup out to Graham.

"Tea is served."

12

Getting to know you

Graham shared a small terraced house with Pete and Mike on Tenbury Road. It was a three-bed, but only just. The two main bedrooms were of a normal size, but the third was a box room, meaning that it could only just accommodate a single bed. They drew lots for this when they moved in, and Pete had drawn the short straw.

The house had a TV in the lounge, together with a sagging threadbare sofa and two floor cushions. The boys had fixed the sofa by putting a piece of chipboard stolen from a local building site under the cushions. Anyone who sat down quickly on the sofa would get a firm jolt to the spine, but at least they didn't have to sit with their knees up to their chin. The presence of the TV meant the house attracted a small but differing crowd, depending on what was showing.

When the football was on, Mike and his mates would sit on the sofa and sprawl on floor cushions drinking cans of beer and eating crisps. The next day the lounge looked like a grenade had been thrown in it and Mike would grudgingly tidy it up after Graham and Pete had shouted at him.

Graham had resisted bringing Liz round, preferring to go to her room, which was always neat and tidy, and smelt nice. It had got to the stage, however, that he felt he had to invite her round to his place, or it would look like he was trying to hide something. They had both decided that tonight they would go round to his place, but he had insisted that the boys clean the house first.

After an hour's cleaning, the kitchen looked less of a biohazard, and by the time they had put the pans and dishes away and washed the sink, it was acceptable. The bathroom took a bit longer, but after a brief argument followed by a concerted effort, it was done. By the time Graham had vacuumed the carpet and opened the windows to let some fresh air in, the house looked good as new(ish).

***

Graham and Liz had been out to a new Chinese restaurant which had opened last week. Liz had been given a 25 per cent discount voucher as she was leaving the library and thought it would be good to try. Graham had told her he had eaten Chinese takeaway several times but had never been to a Chinese restaurant as such. Liz thought it would be an interesting experience as well as a nice meal, hopefully.

As they were shown to their table, Graham looked around at the décor and commented on the wooden screens separating the tables.

"It's fretwork," said Liz, "nice, isn't it?"

"Yes," he said. "Look at that one, there's a bird and some flowers."

"They used to be carved in hardwood and often told a story."

The waitress came and placed two cups down. "Green tea?"

"Yes, please," they both replied. Liz smiled at Graham and raised her eyebrows slightly.

The waitress bowed, leaving the menus.

Graham was looking for familiar dishes while Liz wanted to try something new. Liz ended up with tofu in black bean sauce with mixed vegetables and egg fried rice, Graham with chicken sweet and sour and plain rice. He ordered rice crackers and wontons, thinking that he may not have enough. Both meals came with wooden chopsticks. Liz broke hers open and picked up a piece of tofu with them, popping it into her mouth. Graham stared in silence. Liz stopped mid-mouthful.

"What?" she said.

"You can use chopsticks."

"Yes, why, can't you?"

"I've never tried, how do you do it?"

"Like this, look."

She gripped one chopstick in the middle between her finger and thumb and waited for Graham to do the same. Then she slid the other chopstick into the gap formed by her thumb and index finger and pressed it between her middle finger and the inside of her thumb.

"There you go." She showed him how to use them and he practised picking up prawn crackers.

"So, how did you learn to use chopsticks?" he asked.

"I worked in a superstore in the holidays before uni and we had a sampling display of Chinese snacks, so we all played around trying it. Became quite an expert eventually!"

"I'll say, you continue to amaze me." Every time he said something like this, it made her feel warm and cosseted as though a big fluffy dressing gown had been wrapped around her. She just prayed she could maintain this feeling and not spoil things between them.

They chatted throughout the meal and there were lots of jokes and laughs. At one stage Liz gripped Graham's nose with her chopsticks, and he balanced a prawn cracker on her head, daring her to stand up without it falling off. When they finished the meal and had split the bill, they headed off towards the bus stop.

As they were walking up to the bus Graham said, "You can come back to my place if you like. Only if you want to, I'm not suggesting anything… you know." She could tell in his voice he was nervous.

"Yes, OK. I'd like to see your place." Liz was now feeling nervous as well. When it was her room she felt in control, but the thought of losing that control sent her mind into turmoil. What should she do if he came on to her? Part of her wanted him to, but she was so afraid she thought she might panic or, at worse, even black out. The thought of him having to pick her off the floor was just too much. Her heart was pounding. Suddenly, she realised he was still speaking to her.

"I share with two lads, so it's not as good as yours."

"I'm sure I'll cope." She had seen a few student houses where there were just men. If girlfriends made a regular appearance, they were OK, but when the boys were left to themselves the houses sometimes lacked something. Hygiene, normally.

He put his key in the lock and opened the door, praying there was nothing offensive to see. The hallway was quiet and dark. He could hear music coming from Pete's room. As he led the way climbing the stairs, Pete opened his door, holding a mug in his hand.

"Oh, hi," he said to Graham.

"This is Liz."

"Hi, nice to meet you."

Graham opened his bedroom door and switched the light on.

"Welcome to my world," he said.

"Very nice." Liz noted that the carpet had been recently vacuumed and the surface dusted, and smiled inwardly.

"It's got a big window with a view over the garden which is good in the summer. I sometimes get a squirrel who jumps from the tree branch onto the windowsill."

"Bet you feed it."

"Of course, peanuts from the pet food shop."

"You old softy."

"Guilty as charged."

Graham turned from the window to find Liz close

behind him. They stood facing each other, and she looked directly into his eyes and smiled slightly. He put his hand up to the side of her face and pushed a lock of hair back from her eye. Her breathing became short, and she thought her heart was about to explode.

"It's a bit unmanageable," she said, taking his hand in hers and slotting her straight fingers between his.

"Can I kiss you?" he said softly. Oh God, she thought. I just have to jump in, now or never.

"You may, kind sir."

He kissed her gently on the lips and held her cautiously on the shoulders. She pulled him close and kissed him more firmly; she had to commit totally, she thought. They sat back on the bed and the kissing got more passionate, then they were lying side by side. Liz slipped her pullover over her head, revealing a black T-shirt with a diamanté leaf on it. Graham held her and kissed her neck; she threw her head back and gripped his shoulder with her fingertips.

"Stop, stop!" she said. "Time out, take five." She propped herself on one elbow, breathing deeply.

"What's wrong, did I hurt you?"

"No, it's all good, I just need a minute." Her heart was racing and her breathing short and stifled. Oh God, she thought, please don't black out. Please, please, please. She focused, trying to steady her breathing, remembering her mindfulness techniques. Notice your surroundings, feel the roughness of the bed, the folds of your blouse. Notice the lampshade and the light, feel his shirt.

She lay down facing Graham, studying his face. Noticing his eyes and his eyebrows, his cheeks, nose, and mouth.

"I find the physical stuff difficult," said Liz. "I want to do it and I am enjoying it, but…"

"But what? Is there someone else?"

"What? God, no, it's nothing like that. In my first year I had a bit of a nightmare experience and it's taking me a bit to get over it. That's all. I'll be OK, I just need to slow down a bit."

"Savour the moment, then."

"Yes, can we?"

"Definitely. I'd wait forever for you, girl."

"Hmm, I was thinking more like half an hour, but anyway." They both laughed.

"Should I make tea?"

"No, just hold me, you're a good holder."

They lay on Graham's bed, holding each other. They chatted and laughed, giggled, and kissed intermittently. Liz wasn't really sure how to start. Telling your boyfriend that you had been raped and filling in all the graphic details of the aftermath would be a real downer. In her somewhat limited experience, she thought this was just about guaranteed to stymie the relationship. She had to say something to explain her behaviour.

"I was a bit innocent when I came to uni. At the time I didn't think so, having worked in a department store over the summer, but then comparing to what some of the other girls had done or been through, I now realise that I was. I tried to fit in by going to a party and drinking. Too much glühwein, I'm afraid."

"We've all been there. Drinking and then regretting your behaviour, or whatever."

"Yes, but for me it was more a case of being taken advantage of and then having no memory of what really happened."

"What do you mean?"

Liz looked at Graham, into his eyes, searching his face. He really was a nice guy. Could they not just stay as they were, on this warm bed, cuddling forever. If she told him, it would change everything. She couldn't go back and change what had happened, but she could choose not to let it affect her now.

"Oh, just morning-after stuff. Is that tea still on offer?"

"Certainly is."

She knew she had killed the moment, and she knew she had chosen not to be brave. Something inside her was silently crying, but she could not reach it to let it out; it was buried too deep. They lay entwined together on the bed, and eventually dosed off to wake with the early-morning sun streaming through the windows.

***

As it was Saturday, they agreed to spend the day together. Liz nipped home to shower and change and Graham headed to the bathroom to get in before the others woke up. They agreed to meet at the coffee shop by the library at 11am. As Liz walked towards the library entrance, she saw Graham approaching from the other direction, and they smiled to each other as they got closer.

"What timing," she said.

He placed his hand on her shoulder and kissed her forehead. It felt good, she thought. She felt cared for.

"Drink?" he said.

"No, let's walk into town. We can go through the park. That big sports shop has a sale on, and the organic guy is at the market on Saturdays."

"Sounds like a plan."

As they walked, they chatted, Liz impressing Graham with her knowledge of tree types.

"How you know it's an elm?"

"If you look at the sides of the leaf, they join the stem at distinct levels, called an asymmetrical base, according to my A level Biology teacher."

Although they were both at the same university studying for degrees, Liz seemed to have a broader knowledge than Graham, and she guessed it was just a boy thing. She was studying sports science, he computer science, and they both knew stuff from their own courses. Graham had very little general knowledge, Liz thought, but get him on to the subject of tech and he was away.

They looked around the market, where Liz bought brown rice and tofu, and Graham chocolate nuts, which he proceeded to eat straight away. At the sports shop, Liz tried on a pair of running shoes and Graham bought a headband for the coming winter. They walked back to Graham's house and up to his room. On the upstairs landing they met Mike standing in a pair of boxer shorts with a cowboy hat on his head and carrying a can of beer with an exceptionally long, curly plastic straw sticking out of it.

"Bloody hell," he said, stopping suddenly and looking at Liz with his mouth slightly open.

"This is Mike," said Graham. Mike continued to stare, and Liz tried not to laugh.

"He does sometimes speak, but he's a bit choosy."

"Hi, yeah, hello. I mean nice to meet you," said Mike, turning rapidly and heading for his room.

He closed the door quickly, and they heard muffled voices from inside the room.

"Bloody hell, she's gorgeous!"

"I told you."

"I apologise for my housemates, they lack functioning brains," said Graham, opening the door to his room. "Let's hide in here."

Liz was smiling now, and Graham let them both into his room, holding the door for her. He pushed it closed and turned to face her. She looked at him and put her hand on his shoulder. Liz had been thinking long and hard over the night and all morning as she walked with Graham. Isabella had said in one of her counselling sessions that she would know when it was right to move on. Don't rush, she had said, let things unfold naturally. She had taken time since the party and practised all of the self-help techniques. She was feeling better in herself and no longer had nightmares. She had panicked a bit with Graham when they were first alone, but now found she could control herself.

"Would you do something for me?" she said, her eyes flicking over his face.

"Yes, sure, what is it?"

"Make love to me."

13

Passion

Liz didn't know what would happen, but she did know she had to try. She had a flashback to a pizza restaurant with her parents after her exams had finished at school. They were joking about her having a shandy and not being eighteen and allowed to drink alcohol. Her mum had said no, but her dad had wanted her to try, and had said sometimes you just have to take a risk. Well, now that was exactly what she was doing. Do or die, she thought, and she lifted her head towards Graham with an expectant look on her face.

Graham took Liz's head in his hands, holding her gently, and kissed her, first lightly and then more strongly. She liked that he smelt of shaving cream and tasted of spearmint, and she looked at him with her eyes flicking over his face. His skin was rougher than hers and his face felt slightly prickly where his stubble was growing through. He pulled her firmly against himself, making their two bodies into one. He felt warm and full of life to her, as though he was melting something cold which lay deep inside her.

"God, I'm really turned on," he said.

"I can tell."

Liz liked the fact that he was turned on by her. It gave her confidence, and she really needed that now. She remembered a coach saying at school when they were doing hurdling, at take off your foot pushes the floor, and at landing your foot contacts the floor again. In the middle, you just float. She was floating now, she had pushed off and hoped she would land OK, but that was unknown. She had never been this close to a man (well, intentionally anyway), and she was both nervous and excited – buzzing, she would later call it.

"It's a male thing," said Graham, and Liz smiled, deciding that she quite liked this man.

She knew she had to keep going. If she had doubts or paused, her fear might catch up with her and take over. It's just like running, she thought, mind over body. Dig in. She could do this because she had done it hundreds of times before. Not with a man in a bedroom, but on long runs on the road. Up hills with the wind and rain beating in her face. Dig in and keep going, make the mind tell the body what to do.

Liz smiled and raised her eyebrows slightly. Stepping back, she pulled her sweater over her head. It was an act of liberation, an expression of intent. She noticed his eyes flick over her stretched T-shirt and she loved it. She began unbuttoning his shirt, feeling nervous and excited.

She realised that she had never really seen a man naked. Swimming pools and sauna and that was about all. She took her time savouring every moment, noticing the wispy hairs on his chest and the paleness of his skin. She lightly scratched her fingernails across his chest. Take your time, she said to herself. It's going to be OK.

"Not much muscle, I'm afraid," he said.

"I like you as you are, lean and sinewy."

Pulling his shirt up out of his trousers, she noticed the darker hair on his lower stomach. She knew what lay lower down and was excited, not just sexually but to realise that she was not nervous. Liz couldn't believe she was taking the lead, but she was so turned on, all her self-doubts were beginning to evaporate. Where was this confidence coming from? She pushed him gently down onto the bed.

"I put clean sheets on," he said.

"Considerate and presumptuous."

"No, just hopeful." Holding his arms, she smiled and moved back slightly, taking a brief pause to look at Graham.

"This is the first real time for me," she said.

"I know, me too, to be honest. Well, not the first, but the first I really cared about."

She smiled at him and finished unbuttoning his shirt, pulling it off. Lifting her T-shirt off in a single overhead action, she reached behind her to unclip her bra. She felt good. She was breathing deeply, but this time not through fear; it was passion. He pulled her so close that they melted together. Skin, body heat, limbs, hair merging into one new shape.

She stood up quickly and unzipped her jeans, wiggling them down, hopping from foot to foot, giggling as she did. He pulled his jeans down and then sat on the side of the bed to take them off. They fell together on the bed, sharing bodily warmth.

"Your skin feels so good," she said. She lightly touched his shoulder with her teeth, "I could eat you." His skin tasted slightly salty and smelt of body spray.

"Please don't, I'm delicate."

"Possibly, but delicious, I think." She thought that she would burst. The relief of not blacking out, the feelings raging in her body, the sheer fun of the moment all merged into one.

They kissed again.

She slipped her pants off and threw them on the floor. He touched her buttocks, drawing his fingertips lightly across the skin.

"You score highly in the bum stakes," he said, and she laughed.

"It's all the running. Most girls start running to tone their legs and get a nice bum. Any women's magazine will tell you this."

"I've obviously been remiss at reading women's magazines, Ms McClennan."

"Obviously, Mr Edwards."

He stood up and reached into his bedside cabinet, "I have condoms."

Liz had been hoping he had some and cursing herself for not having one in her bag. Tracey had shouted at her as she left the house, "Nice girls carry condoms!" Liz had laughed but had not wanted to appear too keen, so hadn't taken her advice. She watched as he opened the new packet.

"Placed close at hand, I see."

"Yes, but very rarely used."

She smiled as he slipped his trunks off and lay down with her. Having never really seen a naked man before up close, she was conscious that her eyes were wandering, but so were his. She took her time to explore the contours of his body with her fingers. They pulled close together, feeling heat and passion but not knowing whose body felt what. Her whole body felt on fire, and as he entered her, she let out a gentle gasp. She tried to relax, fearful that she would panic. She told herself, I am not having sex; I am making love. It's not any man, it's Graham. She knew girls at uni who only went out to find a man and have sex. They compared notes and gave them scores. She didn't want that. She wanted Graham, with his *Star Trek* poster on the wall and his funny housemates. Was she damaged goods? She knew she probably was, but she would allow Graham to help repair her. She felt his skin rub against hers, his muscles tense and release. She sensed his hot breath and saw a light sweat forming on his forehead. She let go of the memories of that night and the days after. The fear, the guilt, the regret gradually evaporated with every movement their bodies made. Her thoughts began to stop, she felt primeval. She felt linked to millions of women across the world, millions through time. I am woman, and I am free.

Afterwards, they lay in a hot sweating mass. Liz could feel Graham's breathing as his ribs pressed against hers, his stomach moving up and down. She felt they were completely at one with each other. It was the first time she had been this close to another human being; she could almost read his thoughts. She lay with her legs casually apart, her hand on his hip. Liz didn't feel embarrassed; it seemed so natural. Graham looked at her and ran a finger over a bead of sweat on her shoulder; she smiled and said, "I think I need a shower."

"Me too, but later."

They talked gently for about half an hour, not even knowing what they talked about. Later, she knew things about Graham, not knowing when he told her. Liz closed her eyes, and he drew the quilt over her. It reminded her of her dad putting her to bed. She heard him get up and put his jeans on, gently rustling. He quietly opened the door and slipped out. When he came back, he crept over to the bed and sat on its edge. She felt him watching her and it made her feel appreciated. She had a friend, companion, and lover, and it felt good. She still felt a cold darkness inside her and knew it would take time. The ice had begun to melt, drip by drip.

14

Everything ends

Liz and Graham were now an item. Everyone recognised the unlikely couple; he the gangly male, she the striking but shy female. They were seen in the coffee shop and the library, walking through campus, and getting off buses. As the seasons changed, they went from shorts and T-shirts to thick pullovers and padded coats. They visited each other's rooms, Liz getting to know Graham's housemates, and Graham often appearing in Liz's kitchen, eating toast or washing their dishes. For six months they helped each other grow, becoming confident final-year students. No longer hesitant and awkward, they were comfortable in each other's company.

Graham opened a bleary eye to see Liz getting dressed.

"Where are you going?"

"You know where I'm going, I told you. I'm doing some off-road training with Martha. We're trying for the cross-country championships."

"But I thought you wanted to go to that café for the all-day breakfast."

"No, you wanted to go to the café for the all-day breakfast. Have you ever thought that your life revolves around your stomach?"

"I like eating."

"Tell me about it. I'll be off, I'll see you later in the week."

"What?!"

Liz closed the door and jogged down the stairs, carrying her kit bag over one shoulder. She hated it when they argued, and thought she sometimes sounded like an old housewife rather than a young uni student. All she wanted was for Graham to listen occasionally to what she was saying. She enjoyed being with him. She still felt a twinge of fear occasionally, but she was getting better. In the early days of their relationship, she had been surprised at how much she had enjoyed the sex. She had no incidences of panic or blackouts, which she had been afraid of. At night she still sometimes had dreams; it was as though she had separated sex from the fear somehow. But he seemed to focus only on what he wanted to do, and when she had mentioned this to Tracey and Suzanne, they had simply said that was the nature of men. She was going to make an effort; she shouldn't have just left but had felt hurt that he hadn't listened to her last night, and she was already late.

Graham heard the front door close. Scratching his head, he got up and began rooting in his bag to find a leaflet he had picked up in the computer lab. A couple of guys had formed a club to build computers together and, as Graham had built his last year, he thought it might be an opportunity to upgrade the spec. They were meeting at 10.30am, so he had time to shower and get a bit of breakfast before he met them.

***

Liz persuaded Graham that he should join in with her yoga class, after much cajoling. She had begun this a couple of months ago while using the weight-training gym, having read a running magazine article about it. It said that yoga could help runners by increasing flexibility, relaxing them, and helping recovery. This was enough to pique her interest and, seeing a group of girls in a yoga class at the uni sports centre, she had signed up. Initially, she found it a bit hard and tended to go to the back of the class to follow a couple of the more experienced girls who stood in front. The instructor was incredibly good, coming round and checking everybody's position and correcting them if they were a bit wonky. Over the weeks and months, she had improved and had taken to practising a few postures by herself in her bedroom throughout the week. She had gradually moved from the back to the middle of the class as she gained confidence.

Recently, some of the girls had started to bring boyfriends, and Liz thought it would be a good idea for Graham to try, as his flexibility was notoriously poor. To avoid embarrassment, she tried to teach him a few simple poses herself so that when he went to the class, he was less likely to fail. Over the months Liz had learnt that Graham normally enjoyed things he was good at but would quickly give things up if he felt he was being shown up. She also thought it would be good to do things together, because other than training in the gym a few times, they didn't really share experiences. They would go out, return to one of their rooms and have sex, but that was all – it was becoming mundane. In the running club they were always in separate parts of the group, and whenever she had suggested going for a run together, he always said he would just slow her down.

When they attended the class together, Liz stood in the middle, with Graham in the back row with two other men. The idea being the men could copy the more experienced girls. As she was in front of Graham, she didn't actually see him during the class. After class, however, his face was a bit glum.

"How did it go?" she said.

"It was OK, I suppose, but I found some of the postures impossible. When we did that cross-legged one, I couldn't get my knee anywhere near the floor. In the one where you stand on one leg, I kept wobbling. When we practised at home it was easier, but I found the class a bit too fast-paced to be honest."

"I found it difficult to start, but it got easier."

"I suppose. I don't know, I don't really think it's for me. One of the blokes from the computer club does karate, I might try that."

"Which bloke from the computer club?"

"You don't know him. His name's Steve, he's studying photography and journalism."

"But I thought it would be good to do some stuff together."

"We do loads of stuff together."

"No, we drink coffee, have sex, and occasionally go out."

"But I enjoy sex."

"So do I, but there is more to life in a relationship than wham, bam, thank you, ma'am."

"Relationship? Bloody hell, you make it sound as though we're married."

Liz glared at him. She didn't really know what to say. She didn't want to settle down and get married, of course not, but she wanted more than just a load of one-night stands on repeat. Why couldn't they have a closer relationship? She felt close to him in bed and afterwards, but not at other times. She wanted to talk to him and experience things with him, but if she was honest, she felt a bit lost. After the first-year party she found it difficult to make close relationships with men. She had wanted to tell Graham about the rape but thought he would either run away from her like a bolting rabbit or be dismissive. She should talk to him, she knew that, but something always stopped her.

"I'm getting a shower," she said.

***

"I don't know, he just doesn't seem to want to make any effort. It's all become a habit. Meet up for coffee and a chat, back to one of our rooms, have sex, and ditto the next time. The weeks roll into months and half the year has gone already."

Liz was chatting to Suzanne in the toastie bar where Liz was now working two early-evening shifts.

"I mean, I still love him, but it's not the same. A bit of the shine has gone off the relationship."

"It happens with most guys, in my experience. You have to go through a lot of frogs before you find your prince."

"I don't want to spoil things, but I'm not sure what to do to save things."

"Perhaps you can't save it, might be time to just let go. I've done that in the past and it's like a great weight being taken off your shoulders. Or, like running without a ball and chain in your case!"

They both laughed and then Tracey joined them.

"What's occurring, girlies?"

"Relationship advice," said Suzanne. "Graham's being a bit dull."

"He's not, really. I think it's just me with all the stuff I've got on. This job, the cross-country, dissertation year."

"But we're young and untethered," said Tracey.

"I like to have a variety. Different man for different occasions. A bit like outfits!"

"We know," said Liz and Suzanne together.

"Now, John is a strong rugby player and has a great body but struggles a bit in the brain department."

"He's studying medicine," said Suzanne.

"Precisely."

"And Phil is a bit scrawny but great to take to places as

he is bright and good at conversation. I feel I need another one. A sort of all-things-to-all-girls bloke. Someone with a great body, charming, but shuts up when I want him to. And clean, got to be clean. Rich would help, I'm a bit short of cash this term."

"You don't want much, then," said Liz.

"No, just perfection. Strive for excellence, as they say."

"So, girls, anyone for a toastie, we need to push sales," said Liz.

"Mozzarella, pesto, and tomato on sourdough for me," said Suzanne.

"I'm going native. Sausage and bacon on plain white for me. Oh, and mustard. Got to have mustard. I like to taste things on my tongue." She smiled knowingly at Suzanne.

"You're such a tart," said Suzanne.

Liz smiled and looked down at the counter.

***

"How did it go?" said Liz.

"Not bad. I think I'm going to go for it if they come back and offer it to me."

Suzanne had decided to go into teaching and had gone for an interview in Birmingham for a PGCE to allow her to teach in a secondary school.

"The campus is quite nice, and the school of education is a modern red-brick building, quite funky, actually. You get teaching practice in local schools, and they said you frequently get offered a job in one because most of the schools are short-staffed. If you go for an inner-city school, you get a sign-on bonus as well."

"What about you, any more thoughts?"

"I'm split between staying on to do that PhD or going into medicine," said Liz.

"Won't the PhD be better, as it's a studentship? At least you'll be getting some money if it's fully funded. Medicine is just being a student all over again. Five years and you'll be broke."

"I can do a four-year accelerated medicine programme, and then the pay as a doctor is better than a researcher, eventually."

"Still a lot of demanding work, though, no time to play. What does Graham think?"

"I haven't really discussed it with him, to be honest. He's always at his bloody computer club nowadays."

"What do they do there?"

"Tinker with computers, making them more powerful. They've set up a repair service for students, so they earn a bit of money. They also do programming. He's trying to improve the programme he wrote last year."

"Sounds dull to me," said Suzanne. "Dull little boys playing with dull little toys."

"He's quite good at it. Says computers are the future."

"Dull, dull, dull. You're better off without him. Trade him in for a new model. Get a muscly man who can service your every need."

Liz smiled. Perhaps Suzanne was right. Should she finish with Graham? She wasn't sure. She liked him, but they had drifted apart. Suzanne was always saying she should split with him, but she got the feeling that Suzanne was a bit jealous. When Liz hadn't had a boyfriend, she and Suzanne had met up often, but now with Graham they didn't meet up as much and Suzanne had made a few sarcastic comments. Liz had noticed over the years that Suzanne liked things she could control. She was a good friend and had been brilliant when Liz had all the stuff going on in the first year. Occasionally, Liz noticed a controlling personality quirk in Suzanne. If they were in a group, she liked to be the centre of attention and if she was not, she would try to bring the focus back on herself. Liz wondered now whether she was trying to split her up from Graham because it didn't suit Suzanne, or was Liz just reading something into a situation which wasn't there?

***

Liz went for her interviews and got a place on the accelerated medicine course in Liverpool. She was looking forward to it. Although she knew it would be challenging work with lots of study, she liked the idea of the practical aspect and dealing with people. She had enjoyed her sports science degree, but there were lots of periods shut up in a lab and she often felt a bit like a mole in the sunlight when she came out. She thought the practical side of medicine, and especially dealing with people, would be great. Working in the toastie bar she had discovered a new side to herself. She had always been a bit of a loner, studying at school. Alone in the library, and then the running; both had led her along that path. Now, chatting to people at the toastie bar, she had discovered that she was actually a good listener, and people would confide in her. Being Liz, she had looked up bartending tricks when she started at the toastie bar. It said to keep the conversation light-hearted and ask questions, as people often liked to talk about themselves. The aim was to let the customer steer the conversation and build a relationship over time with your regulars. She had tried this and been surprised how much people confided in her and how much she enjoyed listening, with just the odd "really", "that's fantastic", "no, tell me more" to oil the works.

This evening it was the Halloween bash at the bar. There was a big sign saying 'Get your fangs in a tasty toastie' with blood dripping off the letters. Liz had her face painted like a devil and wore a black long-sleeve top, black jeans, and a black plastic cape from a shop in town. Her hair had red colouring, which Suzanne had helped apply, and to finish things off, she had little plastic horns and fangs. Suzanne was a skeleton, and she had brought Tracey, who had a bit of a dominatrix thing going on. She wore knee-length black riding boots and a black plastic top up to her throat with a triangle cut out, revealing her ample cleavage. She carried a riding crop.

"Tracey is expressing her domme side," said Suzanne.

"I had the stuff anyway, so thought I would reuse it."

Liz looked on blankly.

"Don't ask," said Suzanne.

"What will it be, ladies?" said Liz.

"Specials tonight are cut-off fingers (small sausages with tomato ketchup), or cheese and spider (the spiders in question being finely cut black olives)."

"I think I'll be boring and have my usual pesto and mozzarella," said Suzanne.

"I'm up for the fingers. I like a few small sausages to warm up before the big game," said Tracey.

"I'm not even going to dignify that with a response," said Liz.

"Any men in tonight?" said Suzanne.

"Graham said he might drop in after doing something with his computer mates."

"You're not still barking up that tree, are you?" said Tracey.

"I still like him; things have just gone a bit cool," said Liz.

"Hanging on for grim death more like," said Suzanne.

Liz stayed quiet.

As the night wore on, Liz was busy serving and the volume of chatter increased as more people arrived. The toasties were popular as always. Alcohol was not provided, but a few brought their own, and as more was consumed, the toastie orders got more bizarre. Any combination of the foods they stocked was game, it seemed.

"Can I have cheese and Mars bar?" asked one boy. The trick was to cut the Mars bar in half through the middle and squash it onto the bread, warning the recipient that hot toasted sugar is likely to burn your mouth.

"Damn!" shouted Liz.

"You OK?" said Tracey.

"Cut my hand," she said, holding a folded piece of paper kitchen roll against it.

Suzanne said, "That might need stitches, at least get it looked at. I'll take you to A&E."

"Liz, what's happened?"

She looked up to see Graham. In the crowd she hadn't noticed him sitting in the corner with his computer mates. She looked into his eyes, fear and pleading over her face.

"It's my hand."

"I'll take you to A&E."

"It's OK, I've got it sorted," said Suzanne. "Tracey's mate has a car."

As Liz left the toastie bar with Suzanne and Tracey, she turned to look at Graham. She wanted him with her, with his arm around her shoulder. She fixed her eyes on him, and the last few months peeled away. She still loved him; she knew that now. As the three of them left the toastie bar, she felt like they were wrenching her away from him forever. She wanted to scream and beat her fists. Tears welled up in her eyes, and she felt like the flesh was being ripped from her. The last thing she saw was the look of hurt and loss on Graham's face.

15

Graduation

The end of term was always a bit disorganised. The slow build up to exams left everyone exhausted, and the campus was quite empty as students swotted in their rooms or the library. Coffee shops were often deserted except for the odd student rich enough to own a laptop. Once exams had finished there was an explosion of activity. Being summer, lawns were full of groups of students. Skirts were pulled up, shirts taken off and bra tops were in abundance. Radios blared out the top twenty and groups gathered for small, disorganised ball games. Five-a-side and volleyball being the order of the day. Rooms were cleared, and cases, boxes, and house plants appeared at the bottom of stairwells, waiting for car-driving parents to pick up students with luggage. Those less fortunate would struggle onto buses and trains to be whisked back to the family home.

Liz struggled down the stairs carrying a heavy box with the Chinese teapot balanced precariously on top. This was the last of her things, and stacking them with other people's stuff in the stairwell of their student house, they looked small and incidental. Yet, each piece had memories attached, and over the coming years, they would take her back to aspects of her life in Leeds. For now, she was in a rush.

"You done, kid?" said Suzanne.

"Just about, need to nip to the library to return these books and then I'm good."

As she closed the door and headed off, her mind wandered back over the last two weeks. She was thankful that she hadn't needed stitches in her hand when she cut it but couldn't get the look on Graham's face that night out of her mind. He had looked so hurt, almost like a little boy. She had so much to do over the following weeks and hadn't seen him. It had all been a bit of a whirlwind, going out with the girls from the house, closing up the toastie bar and seeing her running club gang, and she hadn't seen Graham. She really didn't know where she stood. They had grown distant, and as it was the end of term, was that it? Did things simply come to a natural end, that is what Tracey and Suzanne had done, suggesting that you had to move on. They were all moving on to other things and looking forward to it, but she still had a twang of guilt that she hadn't contacted him. Perhaps he simply wasn't interested anymore, and that was fine, but she didn't know.

***

"Suzanne!" She stopped and turned.

"Graham, how's it going?"

"I'm fine. Just looking for Liz, have you seen l

"Last seen drinking coffee at my place and e; chocolate biscuits."

"And where might I find her now?"

"She was off to the library to take some books back, that was about an hour ago, so she could be anywhere by now."

"OK, if you see her, can you tell her I was looking for her?"

"Will do. Bye, computer nerd."

"Bye, sex pot."

They both smiled and went their separate ways.

Next day, Graham was all packed up and waiting for his parents to arrive. He went round to Liz's place but she had already moved out. Suzanne came down the stairs with a box in her hands. She looked at him for a moment in silence.

"You missed her, I'm afraid. Left earlier this morning."

Graham just stared at her.

"Gone?"

"Afraid so."

"But did you tell her I was looking for her?"

"Sure did."

Graham stared in silence, pain and disbelief on his face.

"Oh, OK. My folks are coming for me in about an hour anyhow."

Suzanne gave a shallow smile and felt the hairs on the back of her neck stand up.

***

"I miss Graham in some ways. I guess he just wanted to move on."

"Someone told me he got offered a scholarship to do a master's in the States."

"Not surprised, he was good with computing stuff. Bet he'll do well."

Liz and Suzanne were sitting by the pool, Liz with her straw hat over her head, Suzanne sipping a glass of sangria. They had travelled to Spain to stay in Tracey's parents' holiday villa on the Costa Brava. Originally, they had planned to fly, but as it had been too expensive, they had caught the bus. They travelled overnight from London to Barcelona and then caught another bus to Gerona. It had been cheap, but after sitting and then sleeping in their seats for one and a half days, they had emerged chair-shaped. Liz had found the walk from the taxis up the hill to the villa quite relieving and felt that her circulation was actually working again by the time they reached the front door. They hadn't even bothered to unpack, just opening their cases on the bed and taking out their swimming costumes. Having barely seen daylight for the entire year in Leeds, the Mediterranean sun was just too inviting.

"He was never good enough for you, girlie, you can do better."

"Don't say that, I liked him. Just because he wasn't one of your standard muscly rugby players."

"A girl needs a man with muscle. They can carry your cases, make you feel secure in times of danger, and do the business in the boudoir."

"How do you know if he could do the business in the boudoir, as you say?"

"Well, could he?"

"I have no complaints, thank you very much."

They both fell silent. Liz casting her mind back to the times she spent in Graham's room. They were good times, she thought. Suzanne, for her part, was feeling a pang of guilt for not telling Liz that Graham was looking for her on the last day. If it came up, she would say that with all the rushing around, she simply forgot. Anyway, she had wanted Liz to come to Spain with her, and if she had stayed with Graham, the two of them would probably have done something together over the summer and Suzanne would have been left by herself.

Liz got up and began swimming. Suzanne looked on, envious of her long, lean physique and practised stroke. Suzanne was conscious that the combination of alcohol and biscuits last term had left her with a few extra pounds around the midriff. Still, a tan and a bit of swimming should soon fix that. She could start her teaching course toned and tanned, ready to show a smooth leg to a new crop of fresh-faced male students. Job done.

***

Liz was staying with her parents in a local Premier Inn for graduation. They had all come down the night before and she had an evening meal with them, showing them around the familiar places she knew in the city. It was wonderful to be able to actually point out the places she had only described in letters and on the phone. They had seen her student house, but now she could introduce them to some of her housemates. She took them to the toastie bar and showed them the uni gym and coffee shop. As they walked around campus, they passed groups of others doing much the same thing. Nods of recognition and stops for snippets of conversation. It was as though the kids had opened a secret toy box and were now showing the adults inside.

Liz had arranged to meet with Suzanne and Tracey prior to the graduation and organise where they would meet afterwards. They agreed it should be in the refreshment tent at a particular area so they could find each other in the crowd. Heading off to the ceremony, they were all dressed in gowns and mortar boards, and they were to gather in the right order outside the hall in a covered tunnel formed of tarpaulin. As the presentation would be in subject order, Liz was standing with someone she had only seen a couple of times, as they were in separate groups for lectures and tutorials. They chatted, as they had been thrust together by circumstances but were not friends.

The parents were already seated in the hall and the students edged forwards gradually. As they entered the hall, some parents craned their heads to see, but Liz had issued precise instructions to her parents: no turning around and no standing up. Their seats were all numbered, and each had a programme placed on it, with the list of graduands. Liz spotted her name and chatted to the people either side of her, who she didn't really know but had seen around campus. The degree certificates were to be presented with those receiving a bachelor's, like Liz, going first, followed by students receiving master's degrees and then doctorates. Liz looked around briefly but couldn't see her parents.

As the ceremony began, the Dean made a speech and then each row of students filed out and gathered together at the left of the stage as they had been instructed to do in a rehearsal at the end of term. The drill was simple. A student's name was called, and they walked to the centre of the stage, holding their hands together in front of them. When they reached the Dean, he would clasp their hands and present their certificate. They turned briefly towards the audience for a photograph and then continued to walk across the stage to come down the right-hand stairs and back to their seat. Once the student had received their certificate and was walking away from the Dean, the next student's name would be called, and they set off up the left-hand steps. Barring trips, all should go smoothly, giving everyone their brief time in the spotlight to be photographed and immortalised in a picture frame to stand in their parents' house and be remembered with pride. A rite of passage and finale to three years' demanding work.

Liz got a little more nervous as the rows in front of her had completed their graduation. When it came to her row standing and moving forward to the left side of the stage, she had butterflies in her stomach and wobbly legs. She hoped her dress wouldn't snag or fly up and she wouldn't trip over her heels as she walked. Her name was called, Elizabeth Mary McClennan. She went up the stairs, heart pounding, and walked across the stage standing tall. She touched the Dean's hand, received her certificate, turned briefly towards the audience for her photograph, and then walked to the other side of the stage down the stairs and back to her seat. All, fortunately, without incident, and she breathed a sigh of relief when she sat back in her seat. She smiled at the girl next to her, who grinned in mutual pride and relief.

After the graduation, there were refreshments and groups gathered in little huddles, parents, and students of all varieties. Suzanne, Tracey, and Liz stood for a photograph, and then Liz and Suzanne got Tracey to take theirs and Liz took one of the two of them. They all carried paper plates in the marquee, getting food from the buffet and the single glass of champagne which was provided. As the noise level rose and the champagne was drunk, the odd plate was dropped, and glass smashed frequently, resulting in a cheer and friendly banter. Liz introduced her parents to Suzanne and Tracey, and she met their parents. Memories were shared and people put faces to names. As they all chatted, Liz scanned the room for Graham, but he was nowhere to be seen.

As they left the tent, Liz saw Mike and Pete, Graham's old housemates, talking together.

"Hi, boys, how goes it?"

"Doing well. I'm working for an accounting firm and Pete is doing his master's here."

"What's it in, Pete?"

"Medieval German," he said.

"Really?"

"No, law. It's a qualifying law degree or QLD. You get

to be a solicitor if you haven't studied a bachelor's in law. Aren't you doing accelerated medicine?"

"Yes, that's right. Still studying the body, but from a different perspective. Is Graham here?" Liz asked.

"Graham? No, he's a bit of a star now. Got a scholarship for a master's at Cal Tech so he's soaking up the sun in California. Living the life. Not had much contact with him, to be honest."

Liz felt her heart sink. She had been hoping to see Graham after the summer for graduation. She knew what her mother would say. It's only first love, there are plenty of fish in the sea. But he was a beautiful tropical fish who flashed brightly as he had moved into her life and left a gaping hole when he left. She missed him. When she thought of him, she had a warm feeling deep inside herself. Over the years it diminished, but it never left completely.

16

2010

A chance meeting

Liz jumped out of the taxi, fighting with her brolly to get it up and failing. She had always kept her hair long when she was younger, even trying to straighten it at one stage. It had a natural wave, but in the rain, it could turn into a frizzy mess. Her father used to call her a Gonk, as he thought she looked like one of the popular toy trolls he used to see advertised. Not the best look after a medical conference where she had been the keynote speaker. If he could see her now, he would be proud, she thought. His advice to a gangly, introverted teenager had set her on her path. She could still hear his words, "If you don't know it, look it up." Back then, it had been in a set of eight Collins encyclopaedias which held pride of place in the family glass-fronted bookcase in the front room. The thought gave her a warm fuzzy. Another of her dad's expressions which conjured up feelings of curling up on a winter's Saturday night in front of the TV with the family dog.

Sometimes she wished she could go back to those times. Life had been so simple, or so it had seemed.

"Cats and dogs out here, mate!" A Cockney accent with a hint of public school.

"Bloody hell, not again."

She was pulled out of her reverie by two young men coming through the station door in front of her, one being very animated while the other looked at her, dropping his eyes to her cleavage. She was always amazed at the anonymity of train travel. Just half an hour ago, she had been an idolised keynote speaker receiving a standing ovation from an audience of 250 of her peers. Now, she was being checked out as a passing sex object. She had grown a thick skin as a female trainee in orthopaedic surgery and had vowed never to allow anyone to feel uncomfortable when she led the team in theatre.

Moving her laptop to the other shoulder and rolling her now limp umbrella, she automatically straightened her hair, tucking the right side behind her ear as she had done since her sixth form at school. She couldn't believe she had broken another folding umbrella; she left a trail of them through her life, each one black and compact. She had tried various makes and prices, but the result was always the same. She looked up at the board, scanning for the Manchester train. Platform 14 in ten minutes. She walked quickly, trying not to look as though she was running and set her eyes on the gate. She found that a fixed gaze and rapid pace normally meant people moved out of the way and a crowd would often just divide like the sea for Moses. She had perfected the art of closing herself down since walking for buses throughout her university years. Fasten the coat, bag over the shoulder, look down and walk quickly. At medical school in the latter years, she would talk into her phone, even if she had no calls. Nothing like a bit of assertiveness to get you through. Usually it worked, but occasionally you would get a joker (usually young, male, and overweight) standing in front of you with a broad grin on their face.

"Oh sorry, I was miles away. Didn't see you there!" was her go-to disarming phrase.

Arriving at the gate, she showed her ticket. She made a mental note to learn how to put it on her phone as she now felt like a dinosaur, seeing all the bright young things holding up the QR code on their phones. She was once a bright young thing, but now she guessed she simply looked middle-aged; where had the years gone?

Liz walked to the first open door and stepped through, heading for her seat. It was a small miracle that the seat reservation system was actually working today. She stood up and slipped her jacket off, turning it inside out and folding it neatly before placing it on the overhead rack. The feel of the coat lining rubbing smoothly against the back of her hand took her back to those train journeys to Bath in her youth. She had loved those journeys. Mum would always make her count sheep in the fields, and they would have a competition to count the number of minutes that passed until they went under the next footbridge. Her mum was the one who always taught her to fold her coat inside out on trains so the outside wouldn't get bits of dirt or fluff on it. As a child, she had never asked why it was better to get fluff on the inside of the coat rather than the outside. Perhaps the shiny lining wouldn't pick it up, or, more likely with her mother, outside appearance was more important. To Liz's mum, appearance was everything. What would the neighbours think? Mum would often say. What, indeed.

She took her laptop out and placed it on the table, although she did not intend to do any work straight away as the last two days had left her shattered. At least her seat was next to the window, so she wouldn't have to keep standing up to let people in and out. Gazing out of the window at the platform, the closet-like stillness inside the carriage contrasted sharply with the jostling still going on outside. She could see all the movements, cases being dragged, a child crying, an elderly man tapping a walking stick, but the sounds were muffled and distant to her now. If only it were that simple to cut out all life stresses; just close the door on them. She had read a personal-growth book once which talked about watertight compartments (apparently the author had been on a submarine). The theory was that you could simply visualise a door closing in your mind and leave the stresses on the other side. They were still there, but they did not affect you. She had tried it and then forgotten all about it, like so many things. Perhaps it was time to restart some of the personal-growth techniques she had once used. The alcohol at the conference had triggered something in her and she realised she had never healed completely after university. She made a mental note to start now.

She saw the platform moving backwards before she felt the train start. Raindrops slowly moved down the window, trailing lines behind them, and were pressed back as the train increased its speed and left the shelter of the station. Ever since she was a young child, she thought there was a certain romance about train travel. She recognised the dirt and noise, of course, but equally there was something grounding about travelling by train, which she never got in a car. Occasionally, when changing trains, she would just sit on a small station platform after the train had gone, bathing in the silence it left behind. It was like a meditation to her, with the noise and rushing moving away and layer upon layer of stillness descending. Like cotton sheets floating down on her when she played with her cousins in the summer holidays all those years ago.

"Welcome on board this 18.05 train to Manchester. Our next stop will be Milton Keynes."

She once considered teaching for the Open University in Milton Keynes and went for a meeting there, staying at a ghastly cheap hotel whose restaurant was part of a kids' play barn, smelling of sticky sweets and sick. A town of straight streets and perfect roundabouts was her abiding memory. All too prinked for her. She liked open air and country smells. Anything too organised made her feel suffocated. Jeans, trainers, and a comfy top at home nowadays. She tried to avoid dresses in favour of smart trousers at work. The on-board train announcement had progressed to a list of delicacies available in the on-board shop.

"Hot drinks and snacks, wines, beers, and spirits, and toasted sandwiches."

All very appetising for overweight businessmen in grey suits, and groups of young girls returning from a London shopping trip needing to soak up excessive alcohol, she thought.

Looking out of the window again, she caught her reflection against the dark background of the tunnel they now travelled through. Silver-grey hair, when it used to be fair. Wrinkles under her eyes, and cheeks a little saggy. Still, she wasn't bad. Regular jogging and tasteful make-up meant she still caught the occasional man staring, although she didn't know whether she could be bothered anymore. It had been ages, and she had lost the taste even for socialising, never mind sex. A hot milky Earl Grey tea and an enjoyable book were the sum of her entertainment nowadays.

Having no energy to work on her ever-present laptop, she picked up a slightly battered magazine left by a previous passenger and aimlessly flicked through the pages. Donald Trump (boring), TV programmes (all past), crossword (already filled out), and then her eyes settled on an article entitled 'Solo living'. Apparently today, more women in their forties and fifties were now living alone and this could be "incredibly enriching and liberating". She didn't feel enriched or liberated, but slightly sad and a bit bored with life, if she was honest. Was it OK to feel lonely? She folded over the corner of the article page and closed the magazine. She would take it with her for later.

As the train stopped at Milton Keynes, there was a disruption to her calm as the outside world invaded the sanctuary of the carriage. Three people got on scanning the carriage for empty seats. Standard practice was to not make eye contact and hope they would pick another table seat. Avoiding eye contact was a technique learnt at school and perfected at university. The key was to look engrossed in your work as though you really hadn't noticed the fact that the train had stopped, all the doors had opened, and several people had got on and were now struggling up the aisle with large cases. Bad luck. A man stopped and was now looking expectantly at the seat opposite.

"Is this seat taken?"

No, but I would prefer you didn't take it because I don't want to have to look at you all the way to Manchester. If you do take it, don't you dare order a pepperoni panini, as the smell will make me throw up, Liz thought.

"No, please. You're fine." Said with a well-practised gentle smile.

He sat down and went through the standard ritual of taking a laptop out of his backpack (more modern than hers, she noted) and booting it up. Earbuds as well, she noticed, so he was probably going to watch a film. Nice pullover, though, looked like Merino, and clean white T-shirt underneath. Sleeves pulled up to mid-forearm, so has an action-man opinion of himself. Sports watch – jogger? Perhaps uses the gym, mid-forties, I'd say. Stop it! Ever since she was about fourteen, she'd done this. Analyse everyone and judge them. He was probably happily married with two kids and a Labrador, drove a Range Rover, and lived in a leafy suburb somewhere. Should she speak or not? She was never sure when travelling. You sit close to a person and never know whether you should interact. In any other situation, if someone was in your personal space, you would say something, but not lifts or public transport, it seemed. An unwritten law. Pretend they are not there and protect yourself with an imaginary shell.

"Do you know which direction the shop is?" he said.

Oh, no. Please no toasties!

"I think it's through the next carriage towards the back of the train." Said with the same friendly smile.

"OK, thanks. Can I get you anything?"

Hmm. Considerate too, and he made eye contact.

"No, I'm fine, thanks."

But she really wasn't. She had an illustrious career, but she was lonely, and life held no excitement anymore; she often felt lethargic and permanently slightly depressed when she was away from work. Days rolled on and time ticked away. And for what? She had a nice house, a flashy car and everyone thought she was a success. But inside, she still wanted to be back on the sofa in her childhood home, curled up with the family.

"No problem."

And at that, action man got up and walked away. As he stood, she noted his slim-fit jeans and thought the white and grey Nike trainers were tasteful but not over the top. This situation had potential, and if she were in her twenties, she might have made an effort. Turned on the smile, laughed at his jokes, been oh so interested in what he was saying. She closed her eyes and dosed briefly, remembering times at uni when she caught men's eyes travelling up and down her long legs.

When she opened her eyes, he was sitting quietly, sipping his coffee and working on his computer.

"How do you spell femur? Is it E-R or U-R – it doesn't come up on my spellchecker for some reason."

"U-R."

"Yes, that looks better now that I've typed it. Someone at work fell off a bike and got a fractured femur and has had to have a hip replacement, apparently. Sounds like a nightmare."

Liz listened, made a polite hmm sound to show empathy, but said nothing. She opened her laptop and fired up the screen to look at her slides and tweak them after her presentation. Debriefing, she called it with her students.

"Good evening, ladies and gentlemen… and thank you for travelling with us. My name is Gerard… and I would like to remind you of our on-board buffet service… situated between coaches F and G towards the back of the train. The buffet car will close in ten minutes… after we pass through Stoke-on-Trent… We will be arriving in Stoke-on-Trent in ten mins. Stoke-on-Trent our next station stock… I mean stop. Our next station stop. It's been a long day!"

Liz smiled to herself and looked up to see several other passengers doing the same. She loved the random camaraderie you got on trains. A shared suffering, she supposed.

"Train announcements are always entertaining," said her opposite number.

"Yes, I have known several prize ones," she replied.

"What is it you're working on?" he said.

"Oh, just some slides for a lecture, how about you?"

"Checking emails and trying to sort out personnel. I've got someone off, he with the hip replacement, and need to cover his workload. Always a nightmare. What is it you do?"

"I'm an orthopaedic surgeon – always a conversation stopper!"

"Ha! Hence you knew how to spell femur."

"Precisely, I write it a lot in any given day. What about you?"

"I'm a buyer for an engineering company. My section makes components for offshore wind turbines which is pretty big at the moment as you can imagine."

"Sounds exciting. Do you ever get to visit them, by boat, or helicopter, or whatever?"

"I have done. It feels quite 'special forces' flying in a helicopter over a wind turbine in the North Sea. Although this is tempered by constantly trying not to appear as though I am about to throw up. I've had travel sickness since I was a kid."

"So, not good when the train starts to tilt, then."

"Tell me about it. I have to look up from my computer screen and fix my eyes on something distant just to stay alive."

Liz grinned and realised she was having a pleasant conversation with someone about day-to-day things other than orthopaedic surgery. She was certainly developing a bit of a warm fuzzy, she noticed, to her surprise.

"Stockport, Stockport our next station stop!"

"That's me. I had lost all track of time! I'm Mark, by the way. It's been great to meet you, and I really enjoyed the chat."

"Liz, nice to meet you."

Mark packed his laptop up and crumpled his coffee cup into his hand, reaching across to the bin on the opposite side of the carriage to put it in. He stood up and slipped his laptop bag over his shoulder and moved forward to get into the queue of people ready to disembark. Liz went back to her laptop.

"Sorry, don't want to be weird, but if you fancy getting a coffee sometime, that's my contact email."

It was Mark who had walked back from the train door and was placing his business card on the table.

"I don't have anything other than a cheesy work card, but the email will get me, and I've written my mobile on the back."

Liz looked up with what she was aware was a slightly surprised look on her face and consciously changed it to a thin smile. Mark held up his hands in mock surrender.

"Sorry, as I said, trying not to be weird."

He rejoined the queue of people now getting off.

As the train pulled out of the station heading for Manchester, Liz looked at the card sitting on the desk in front of her. She knew she had an appalling social life, and she really did want to meet someone outside her insular circle of medics. But meeting a man on a train? It was just so Mills and Boon, and she thought perhaps slightly creepy. He might be a murderer or rapist or simply have a wife and two kids and want a bit on the side. No, she would leave the card precisely where it was and file the memory away under 'interesting but could be odd'.

"Manchester Piccadilly, our final station stop. Please ensure you take all belongings with you."

Liz packed her laptop into her bag, stool up and pulled her coat down from the overhead rack. Unfolding it, she slipped her arms into the sleeves and fastened it against the inevitable Manchester rain. She would not bother with a taxi, as her flat was only a short distance from the station and the traffic would be hell around the station anyway.

She joined the queue standing in the carriage corridor as the train slowed down to stop. Suddenly the train jerked forward, and she was pulled off balance. She put her hand down on the table to steady herself and her hand landed right next to the business card. She had a flashback to a personal-growth weekend retreat at her second university and a talk on meaningful coincidences. She hadn't used the technique in years, but on an impulse, she picked up the card and put it into her inside coat pocket, hoping nobody had seen. Stepping off the train, she headed for the station exit, feeling slightly guilty.

17

Should I or shouldn't I?

Liz slipped off her jacket and put it on the back of a chair.
"OK, let's go through examination of the hip joint quickly and then we can move on. Denise, history, and red flags."

"Slow onset pain with exacerbation due to increased overload. Heavy shopping bags, prolonged standing, long hill walks, or whatever. Red flags age, sleep disturbance, increasing pain, recent infection, history of carcinoma, trauma."

"Good. Pete, objective examination."

"Look, feel, move. Change in contour, localised pain to palpation, site, and type. Range of motion typically capsular pattern with reduced range to flexion and adduction. Harder end-feel to joint."

"OK, but you both focused only on the hip. Remember to clear the spine and consider medical conditions in the iliac fossa. Pain referral from the lumbar spine or pelvis into the hip region, or visceral referral into the area. Is the hip an isolated pain, or part of a pattern of several pains, suggesting a systemic rheumatological condition?"

They chatted for a while, Liz demonstrating the standard hip exam, for Denise to practise on Pete, and then they reversed so they both had a chance to play both doctor and patient. Liz corrected their hand position and body stance to avoid too much strain on the practitioner and to make things more comfortable for the patient. When she was happy, they moved on.

"So, if we are considering osteoarthritis, do we scan?"

"No, not according to NICE," said Pete.

"Yes and no," said Denise.

"OK, explain," said Liz.

"Routine X-ray is not needed to confirm the diagnosis, clinical features are usually enough. But X-ray might be needed to exclude other conditions, or if there is a sudden worsening of symptoms."

"Spot on. The clinical examination, and especially the history, is usually the strongest indicator. Don't forget that includes psychosocial factors, not just hands-on stuff. Quality of life might be poor with a good X-ray and equally might be good with a poor X-ray. Mood, relationships, housing are all social factors to be considered. Let's get away from pure pathomechanics, which was the only thing emphasised when I trained. Humans are not just machines."

This was one of her favourite lines. Although she was an orthopaedic surgeon dealing daily with bones, she was well aware that non-structural factors were important. She was lead author on a number of papers that argued for non-surgical management of hip osteoarthritis whenever possible and had lectured widely on the error of relying solely on X-rays to make a diagnosis that may ultimately lead to surgery. She often thought she would have been better training as a physio rather than a surgeon, because exercise was her thing.

"OK, let's wrap up. Anyone going to the coffee shop?"

"I'm up for one," said Pete.

"I've got to go to ward 10B," said Denise, "so I'll have to cry off."

Pete and Liz packed up their things and walked down the corridor.

"So, how are things, Pete?" said Liz.

"Not so bad. Work's going OK, to be honest, but home life is a bit stressed."

"How's that?" said Liz.

"Same old, same old, I'm afraid. Working all hours and not enough time for home."

"Hmm, how's the baby?"

"She's OK, sleeping through now, at least. But no one told me a young baby would be 24/7 and Gemma was suffering for a bit from post-natal depression, I think. All our energy goes on the baby and none on ourselves, so things between us are a bit rough at the moment, sad to say."

"That's a familiar story. I remember last year when Sue Arnold came back from maternity leave, she was a changed woman. Unfortunately, most of the healthcare focuses on the baby and very little on the young mum. I'm sorry, but you joined a profession which is good at treatment but appalling at wellness. Welcome to the club."

Liz and Pete walked in silence into the coffee shop; he ordered a cappuccino, she a green tea. Liz had a flashback to her university years when her boyfriend at the time, Graham, had always drunk cappuccinos in the coffee shop, only to admit later that he really hated coffee and preferred green tea. When she had produced it in her student room, it had led to other things. She missed her student days, as did many people, she supposed. It had all seemed so simple. Only herself to focus on, and any problems revolved around studies, bus times, going out and what to eat. But she always had people around her at an equal social level. She could just drop into a friend's room for a chat, and they would just appear at her door to do the same. Nowadays everyone wanted Ms McClennan. They would chat about some clinical problem or research finding and then go. She was the boss, and nobody cared about Liz the person. If they asked about her weekend, she felt they were only half listening, going through the motions. She was Ms McClennan, a leading light in her profession, never just Liz as she had been at uni.

Pete's bleep went off, so he had to go, and Liz finished her tea. As she was going, she reached into her coat pocket for a tissue and, as she pulled it out, a card fell onto the floor. It was the business card she had been given a week ago on the train back from London, from Mark Smith. She looked at it and thought about screwing it up and just putting it in the bin. That's what Dr McClennan would do, but what about Liz from uni? She wouldn't be sure, and would dither a bit, but eventually she would phone and go slightly pink if he answered. Could she dig deep inside herself, through all the layers of learning and responsibility. The defensive barriers put up, the successes and failure, the celebrations, and disappointments. She walked out of the coffee shop along the corridor to her car, passing several people as she did.

"Ms McClennan?"

"Not now, I'm in a bit of a rush."

"Dr McClennan."

"I'll catch you later."

She beeped her car, opened the door, and sat inside. For several seconds, she just looked at the card. She got her phone out and breathed slowly, closing her eyes. Digging deep within herself, she travelled back and found student Liz. The shy, leggy runner. She dialled the number and pressed the green button, noticing that she had a tear in her eye. Pull yourself together, she thought.

Three rings and the call was picked up.

"Not again! The drawing needs to be scrapped and redone; they can't just be changed. Suck it up and get it done."

She sat silent for a second. "Hello."

"Who is this?"

"Oh, hi, is that Mark?"

"Yes."

"This is Liz McClennan. We met on a train from London to Manchester and you left me your card. Just wondered if you wanted to grab that coffee. If you were just being polite at the time and are now cringing in regret, that's fine. I'll understand."

"Oh God, I'm so sorry, I don't normally answer the phone like that, I thought you were somebody else," he said in a softer tone.

"No problem, these things happen."

Silence.

"Yes, coffee, would be great and I'm not cringing in regret! Glad you phoned, actually. A coffee and chat would be brilliant. I'm in Manchester on Monday afternoon if that's any good. Failing that, how about one evening?"

"Days are not good for me, but I could do an early evening. How about Tuesday, about 5.30 or 6.00?"

"5.30 on Tuesday works for me. There's a coffee shop across from the station, the one with the old bike hanging in the window, what about there?"

"I know the one. Not been in, but I'll see you there."

"Look forward to it. I'll wear a red carnation in my lapel just in case you have forgotten what I look like!"

"If you can get a carnation at this time of the year, you're a very clever man."

She hung up. I can't believe I just did that, she thought. I just asked a man out for a coffee, who I met on a train and have only spoken to for about twenty minutes. She was nervous and excited at the same time.

***

Liz arrived at the coffee shop and stood across the road looking for a while. She wondered what the old bike was doing. It was painted bright red all over, tyres as well. Clearly some artistic statement which she did not get.

I'm obviously too old, not hip enough or simply unartistic, she thought. There were a few people inside, so she would not feel too exposed, and being near the station, there were several women sitting by themselves, some checking mobiles, others on computers. She pushed the door open and quickly scanned the floor to see if she recognised anyone. In the corner sat a man reading a paper. As she looked, he lowered the paper, and she recognised it to be Mark, with a coffee mug in front of him. He reached down for something at one side, sat up again and placed a single red carnation on the table opposite him. With a flourish, he opened his hands, turning his palms upwards, and met her eyes with a gentle smile.

It was such a lovely gesture that she started to laugh and put her hand over her mouth as she did so. Catching the barista's attention, she ordered a green tea. She paid for it and carried it over to Mark.

"So, a clever man, indeed."

He half stood and bowed slightly.

"Nice to see you again, and sorry for the tone on the phone call, I had a nightmare of a day."

"We all have those. Did you get your drawing redone?"

"Yes, but not without more trauma."

"Windmills, isn't it, you said on the train."

"Yes, I was an engineer, now in the planning and operations stages of projects. Sometimes I long for the days when I simply got my hands dirty. And you're an orthopaedic surgeon, you said."

"That's right, for my sins."

"Tell you what, as we have both probably had our fill of our jobs, why don't we talk about everything but."

"Sounds like a good plan to me. A conversation about things other than surgery or medicine would be very welcome."

"And I promise not to mention turbines, wind farms, or anything related."

"Done."

"So, hobbies?" said Mark.

"Running and yoga, that's about all."

"So, no crochet or flower arranging, then."

"Sadly not, I'm an active girl. What about you?"

"Bit of gym work. Used to do karate but haven't in years. Jogging when I'm staying in a hotel. Play the guitar a bit."

"Really. What sort? Are you a heavy rock bassist or a budding Knopfler?"

"Acoustic. I twang and sing incredibly old Simon and Garfunkel songs very poorly."

"Showing your age there. I bet none of my staff under thirty have heard of 'Bridge Over Troubled Water.'"

"Philistines."

They chatted for about an hour, both enjoying talking to someone about things other than work. They recalled a few shared experiences, remembering TV programmes and pop music from the 1990s. It felt comfortable. Liz wondered what would happen at the end of the evening. Did she want to see Mark again and would he want to see her, or was this just a social chat and bit of networking? She wasn't sure what she wanted.

"Right then, time to go, I suppose," he said.

"Yep, we both have work in the morning."

"Listen, I'd love to do this again, but don't want to be pushy. To be honest, I'm not sure what the form is nowadays with internet dating, apps, and stuff. In my day you just went out for a pint. It all seemed uncomplicated. If you fancy doing something, I don't know, going hillwalking or catching a film, or whatever, I'd love that, but I'll leave it up to you. I'm a bit out of practice, I'm afraid, when it comes to relationship stuff."

Liz looked at Mark and smiled. She saw a mild, gentle man and kindred spirit. But is that what she wanted? She really didn't know. If she were honest with herself, she was comfortable in her own company. She could go out for meals by herself and sit quietly with a book. Her exercise routine was essentially solo, and her job? Well, her job put a barrier around her. She performed an act. Healer, teacher, mentor, but never really friend.

***

Liz was based at the Royal, a bright shiny new hospital which had been built on the grounds of an old Victorian red-brick monolith. It had the most up-to-date facilities, and her surgical rooms were the envy of many of her colleagues. However, although most of her clinics were based at the Royal, once a fortnight she went to the Community Hospital, a small, often-unnoticed building to the outskirts of the city. She quite liked the intimate feel of the Community Hospital with its ageing wards and peeling paint, but it had another hidden secret. During the formative years of the NHS, a number of postgraduate educational facilities had been established across the country. These had gradually dwindled over the decades until now only two were left, and one was at the Community Hospital. It ran postgraduate courses for all medical and therapy professions but focused on rehabilitation. Liz herself had presented several courses and been to numerous lectures within her own field. The postgrad centre at the Community Hospital could organise anything. However, because it was cross-professional, you could also go on courses outside your own area and that could be hugely entertaining. The psychology department in particular would often organise very strange lectures and single-day courses. Liz, together with a core of others, lapped these up. They called them the alternative courses and there was a group of about thirty professionals who attended them in dribs and drabs. Over the years, they had called themselves the Altos, and really only met on the courses and the lunch and coffee breaks they involved. There was Dave, a physio, Liz herself, Sheila, a senior sister, and Barry, an occupational health nurse. Liz went on anything that piqued her interest. She had done tai chi for balance, although there was nothing wrong with her balance, and several mindfulness courses. She even did Tibetan chanting and chakra healing using singing bowls. That particular workshop had been run by a young man with a shaven head and goatee beard called Sebastian-Ray. At lunch break one of the other students whispered to her that Sebastian-Ray had formerly been called Doug Janes and she recognised him from the fish stall at the local indoor market. Today, however, the lecture was on loneliness and solitude. Several of them had agreed to attend this because the lecturer came to the end of one of their yoga classes to promote his workshop. When he had said there was a difference between loneliness and solitude, Liz and Denise had looked at each other and frowned, with Liz mouthing is there? Sheila had said solitude for her was sleeping in a separate bed to her husband when he snored, and they had both stifled giggles like two schoolgirls.

Liz actually learnt a few things from the talk. Although related, apparently solitude is something which you choose, while loneliness is often forced upon you. She was familiar with both but had not realised they were separate and found the talk quite enlightening. It seemed to switch on a light bulb in her mind. Solitude was the tranquil, peaceful state she sought with her yoga and meditation and was essentially positive. Loneliness, on the other hand, was negative and imposed through social isolation and lack of close relationships. It gave feelings of emptiness and sadness and in extreme cases even despair, said the tutor, all of which Liz felt she had experienced over the years. She could certainly identify with this. She enjoyed her meditation and looked forward to it, but often felt isolated from others by her position at work and alone, especially at weekends. One of the points that really gelled with her was that loneliness could occur even when you were surrounded by others if your connection to them was superficial or unproductive. Knowing this, she decided to act; she needed a close friend away from her work, and she thought Mark just might fit the bill.

***

Liz had phoned Mark, and they agreed to go for a long walk around a local woodland park. She had tossed up between a walk and a run but thought that in all probability she would outrun him. Even though he appeared to be a kind and gentle man, he still had a male ego which would be by its very nature quite fragile. When she arrived, he was taking his coat out of the back of his car and out jumped a black Labrador.

"Sorry, should have checked. You OK with dogs?"

"Love them, especially Labs," she said, fondling the dog's ears.

"This is Milly, she's not mine but my neighbours'. I walk her occasionally for them."

As they began their walk, Liz noticed Mark looked quite the action man in a thick jumper with leather patches. She noticed he had pulled his sleeves up and had nice forearms. She had always been a bit of a forearm girl. She had chosen to wear walking shoes rather than boots, as they were walking in the woods and it was dry. A cropped padded jacket with thick running tights below and a head warmer completed the look. The effect was to emphasise her bum, which she was pleased to notice his eyes strayed towards several times during the walk. Still got it, girl.

They walked and chatted; their conversation being

punctuated by each of them throwing sticks for Milly. The dog liked to hold on to the stick and then drop it at Liz's feet so she would try to pick it up. Usually, Milly would grab it again and Liz would wrestle her for it, throwing it into the bushes so she would have to snuffle around to find it. Eventually Milly got tired of bringing the sticks back and simply chose the biggest, most cumbersome one to walk with, acting like a snow plough to people approaching from the opposite direction. If they stopped to chat to people, Milly would look on with doleful eyes and occasionally drop her stick to smell someone's crotch.

"Sorry, she has no manners," Mark would say, trying and usually failing to push the dog away.

Liz found out that Mark had been married and was now divorced. His ex-wife had been a personnel assistant working in HR when he first moved to his Leeds company. He had been intimidated by her, as she was picked up from work by a famous footballer in a Porsche. Later in the year he had found her crying in the car park after her boyfriend had hit her. He had consoled her and sworn not to tell anyone in the company about it. One thing had led to another, as they say, and they had dated and eventually married. The marriage didn't work out and they split up after five years. There were no children.

"How about you, what's your relationship story?" asked Mark.

"Very boring, I'm afraid. Had a first-love relationship in the last year of university and we both went separate ways, he to computing and me to medicine. Couple of flings throughout my career but nothing special. Most of my time has been spent studying and building a career in a male-dominated profession. Female orthopaedic surgeons are few and far between. I've been a bit all work and no play, and time moves on, I'm afraid."

They got to the end of the path to find a small coffee shop set up. A van and some wooden tables, but it was very welcome. They got drinks and a piece of cake, Liz a flapjack and Mark a brownie, and sat down. Milly stared at Liz with saliva dripping from her mouth until she realised she wasn't going to get anything, so curled up under her seat.

"So, what's on the agenda for the rest of your weekend?" said Liz.

"I'll get Milly back and then grab a bite to eat, I'm off to London tomorrow. Catching a 7.30am train."

Liz nodded and kept quiet for a while. "If you want, you can stay at my place to make the early start easier. I've got a spare room which girlfriends often use."

"Are you sure?"

"Yes, we could eat out or I could cook something."

"You can cook as well as doing surgery?"

She laughed.

"Yes, basically the same thing. You use tools and follow a set of predefined steps. When something goes wrong, you improvise."

"But not with veg, I'm guessing. Tell you what, I can help out in the kitchen. I promise to follow your orders. I'm an engineer, I'm very precise with tools."

"It's a deal."

"I'll report for duty at what, 6.30?"

"Sounds good, I'll do a bit of shopping and change."

"And I'll get doggo back home and get a shower. What's on the menu?"

"Veggie OK?"

"Perfect for me."

"OK then, it's an old favourite. Coconut and sweet potato curry with brown rice. Spinach dahl and green salad. I'll bung a couple of samosas and onion bhajis in for good measure, bought from a supermarket, not homemade, I'm afraid."

"Brilliant, see you at half six."

Liz gave Milly the end of her flapjack, making a friend for life, and they got up and walked back. Liz talked about the recipe as she went. Mark listened and thought, this woman is lovely. There was a familiarity about her which he found appealing.

18

Recipe

Mark arrived at Liz's flat on Minshull Street at 6.30pm with a bottle of wine in one hand. He pressed the entrance buzzer.

"Hello."

"Hi, Liz. I come bearing wine."

"Come on up, I'm on the third floor."

As he passed the desk, the concierge said, "Good evening, sir." Mark felt himself being appraised, especially as he had an overnight bag.

"Hi," he replied.

He pressed the lift button and went up to the third floor. Liz was standing at her door.

"Welcome to my humble abode," Liz said. "The spare room's through there if you want to dump your bag. I'm in the kitchen creating mayhem."

Mark put his bag in the spare room and followed Liz through to the kitchen, putting his wine on one of the surfaces.

"I met your concierge. Not sure he approved."

"Tom? He's just an old soldier who keeps us all in our place. He's quite a reassuring figure to come home to on a dark and rainy Manchester night."

"Yes, I can see that. The building has a nice heavy glass entry door as well. If I'm not mistaken, it's tempered laminated frameless glass with a top and floor mount system."

"Ah, you can't take the engineer out of the boy!"

"Guilty as charged."

"So, what should I do, miss."

"Well, my boy, you could chop up the sweet potato while I top and tail the green beans. I'll toss you for the privilege of slicing the courgette and bunging in the coconut milk. I've fried the onion and garlic for the dahl and added the turmeric and cumin. Just about to make up the stock."

They chopped and sliced as they chatted, Mark eating bits of raw sweet potato. Liz added the lentils and stock to the onions for the dahl and then put the brown rice on to simmer.

"Let it all cook for a bit and then we'll put the samosas and bhajis in the oven. Shall we crack open the wine?"

"I'm a dab hand with a corkscrew," said Mark. "It's all to do with force moments and leverage."

Liz was silent for a time while she arranged samosas on a metal tray. She still had a slight resistance to drinking alcohol, and were she by herself, she would not drink. Over the years she had become a bit better, but her thoughts always went back to the freshers' party at uni when she smelt alcohol. She tried not to let it dictate her behaviour, it was just that not drinking had now become a habit with her.

"Did you know that corkscrew thinking is a thing," said Liz.

"What? No."

"I heard it at a lecture once. Apparently, it was something Winston Churchill championed in the Second World War. Trying to get people away from linear thinking. Creative problem solving and emotional intelligence skills, so it seems."

Mark filled two wine glasses.

"Well, I'll drink to that," he said and offered Liz a glass.

They took the plates through to the dining room in relays, and Liz selected some music.

"Any objection to Van Morrison?" she said.

"Van the man, God bless him. Still have *Astral Weeks* on vinyl."

"Me too. Saw him live once, many moons ago."

As they ate, they chatted, and Liz explained exactly what an orthopaedic surgeon did.

"I'm a hip girl. Most surgeons nowadays specialise on one area. Shoulders, hips, knees, foot, and ankle, or whatever. It makes keeping up with changes in methods and research easier."

"I can't imagine the length of training you have to go through."

"It's tough, but you surround yourself with people who are doing the same, so you just get caught up in it. But it's just like any other job, really. It has this whole romantic image surrounding it from TV series and stuff, but at the end of the day you learn techniques and put them into practice like anything else. It would be the same learning to type or operate a road drill, I suppose. Also, there are the personalities to contend with. An operating theatre is just like an office in that respect, everyone has home stuff going on. Problems with the kids, partner stuff, or whatever. It's all very human."

"So how did you get into engineering?"

"I was a YTS kid and worked up through the ranks. HNC, degree, and lots of professional training. I mucked up my A levels at school so couldn't go to university. Had a few lowly jobs and met a few dodgy characters. YTS saved me, I suppose. Put me back on a straight path. Later discovered I was dyslexic which partially explained my trouble at school, but it wasn't a thing then. Nobody identified it until I began my degree course."

"That's a familiar story, I'm afraid. Lots of boys especially, fall through the net."

They packed the dishes away and stacked them into the dishwasher.

"This is a nice flat," said Mark.

"Yes, fortunately I bought it before the prices went sky high. It's convenient, but quite tucked away so not too noisy. I'll give you a quick tour if you like, not much to see. Three beds, the main one is ensuite. This one is small, so I use it as my office. Bathroom and shower. Kitchen and dining room you've seen. Downstairs we have a baggage room and small gym which is handy. Treadmill, bike, rower, and a small multigym. Few dumbbells and mats and stuff. I'm one of the few people to use it, I think, and then only occasionally. I've got membership to Pheons through work. They have every bit of kit you could want and a nice pool and sauna suite, so I go there. On a fine day it's walkable, just two blocks, and when it's pouring down there's an underground car park with a lift which brings you up inside the gym."

"You're in Leeds, you said?"

"That's right. I rented a flat when I first moved there with my job. It is an old mill development, quite nice. They had a scheme where you could buy it when you had been in for five years and that's what I did. My first flat was a two-bed, and I sold that and moved into a bigger one in the same block. I've been there for twenty years. The area around has been modernised and is now a fashionable spot, but when I moved in, the mill was one of the first things to be done up and everything around was old Leeds. Terraces and corner shops. Some houses had their electric cables on the outside and there were even some original cobbled streets. They did the whole place up and relayed the cobbles to make it arty. The claim is that cobbles make it easier for pedestrians to hear cars approaching. They seal them with asphalt to make a continuous surface nowadays."

"And you went to the uni to do your degree?"

"No, the HNC conversion was at the old technical college which joined with the poly and then became the met. You would have been at the old red-brick traditional uni."

Liz was silent in thought for a while.

"So, we would have been in Leeds roughly the same time, working it out. You will have finished your YTS and moved to Leeds when I went up to uni. I would have been a fresher."

Mark was silent for a while, his thoughts clearly miles away.

"Sorry, yes, we might have walked past each other in the street!"

"Right, well, I think I'll turn in. Early one for me in the morning," said Mark.

Liz looked at him for a while, he seemed to have gone a bit cold. She wasn't sure what she had said.

"If you're happy in the spare bed, that's fine, but you can come in with me if you like. Just to sleep though, nothing else. Let's be adult about this. Shared bodily warmth and all that." She had no idea why she had said this. After all this time, she still wasn't cautious. She had met a guy on a train for God's sake, gone for coffee, a walk, and had a meal, and now she had brought him back to her place and asked him to sleep with her. She had resolved to move on, but was this too quick?

"I'd like that. I will be a true gentleman and honour your chastity. Lead on."

***

Mark lay on his back, in his underwear in case things got out of control. Liz was wearing shorts and a T-shirt and had turned towards him and placed her head on his chest. They were chatting as she caressed his chest, as it seemed the thing to do.

"The marriage didn't work, I suppose, because I was a

bit star-struck to begin," said Mark. "Looking back, I think she was a bit of a trophy wife. She had been with a famous footballer and now she was with me and all that. Young men are a bit stupid, really."

"So are young women, believe me. It's just part of life, Venus and Mars, as they say."

"Eventually I realised she was a bit shallow. That sounds like a terrible thing to say, and the marriage failure was not all on her, if I'm honest, far from it."

Mark turned over to face Liz.

"The thing is, it really affected me. I didn't think it would, but it did. Guilt, failure, lots of stuff going on in my head. It's common for men to talk about mental health nowadays but back then it was just suck it up and move on. Looking back, I struggled when I really should have sought some help."

They lay silent for a while, Liz looking at Mark.

"I was raped in my fresher year."

She just came out with it, she didn't know why. She had never told any boyfriend before. After the conference she realised she had been bottling things up all these years and it had been eating away at her, stopping her from moving on. She was a forty-six-year-old woman with a nineteen-year-old's problems.

"Bloody hell," Mark said, and deep down inside, a fear was rising. Something dark and unseen but still there.

"It was at a party. I was young and innocent and never really drank. I went to the party to try to get in with the popular set and my drink was spiked. I ended up in a bedroom not really knowing what had happened, and my friends took me home. Like you, I didn't really think it had affected me. I didn't really think anything, to be honest, until the next day. I'd never had sex, and it was a friend whose mum was a nurse who worked it out and they took me to a SARC centre. Tests, counselling, and stuff. It helped. They taught me some techniques, mindfulness and what have you. I think it helped more because I didn't recognise that I needed help. I suppose when you know something is the matter with you, you're halfway there, but if you don't, it eats away at you, silently affecting everything you do."

"Yes, I've found relationships difficult since the divorce. It's like, why bother. Life is just easier by myself." His heart was pounding, breath short.

"I know, I know, totally. But now, lying here, this feels so good. Relationships are part of life's great patchwork. You can do without them, but they're fun to have. It's like food. You can survive on nutrient-rich drinks, but eating a meal is so much better."

"You're right. And on that note, let's get some sleep," Mark said.

He lay there with his eyes closed and thoughts drifted in and out of his head. He knew he wouldn't sleep, but he had to keep calm and appear to.

19

Cobblestones and Mills

"It's owned by the Portside trust who bought up a number of old mills in the area. Saved the heritage really by converting the buildings and using them for flats rather than flattening the lot. Originally it was a Victorian flax mill, and they took down the broken bits, repaired what they could and built the new section on in a matching brick colour."

Mark and Liz were standing outside Mark's flat in Leeds, having come over for the day. They had gone hillwalking and agreed to drop off at his place to see his flat.

"When I moved in, it was all old terraces in the immediate area in that direction and suburbia over there. The terraces were gutted and modernised, so they all matched, and the cobbles were relaid. The trouble is, it has become very fashionable, a bit like Notting Hill in London, and the local people no longer live here. It's all aspiring young professionals. We can walk around a bit if you like, there are some coffee shops and a new veggie restaurant in that direction."

"I like a good veggie restaurant, takes me back to my student days. Thick soup and a bread roll to fill you up all day," Liz replied.

"Yes, and brownies. I like a nice brownie, especially when they have solid bits of chocolate in them."

"Are you having cake fantasies?"

"It's all the hillwalking. A man's got to eat."

They chatted as they walked, Mark pointing out the changes that had occurred since he moved in. As they turned the corner, they saw nicer houses and wider pavements. Many of the houses had been extended with additional rooms for growing children or grandparents, they guessed.

"This is a nicer area, or at least it was when I moved in. With the terraces being modernised, this area is a bit more of a patchwork. Families mainly, whereas the terraces are young couples. When I first arrived in Leeds, I remember going to a party in one of these houses, can't remember which."

As they walked on, Mark stopped and turned, suddenly feeling a shudder pass over himself.

"Hang about, I think it was this house. Yes, I remember some drunk students swinging around the tree when we left." His mind was travelling backwards.

Liz was smiling and looking at Mark as he talked. She turned to look at the house he was indicating and froze. She stood still and went as white as a sheet.

"Liz, are you OK?"

"I... I...."

"What is it?"

"Remember I said I went to a party in the first term and was raped when my drink was spiked?"

Mark looked at her and his face froze.

"You're not serious."

"It was here."

Time was slowing down for Mark – each thought turned like a rusty mechanical clock. He looked at Liz.

"Bloody hell, come on, let's go to the coffee shop and sit down. You need a coffee and a cake or something, you look bloody awful."

They headed off towards the coffee shop, Mark leading the way and breathing quickly. Short, shallow breaths. When Liz was settled with a coffee and cake, she was a little less white.

"That really brought things back," said Liz. "Not so much the event but the feelings after. It seems crazy but the rape itself is not such a big thing to me. Or rather, the physical act was not a big thing. I went to a student party, got a bit drunk and had sex. It happens hundreds of times, I suppose. But it is the fact that someone deliberately targeted a girl – OK, it was me – but targeting any girl is just so sick. And then afterwards, it's like you said, it is the way you feel about it is so surprising. I felt guilt – for what? I don't know, I really can't explain my feelings, but they were real and affected me for the next year or two. Occasionally, I still have little mini flashbacks. I was at a conference and after I had spoken, one of the organisers was congratulating me and held out a glass of sherry. Just the smell of alcohol triggered something, it's crazy."

"Well, you're the medical person, not me, but someone once explained it to me like this. If someone puts a cut lemon under your nose, your mouth will water. Even if you try to stop it happening by controlling your thoughts, your mouth will still water. Your reaction is not your fault, we are simply hardwired that way."

"You're right, associative learning, I think it's called. Actually, that's rather good, I might steal that for one of my lectures!"

They both smiled, and the mood lightened a bit. Liz played with a sachet of sugar for a while, obviously thinking.

"So, you went to a student party at that house? God, I hope it wasn't the same one, that would be spooky."

Mark shifted on his chair. "Long time ago now, and I can't remember much about it, to be honest. I went with a dodgy ex-acquaintance from back home called Neil. I had lost touch with him, thank God, but he phoned me out of the blue and invited himself to sleep on my floor because his girlfriend had thrown him out. He found out about the party because some neighbour in the street had been invited or something. Anyway, we walked over, and I met some engineering students from Leeds Uni and we chatted. A few girls were dancing in the middle of the room. I remember one was going a bit crazy and the uni students were all looking at her because the disco lights went through her summer dress, and you could see her knickers. They were incredibly young. I think Neil danced at some stage, actually, the arse. He was such a loser, he took cans which I had to buy for him, and then I saw him drinking someone else's vodka in the kitchen. He left the next day, and I heard nothing from him again. My mum sent me a press cutting when I was working in Germany, actually, so it would have been about four years later, saying he had been locked up for theft and drugs or something."

Liz had remained silent as Mark spoke.

"Mark."

He was looking out of the window, lost in his thoughts.

"Mark."

"Sorry, what? I was miles away."

"I think it was me at the party."

He just stared at her in silence with his mouth slightly open. His mouth moved, but no sound came out initially.

"You... at the party?"

"I was the one dancing in the summer dress. My friends had told me they could see through it. The boy who offered the can, I think that's what happened to me. It was all a bit hazy afterwards. I went upstairs to use the toilet but felt dizzy and can't remember much after that. I remember flashes. The boy putting his hand up my skirt, the ceiling of the bedroom, and waking up when Suzanne, my friend from uni, was speaking to me. They took me home in a boy's car, and it was not until the next morning that I realised something was wrong. I went to a sexual assault centre in the hospital, and they measured elevated levels of alcohol in my blood, indicating that my drink was likely spiked, probably with vodka as it is relatively tasteless."

"Oh shit. I remember hearing a conversation between Neil and Ted, an even more dodgy character I once shared a house with. I was walking up the stairs and they were in the living room. I overhead them joking about spiking a girl's drink."

Mark was now white and began to sweat.

"No, no, no! That's why he left the next day without saying anything." Mark's heart was racing.

"It's in the past, and we should let it go," said Liz.

"But he might still be around. We should go to the police or something." He was beginning to hyperventilate.

"No."

"They could question him; I can tell them what I know."

"No, Mark, are you OK?"

"Your description of events coupled with mine."

"No, Mark, calm down and try to breathe normally. Settle, slow your breathing. All it will do is bring back unpleasant memories," Liz said calmly. "It was twenty years ago. Wickedness was done but cannot be undone. By revisiting things, we will simply relive the events and that is too hurtful. The best thing we can do is move on. One thing that all this yoga and mindfulness stuff has taught me is you cannot change the past, but you can choose what we do now. The present moment is where we live. Alternative as that may seem, it is true. Let's pay the bill and head back."

Mark was still breathing strangely. Rapid, short, shallow breaths.

20

My friend, how are you?

Liz sat on the London to Manchester train, having attended a Royal College meeting, which, as always, was exceptionally long and very boring. At one point she just wanted to stand up and shout, "Just shut up!" People seem to have the ability to say one hundred words when only ten were needed. It was as though they bathed in the glory of the limelight given out by the other people around the table looking at them.

After her trip to Leeds, her mind had kept wandering back to the conversation in the coffee shop with Mark. In some ways, it added closure for her. She had occasionally wondered in the back of her mind if what happened to her was real. It was as though a little voice was speaking just out of range. Really? it would say. But now, following the conversation with Mark, it had made it real and, in some ways, less threatening. It had brought it out of the darkness and into the light. She dealt with real things every day of her life as a surgeon. If someone had pain and you X-rayed their hip, you might find bone changes. It was real, not imaginary. She had seen the effect this had on patients many times. It was a sense of relief on their faces as it occurred to them that they were not making it up. It was real, not just in their mind. Validating the patient's pain, she had once written in a paper. She felt the same now. It was a real man with a name who had done this to her.

As she sat and allowed her mind to wander, she was aware of the normal train things around her. How many times had she made this journey, she thought. Many dozens, she assumed, and all slightly different. Today the electronic seat reservation system had worked, and she was sitting in the seat numbered on her ticket. Not only that, but so far, the train was on time. She had lost count of the number of delayed journeys she had been on through lack of a driver, leaves on the line, or other seemingly simple things that could go wrong.

As she thought back to the coffee shop conversation, her mind stepped further back to the morning after the party at university. It had been Suzanne who went with her to the police station and then suggested the SARC centre. She had held her hand throughout the entire process and remained a friend for the rest of her university life. She wondered where she was now and what she was doing. When Liz had gone into medicine, Suzanne had gone into teaching. They kept in touch for a while but then she became submerged in medical training and the contacts got further and further apart until eventually it was Christmas cards with a small note. Then they lost contact completely. She felt a pang of guilt but also some regret at the number of people she had known and let fall through her fingers over the years. Yes, she had achieved much but at what personal cost? Was life really about a successful career, scientific papers written and professional recognition? What if she had been brought up in the jungle? Those things would be meaningless to her, but social interaction, which would strengthen the bonds of the herd, would be vital. Perhaps life really was an illusion or just a big game, as had been suggested on one of her many alternative workshops. And if it was a game, was she really winning or had she started to lose from the day of the party? Was her reaction to what had happened the main problem rather than the event itself? She often found this with patients. Some, after hip replacement surgery, would simply start walking and even jogging and return to their daily lives with no effort at all. Others, having exactly the same operation and the same bright clinical future, would make slow progress and end up almost disabled. The difference the research had shown her was not physical. The bone changes and the surgical technique they required were the same in both cases. It was the psychosocial factors which made a difference. The patient's thoughts and beliefs and their interaction with others around them. Friends, family, work colleagues.

The physical or biological act of being raped had clearly had an effect. But, in her case, that was small. She knew of cases where venereal disease had been spread, or pregnancy occurred. She knew of violent cases involving internal and external injury. None of this had happened to her, but as she dwelt on that event over twenty years ago, it suddenly occurred to her that it had been like a bowling ball which had knocked her off course. She had retreated into herself and was protective against interactions with others. She had very few boyfriends since, and none had been serious. She had always been an introvert when it came to relationships, but with Graham at university, she felt it really worked. As she reflected on the memory of Graham, there it was again, that same feeling of warmth and longing. She had been capable of love and sexual attraction, but the event of that party, she felt, had knocked her off course. As the event had occurred before her relationship with Graham, she now recognised that it was her reaction which had caused the rest of her life changes. Had she chosen her career path to reinforce her isolation? A woman in a predominantly male world. Was it because the relationship with Graham had split up that she felt hurt and had become more insular? Where was he now, she thought, and what was he doing?

***

The studio assistant clipped the lapel microphone on Graham's collar. He regretted wearing a pullover over a T-shirt now, as a collared shirt would have been easier for her. He always found miking up slightly awkward. Someone (frequently young, female, and attractive) came uncomfortably close, your faces virtually touched, and you had to just sit there looking at some distant object.

"All done, Mr Edwards."

He hated being called Mr Edwards, it always reminded him of his dad. Had he grown into his father? He sometimes wondered.

"Thanks, that's great."

He sat in a chair under bright lights, waiting for the interviewer to appear. He always thought they did this to make a dramatic entrance. Pathetic, really. But then he had little respect for journalists and TV people in general. Over the years, they had accused him of various things. Making too much money, producing things in the third world, not caring about employees, and now it was AI. Artificial intelligence was going to see off the human race.

"So, Graham. May I call you Graham?"

"Sure."

Sure, he thought? When had he become so American? It had happened gradually. He had left England for his scholarship studies at Cal Tech after finishing at Leeds, in a flurry of activity and regret. It had all been so different. Sunshine, people giving lectures in shorts and flip-flops, and huge facilities. The whole computer lab in Leeds would fit into a small office in California. They had the latest computers with the best screens, things he had only seen in computer magazines in Leeds. Everything was new. He went to Disneyland, ate in huge buffet restaurants, swam in the sea, and walked along the beach. But each time he did something, he thought, I wish Liz was here. When he ate in a restaurant, he wondered which foods she would have chosen. As he jogged along the beach, he imagined her sprinting off in front of him and laughing. He had loved and lost.

"General format will be a casual chat," the interviewer was saying.

"Perhaps a bit of history, how the company was set up then, to the future, and what it holds."

Graham pulled himself back and looked at him. Perfect teeth, coiffured hair, and a suntan. He thought they probably produced clones somewhere on a production line. He had lived in the States for twenty years, but still felt very English. He flew back several times to see his parents and a few uni friends in the early years. He had met up with Mike and Pete once, and Pete had come to stay when he was in the States on business. He had kept in touch online with a few friends. At one point someone had started a uni social media site, and he had heard what people were doing and messaged a few. He had seen Suzanne a couple of times on the site but never Liz. Someone had said they had seen her when she was studying medicine, and later someone else thought she was now a surgeon. He often wondered what she was doing, where her life had taken her. She had left without saying anything to him, and it had hurt. Big boys do cry, his mum had once said to him when he was fourteen. He had, although he never told anyone. In the first few weeks in the States, he felt lonely and isolated, but it had not lasted. The excitement of his course and the dream life in California had sucked him up in a whirlwind, and he had never really looked back. But occasionally, just occasionally, his mind would wander even now back to the girl who had been so special.

***

Liz always felt better when the train eventually pulled into Manchester Piccadilly. Familiar surroundings and the noise and bustle of home, she supposed. As soon as she passed Stockport, she began packing her stuff away. Papers folded up and put back in her file, laptop away in her backpack. She reached up to the overhead rack and took her coat down, unfolding it and slipping her arms into the sleeves. Her thin padded jacket was her go-to for train journeys nowadays. Short to sit in when she took a taxi, and when zipped up to her neck, warm enough to stop the cold Manchester drizzle from seeping through. As the train slowed, she got up from her seat and made her way to the door to be at the front of the line. She hated being too far back because the internal sliding doors had once closed and tried to crush her. As the train stopped, and the light changed from red to green, the person at the front pressed the button and the door gave a staccato metallic thud as it unlocked. A bit like a starting pistol, she always thought, and as the door was pushed open, the sudden change in air and noise seemed to suck people out of the train, like beans from a just-opened can. A fast walk to the barrier past courting couples embracing and snippets of greetings from different directions. "Hi", "Good to see you", "How was the journey" drifted by. Everyone had someone to meet them, it seemed. She braced her shoulders against the straps of her backpack, swiped her ticket through the barrier, seeing the light turn green, and headed to the exit. Minshull Street, here I come.

"Liz? Liz!"

She turned and looked inquiringly at the person bearing down on her from across the station. As she looked into her face, she saw her for the first time in twenty years.

"Suzanne? No! What are you doing here! It must be twenty years at least."

"I live just up the road in Rochdale now. Just about to get the tram. Do you fancy a quick coffee or something? My tram leaves in twenty minutes."

"Yes, great. How about Pret, it's just through there and the tram station is down the escalator across from it."

"Great, lead on!"

Liz slipped the backpack onto one shoulder as they entered the coffee shop, noticing Suzanne had a funky cross-body bag in bright red.

"What will you have?" said Liz.

"Mine's a regular mocha, please."

Liz ordered a green tea and smiled inside as she remembered Saturday mornings in Beano's vegetarian café in Leeds all those years ago. She surprised herself by noticing a warm glow at the thought. As she looked at Suzanne, she saw the same eyes she had known twenty years ago. A few extra lines around the eyes and a wisp of grey at the side and fringe, but her friend was still there. As she returned to her seat, Suzanne looked at her and said, "Oh Liz, I've missed you! Do you remember all those late nights listening to Dexys on my old Garrard deck?"

"Too-Rye-Ay. Yes, I remember! Even had the album cover stuck up on the wall with blu tack!"

"And the house, do you remember the house?"

"Carter Street, yes! You, me, Tracey, and big Dave."

"Yes, and you had a room overlooking the street," said Liz.

"I had a lot of good times in that room!"

"You always were a hussy, Ms Davis."

"Not the case. I was very well behaved. Mostly."

"Anyway, what about you and Graham, you dark horse. We all thought you were so prim and proper and then, bang! The odd couple became the campus stars."

Liz smiled at Suzanne and was taken back twenty years.

"You were a good friend," said Liz. "When all that stuff happened to me in the first year. Don't think I would have coped without you."

Suzanne looked into those familiar eyes. She had missed her friend, she really had. But a little memory kept gnawing at her. What she hadn't said in those last few whirlwind days. Time is a great healer, they say. Possibly, but the thought was still there.

"I know, but I felt guilty taking you to the party, and you know."

"I have a story to tell about that," said Liz. "I met a guy who went to that party and thinks he may know who raped me."

"What?"

"It was a chance meeting. On a train of all places, it was so Mills and Boon. We met up later and got chatting, went for a few... Not dates really, but social stuff."

"Have you kissed him?"

"What? No!"

Liz looked at Suzanne quietly for a few seconds.

"But I have slept with him."

"You old tart!"

"No, really. It was just sleeping. With clothes on. For comfort and what have you. Apparently, it's a thing with millennials according to some of my staff."

Suzanne looked in silence.

"It was just sleeping. Shared bodily warmth and company. Really, he's nice. But."

"But what?"

"I don't think I want a relationship. Well, not that sort of relationship. We chat and it feels… Comfortable. Do you know what I mean?"

"No spark, then."

"No, which I quite like. I don't know if it's age or I'm just boring."

"Or you still love Graham."

"What? No. I haven't seen him since uni."

"He's a famous tech millionaire now, you know, I saw an interview on TV a few years back."

"I knew he was successful, but I don't really keep up with tech stuff unless it's medical."

"Ah, his tech stuff appeals to the bright young things."

"That's me out, then. I've only just discovered how to put my train ticket on my phone!"

Suzanne looked at her watch.

"I have to shoot off. Let's meet up again. So much to say!"

They exchanged phone numbers and emails and promised to meet up soon. Liz watched Suzanne take off and followed her coat with its red bag strap until she disappeared down the escalator. Meaningful coincidences, she thought. Another of the Altos lectures.

21

Let's catch up

Suzanne had phoned Liz the next day, full of excitement. She suggested a pizza in Manchester and a good long chat. Liz liked the idea of catching up with her once best friend and felt she needed to chat things over with someone anyhow. She could think of no one in the world she would rather speak to about all the things she had going on. Suzanne had been with her through thick and thin. She knew Suzanne would peel off the years between them very quickly and see right inside her. This is what Liz needed, she thought. Therapy is fine, but sometimes you just needed a friend who has known you forever.

Suzanne was already seated when Liz arrived.

"Well, hello again," Liz said. "Twice in the last twenty years seems a bit much."

They both laughed. Once they were seated and had ordered their food, the interrogation began.

"So," said Suzanne, "tell all."

"Are we talking career, life, or recent revelations?"

"All of the above but start with your career. What happened from the moment you left me, I've had bits and pieces in letters, but now I need it in the flesh, as it were."

"Well, as you know, I had decided to do accelerated medicine at Liverpool. It was a four-year course, quite hard but rewarding. Most of the hospital work was done around Liverpool and the North West. I then went to work in Bradford to begin my surgery training. I went abroad to Canada for two years learning some new techniques and working in a sports medicine department. That was good because I got to train with one of the university teams, and even competed for them in road races. Then back to the UK, this time to Leeds, and worked my way up to consultant post. Various research projects and publications, and that's it really, in a nutshell, all pretty boring, and time seems to have flown by. What about you?"

"Well, we were actually pretty close geographically because I was in Birmingham for a year doing my PGCE, and I then taught geography for two years. It was OK but teaching in a secondary school is a lot about discipline, and not so much about the subject, so I decided to do a TEFL course and went abroad teaching English as a foreign language. Initially, I went to Spain and taught in an English school near Barcelona, and then I went to the States for three years teaching in a small college in New York. That was a pretty exciting life in the Big Apple and all that. Then I came back to the UK and taught at the University of Huddersfield in their geography department. And that's where I am now, teaching in Huddersfield and living near sunny Rochdale. I think your career has been more exciting, don't you?"

They both cut up their pizza and had a sip of wine.

"Well, that's the career bit done, what about the important things? Men," said Suzanne.

"They've been a bit sparse in my case," said Liz. "I've had a couple of short relationships, a few platonic and a few sexual. One guy was ten years younger and the whole thing was quite exhausting. But mainly I've been happy with my own company. Surgery encourages that in a way, lots of study and conferences and the like. Although I suppose recently, I have been reflecting on this. It's probably more my character than the profession. I think I'm coming to recognise that I simply value my solitude."

"And this new man?" said Suzanne.

"Well, he shared my table on a train from London to Manchester and we got chatting. He left his business card asking if I would like to go for a coffee. Now, obviously, my antennae were waving at this point, and I thought, no way. However, just as I was about to leave the train, I stumbled, and my hand fell next to the card he left on the table. Now, you know me and coincidences, I took the card and put it in my pocket and forgot all about it. At a moment when I was feeling a bit low, I reached into my pocket and the card fell out. A meaningful coincidence again, as they say. I plucked up courage, you would have been proud of me and phoned him. We went for a coffee and a hill walk, and then we cooked a meal together. He had an early start the next morning, so I had invited him to use my spare bedroom. Probably a dangerous thing to do with a man you know so little about, but he had a good feeling about him. At the end of the evening, it was me who suggested we share the bed just for company really, as I think he was as lonely as I. And that's it. I haven't seen him again because he went away for the last week to Germany for two months with work. When he comes back, we'll probably meet up again and I'll see how things go. But as I said, I think it's a platonic comfortable relationship rather than one likely to be filled with passion. But I'm honestly OK with that. Anyway, what about you? You were always a bit of a party girl at university," said Liz.

"I had a bit of a run-in my PGCE year and then things gradually calmed down, I suppose. I had a boyfriend who became a live-in partner for about two years, but we eventually drifted apart, and he moved for his job. Luckily, there were no children involved, and we were in rented accommodation, so the split was really quite painless. Since then, I've only had casual relationships. Feeling a bit cautious about commitment, I suppose. I think I've probably had a bit more sex than you by the sound of it, but I certainly haven't been a party girl. Those days have long since gone. I'm currently a singleton living near Rochdale, which I would have thought was a bit sad in my university years, but actually, I quite enjoy it."

"I know what you mean," said Liz. "Living alone has value which when you're younger we just don't see. As the years roll by, it becomes more and more attractive, doesn't it?"

"Yes, when you're young, I think it's a bit of a badge of achievement having a boyfriend in your bed, but as you get older, the entire process seems a bit messy. Whereas once I wanted a couple of glasses of wine and a man for the night, I'm happy to curl up with cocoa and a good film nowadays. My younger self would say I've become a boring old spinster, but I would say don't knock it until you've tried it." They both laughed.

As they had both finished their pizzas, Suzanne said, "Are we going full hog for dessert?"

"I feel we should," said Liz, "as it's only once in twenty years."

They both ordered coffee and cake, chocolate brownie with a dollop of ice cream for Suzanne, and blueberry cheesecake for Liz. The conversation continued and became more intimate.

"So, tell me what happened with this guy and the party," said Suzanne.

"Well, it was really weird. He had a dodgy friend from back home staying with him at the time in Leeds and he apparently got invited to a party, so they both went. He remembered a girl dancing in a summer dress and the light shining through, showing her knickers."

Suzanne burst out laughing, "Oh, I remember. That was so funny, and you didn't care at all at the time. You were footloose and fancy free."

"When we went for a walk in Leeds, he recognised the house where he'd been to the party, and, Suzanne, I'll be honest, it was the same house, and I was stunned into silence. It took me back twenty years in an instant to that walk from the bus stop to the party. Although properties had obviously changed in that time, to me it was like yesterday."

Suzanne looked on in awe, transfixed.

"Mark said he remembered his dodgy mate started dancing with the girl in the middle and then they both disappeared. But he also remembered said dodgy mate bringing a can to the party and then drinking from a vodka bottle in the kitchen. If you remember at the SARC centre, my blood alcohol levels were high, and they said my drink had probably been spiked, most likely with vodka. Putting two and two together, I think it could have been Mark's dodgy mate who spiked the can of drink and offered it to me. To cap it all, Mark remembered a conversation between dodgy mate and another of the guys he shared a house with back home talking one evening about spiking a girl's drink. That was one of the reasons he left the house to start his YTS course. He was livid when I explained what had happened. He got quite upset, and I was a bit worried about him for a while, to be honest, he started hyperventilating."

"Bloody hell, really?"

"He was all for going to the police and what have you, but I don't want to rake things up again, and anyway what is the point after twenty years? They're not going to be able to prove anything. In a way, I find this revelation a bit like closure because always in the back of my mind I've thought did I just make it all up? Now I realise it did actually happen that gives me some control over the memory. Does that sound mad?"

"Not at all, it sounds very human and very Liz."

Suzanne got up and moved around the table to put her arm around Liz's shoulders. Liz put her head on Suzanne's forearm and said, "I have so missed these chats. In one of our rooms, one of us lying on the bed and the other on the floor."

"There will be lots more, I promise."

22

2000

American dream

When Graham had arrived in America, his mind had been a whirlwind. Everything happened so quickly. He had been shattered by events of his last term in Leeds but had decided that the only way forward was to turn over a new leaf and embrace his new life with gusto. He had been offered a scholarship at Cal Tech and the course was amazing. He decided to start selling his computer programme, which he had intended to do through the computer club in Leeds but had never got around to it. It seemed logical to start now he was in America, especially as interest in the programme was instrumental in him gaining the scholarship in the first place. He simply put a notice up on the department wall at the university and got people to contact him. A relatively innocent move which would go down in the annals of computer history. Gradually, the sales built up and he needed another CD writer to copy the programme quickly enough, and eventually ended up with five writers in his ridiculously small flat, churning away all of the day and night. Over the next few years, he expanded from his flat to his friends' garage and the sales continued to increase. Things would pretty much have stayed as they were had he not met Gina.

He often saw her in the university cafeteria but did not know her. At one point, she had worn a black long-sleeved T-shirt and for a split second, he had thought it was Liz until she turned around. Someone said she was studying graphics and had begun to use a new computer graphics programme they were trialling. One day she appeared in Graham's computer lab wanting somebody to look at her faulty desktop which she had brought with her. Ever the British gent, Graham had seen her come into the lab and said, "Can I take that for you, miss?"

She had looked at him with a look of amazement on her face.

"Oh God, you're British!"

"I am," he said, smiling. "What's the problem?"

She explained what had happened, and he took up the challenge, being used to repairing student computers from the club in Leeds. They chatted, Graham being aware that she was more interested in the sound of his accent than what he was actually saying.

"There we go, all fixed. As right as rain now."

"Sorry, what?"

"As right as rain? Just something we say in England."

She smiled, and he thought she looked like a Hollywood star. She had long hair, perfect teeth and make-up which looked as though she was going on a night out rather than studying at a uni. He would have asked her out there and then, but he was too shy.

"Well, thank you," she said.

"You're very welcome."

She waited as though he was about to say something more, but he didn't, so she left.

He saw her again in the cafeteria (he had gone each day in case she appeared) and said his rehearsed line.

"Computer still OK?"

"Yes, brilliant, thanks."

"Can I join you for lunch?" he said, surprising himself with his confidence.

"Yes, great!"

They sat down and chatted. He told her about his work and where he had studied in Leeds. She assumed they all still wore cloth caps and clogs, having read Dickens and seen Lowry prints at school, and he explained that this was not the case. She talked about her home in Texas, and he got the impression that her parents' ranch was only slightly smaller than Yorkshire. He loved it. Everything in America to him was big, the cars, the shops, the land, even her personality. They started to date, and she showed him America. She drove him around in her big car, took him to all the well-known restaurants, where he ate gigantic steaks, huge salads, and pancake stacks. He was living the dream. He went to stay with her at her parents' ranch, rode a horse (just), and tried to lasso a wooden post. She introduced him to her father, who was a Texan businessman. He encouraged Graham to be more businesslike about his computer venture and set him up in an office. He got him to speak to some financial people, and as things grew, he invested money in Graham's company. Under Gina's father's tutorage, he now had a financial director and a human resources lead. The combination of Gina's father's business acumen and Graham's computer skills was explosive, and the company built up rapidly and became one of California's major hits. His computer programme still sold to students, but now there was something new. Computer games, and he got a head start on them.

Gradually, the relationship began to sour. He didn't want to settle down and was conscious that he was now viewed as the future son-in-law. He was very English; she was a big brash Texan. What he had once found attractive and exciting now began to grate on him. He liked English girls, and deep down he still loved Liz, although he would never admit it to anyone. He missed her and kept comparing Gina to Liz, and Gina, in his mind, came up short. Eventually Graham and Gina split up (he later learnt she had married a senator). Over the years he had several short-term relationships but each time they seemed to be in the shade of Liz's light. He knew he still missed her, and he knew he had let her slip through his fingers, but he could not get her out of his mind.

***

Graham hated board meetings, and this one was particularly difficult. For years they had been known as a gaming company and now they had to encompass artificial intelligence. AI was clearly the way forward, although it was in its infancy. Everyone who was anyone in the computer industry was getting into AI, and they really couldn't afford to be left out. When they had moved into the gaming world, they had a huge advantage from Graham's research. It had taken a long time for the rest of the industry to catch up, and by that time, they had carved out a huge market share for themselves. But AI was something they had little experience in. For this reason, Graham had started to hire some AI experts, and he was now proposing to work with another company who specialised in this area. As with all board meetings, he would prefer to talk about the technical side of computing, but the money men held all the strings. He found himself having to justify the frighteningly large cost of moving into AI to people who knew nothing about it.

After an exhausting two hours, the vote had eventually gone his way, and he looked back enviously to meetings when he had started the company, which involved a chat over a few drinks and a sandwich in a local bar. In his opinion, they had achieved more in those meetings than they ever did with the full board.

But now it was all over, he was free to do what he liked best, go down to the computer labs and chat tech with his fellow geeks. A few of his staff were early birds. Jill and Brian ran across town to the lab, showered, and were at their desks before 8am, choosing to leave early. When he saw them, his mind often wandered back to running with Liz at uni. Was she still running, he thought. As he walked around, there were smiles, jokes, and general banter. Dave was hitting balls over the net of the ping-pong table, his mind clearly miles away. He ran a happy crowd, and although nowadays he spent most of his time in meetings, interviews, and planning, the computer labs were where his heart was. It had all started here, or at least in a smaller lab, as the facilities had grown considerably over the years. He had begun programming and basically doing everything himself. Fairly quickly after his master's degree, it became obvious that tasks needed to be divided, and he began to link with artists and designers. Initially, this had been friends and colleagues from Cal Tech, but over the years, he had employed people and head-hunted skilled staff to build a team that was the envy of the industry.

The artists created the game art, programmers debugged the source code, and designers put it all together with the game being accessed by users at several levels. This had been simple to begin with but had increased in complexity over the years. Now it was possible to play online for an entire day and never visit the same part of the game twice. As he walked round, he heard snippets of conversation about spatial relationships, batching, and image compression.

In the middle of the room were three people standing around a 3D model of a new scene of the game world. They were checking it against a blueprint for accuracy and the designer was talking with two artists about fleshing out his ideas to make the world more believable. There were trees, exotic birds, and water reflecting moonlight into a pool. Graham loved this type of collaboration even now and could remember his excitement at seeing artists draw the worlds he had only imagined. He always found the designers useful, as they seemed to be able to bring everything together and drive a project forwards. It was all too easy, in his opinion, for people to end up in silos, working hard but not communicating well with each other.

Over the years, as the game got more complex, several art sets were needed with maps of each. As a player worked through the levels, things got more difficult, but it had been important that the difficulty curve, as it was termed, was even. For a player to succeed at one level and progress to another only to find it far too difficult would lead to them stopping playing the game, which was a disaster in the gaming world.

***

Suzanne was wrapped up in the quilt, looking at Ben as he got dressed. He had striking broad shoulders and a nice bum and was quite tall. All of these features were in his favour. However, there were two things which went against him; firstly, if Suzanne was honest, he was a bit thick. His conversation revolved around baseball and his car, both of which justified a concentration span of about five minutes in Suzanne's view. Secondly, he tended to talk dirty while he was performing. An annoying habit which would often leave Suzanne thinking she should shout, "Just shut up and get on with it," but of course she never did. She would lie there listening to comments of "Oh, baby, you really do it for me", "Come on", "Unbelievable, yes, yes yes!" She once mentally wrote a shopping list while this was going on and he was pumping away, and regularly gave her best Meg Ryan climax act to stop his diatribe. As she lay there, she thought, I think I'll trade him in for a new model. She had a rule that she never went with undergrad students who she was teaching, but there were plenty of postgrads walking around who found her English accent enticing. He gave her a little wave and she dutifully smiled as he closed the door. Bye, bye, Ben, have a nice life.

She reached across to the bedside table, picked up the TV remote, and began flicking through the channels. Sports, car ads, politics; American TV really was rubbish. Soaps, politics, and continuous ads.

"Bloody hell," she said out loud, and fought to find the volume button, sitting up in bed.

And now we're going to meet a Brit who has taken the computer world by storm, please welcome Graham Edwards!

She watched with saucer eyes as the interviewer chatted with Liz's geeky ex-boyfriend. Suzanne knew he had gone to America on a scholarship to do his master's, but clearly, he had gone much further than that.

So, Graham. May I call you Graham?

Of course.

You're a Brit, from Britain.

That's right.

How are you finding California?

Great, love the sunshine. Better than rainy Leeds

That was where you were at university?

Yes, that was for my undergraduate degree and then I went to Cal Tech for my master's.

And now you have a software company called Hard Sofa which is doing pretty well, I understand.

"Hard Sofa! Bloody hell, Graham, I remember that sofa, you geek." Suzanne was now shouting at the TV screen.

So, Leeds. That's all mills and smoking chimneys, I guess.
Well, not now, it's a modern city.

"Oh, God. Bloody Americans," said Suzanne. "It's not all cloth caps and clogs, you dunce."

Five minutes later, as the interview wound up, the interviewer said:

And that was Graham Edwards, the Brit heading up Hard Sofa, a tech company that's really going places!

Suzanne jumped out of bed and picked up the phone, dialling the college admin office.

"Hello, could you get me the number for Hard Sofa, a computer software company, please."

***

Graham unclipped his mic and handed it to the assistant. He disliked interviews but knew they were a necessary evil. His assistant had put a note on his desk simply saying Suzanne from uni telephoned. For a moment he was puzzled and then he remembered the name; Suzanne had been Liz's friend at university and she had always called him computer geek. He wondered why she was phoning but thought he would return her call anyway.

"Hello?"

"Hi, is that Suzanne?"

"Yes. Graham, is that you?"

"Certainly is. How are you?"

"I'm fine. Listen, mate, I saw you on TV yesterday. What's this all about – you became famous?"

"It's a computer game. It uses some techy stuff I was working on for my MSc, and sensibly, someone told me to register the rights in my name."

"So, you're a millionaire and a self-made man, then?"

"Well, not quite, but we sell quite a few programmes."

"Let's do lunch and you can tell me all."

"Sounds good to me, I could do with hearing an English accent to ground me again."

"You know me, English rose, and all that."

They arranged to meet at a restaurant Graham knew. Nice, but not too flash. He arrived first and ordered a lager and sat down at the table. He saw Suzanne arrive in a taxi out of the window and enter the restaurant. He was instantly taken back to his university days, and half expected Liz to be with her, as she had been all those years ago in the student union bar. As she approached, he stood up, went around the table to greet her and gave her a hug.

"Good to see you," he said. "How long has it been?"

"Must be ten years," she replied.

"Yes, end of term, before we all split."

"You to America, it seems."

"That's right. Scholarship boy, that's me. The course was quite good, and I learnt some new coding methods which I tweaked a bit and discovered I could make a relatively unique computer game. It's set in space, has a number of levels, some about discovering things and some about battling creatures – the normal sort of stuff, but it's become very popular because the effects are better than a lot of the other games currently available."

"So, it's a bit like *Star Trek* on computers then," said Suzanne.

"Yes, something like that," said Graham, smiling.

"And people actually buy these games, do they?"

"Yes, they're popular with a certain type of customer – predominantly men in their teens but we've got girls as well. One of the things I'm working on at the moment is to be able to play the game not just against somebody else on the same computer, but to link several computers up, and you can then play the game with somebody else."

"And how would you link the computers up?"

"It's a new development called the World Wide Web, where you link computers through the telephone cable."

"I haven't heard of that."

"No, it started in California and is gradually spreading across the US. Eventually, it's predicted to spread right across the world, so potentially customers could be anywhere."

"So, you're going to be an extremely rich geeky boy, then."

"Certainly, hope so. No, to be honest, I just enjoy the computer stuff, the business side leaves me a bit cold."

"But you've obviously got that going on, though."

"Yes, I had a girlfriend when I first came to America – Gina, whose dad was a Texan businessman, he set me up with a couple of business guys in exchange for investing some money himself. So, I do the computer stuff with a couple of other geeky mates and others do the business side."

"I always knew you'd be a success, you little geek."

"What about you, what have you done since university?"

"When I left, I went to do a PGCE course, and I now teach English. I taught in a secondary school in Bradford for a while and then decided to do TEFL teaching, so went to Spain, taught in a couple of English schools there. From there I took a position in the States and that's where I am now, I've got a two-year contract, essentially teaching English in a private school."

"So, do you see any of the old crowd from university?" Graham said.

"I've seen a few over the years, there's been a few weddings and a couple of get-togethers but that's about all. I went to Spain with Liz when we finished uni and then we kept in contact for a while. We gradually lost contact – she went into medicine and is now becoming a surgeon, I think."

"Well, she always was brainy," said Graham wistfully.

"Do you miss her?"

"To be honest, I do a bit."

Suzanne looked at Graham and was silent.

23

2010

I have a plan

Liz walked through into theatre in her purple scrubs, always a size large to suit her height, tied tight around the waist. They were droopy around her hips, but she wasn't trying to impress anyone on her team. Her theatre shoes were rubber, like her favourite Crocs at home but less comfortable. Her hat was also purple. She had scrubbed for five minutes using Betadine which she found less irritating on the skin than Hibiscrub and better to see if she had missed any skin areas. She wore a visor mask and a pair of surgical gloves. The patient was already prepped and draped. Turned on their side, all Liz could see was part of a shiny yellow limb. As she stood in front of her patient, she said, "How are we?"

Tom, the anaesthetist, said, "All well here, levels are fine."

She knew Tom's wife was called Sue, and they had two children, but other than that, she knew nothing about him. He was a good anaesthetist, but just a face in the background to her.

Liz made a 10-centimetre incision at the top of the hip using her scalpel. She cut through the skin which appeared yellow due to its covering of iodine-impregnated adhesive drape. She favoured an anterior approach, coming from the front of the hip, as she was able to work between the muscles by pushing them apart. Some of her colleagues used a posterior approach from the back of the hip, which was easier, but Liz knew this involved cutting through the backside muscles, leading to a longer recovery, so she reserved this technique for obese patients only. Once through the skin, she exchanged her scalpel for an electric knife to cut deeper into the tissues, passing through fat and fibrous padding tissue. As she worked, she heat-sealed any blood vessels to keep the area relatively dry, the monotonous fizzing sound acting as a background track to her work. Once she could see the white of the thigh bone, Doug, her registrar, used a deep retractor to pull the thick tissue apart. When Doug had started, he had been a bit cocky. He was brought up on a council estate in Bromsgrove and played the working-class hero well enough to attract the less worldly-wise young nurses. Liz knew from his CV that he had gone to a fee-paying school and had attended a crammer in Oxford when he had failed to get the grades he needed to enter medical school the first time around.

As she cut through the thick joint capsule, she saw the characteristic release of watery joint fluid which her theatre nurse suctioned up. Once the supporting tissues were cut, Liz bent the hip and twisted it to separate the ball from the socket. Now she focused on the socket using a round reamer with a surface a bit like a cheese grater to remove the degenerated cartilage, enabling her to fit a trial cup. She moved onto the thigh bone where she removed the ball with a bone saw and widened the bone canal with a conical reamer. She was now ready to put in a trial stem for the ball to fit on.

The operation proceeded like clockwork with measurements taken, computer images adjusted, bones cut, the trial joint introduced, and movements assessed. Tick-tock, tick-tock. A well-practised team working together smoothly. She knew all of them in some way. She had trained most, had team meetings with them all, and met some socially. But she knew she was always distant. If they went for a meal, when she left (always early) the conversation would become more animated as she closed the restaurant door. She knew she would always be the boss and never the friend. There would always be a distance, and it was a one-way street. Sometimes she wished for more.

***

Suzanne had heard Liz mention the conversation she had with Mark about the party where Liz had been raped, and about Neil, the shady character Mark had gone with. It was an incredible coincidence that two people should meet after all this time and find they had attended the same party years ago. But life came up with many surprises, and she saw it as an opportunity to make things up to Liz for what had happened at uni. Liz thought Suzanne had been a good friend, and she had. Mostly.

If she could find this Neil character, it might lead to some type of closure. It was a long shot, but one worth taking. Suzanne felt she had let Liz down by not caring for her when she was a young innocent fresher. If she was honest with herself, when she mentally travelled back to the week of the party, she had had a little devil inside her, tempting her to corrupt Liz a bit. From the moment Liz first opened her door to her in Trentfield Hall, she had felt jealous. When the door opened, she had seen a fresh-faced goddess with magical hair and a body to die for. She had held her breath in disbelief before she pulled herself together. She never fancied girls, but if she did, Liz would have been the one. She had often seen her striding across the campus, not walking normally, but almost floating, oblivious to people looking at her. And she was so innocent. She never noticed boys looking at her, and Suzanne knew Liz could have had any man she wanted. But that was just it, she didn't want them. Chunky rugby players, rich fan boys with flashy cars, fearless army smarmies, all types which Suzanne in her uni days craved – Liz could have had any of them, but she settled for Graham. The geeky computer nerd built like a length of string.

Initially, Suzanne had been happy because she thought everyone would now see Liz as someone with laughable taste in boys and Suzanne would shine beside her. Suzanne would arrive on a white charger, persuading everyone that he was really OK. Liz has strange tastes, she would say, and everyone would laugh together. But that had not happened, the geeky couple had morphed into stars of the university campus. People started joining the running club, girls sought out tall, willowy boys; it was unbelievable. Suzanne had lost control of the situation. Liz had not noticed any of this going on, of course, she was blissfully unaware of the whirlwind she created around her.

In freshers' term, Suzanne knew Liz didn't drink and had never been with a boy, and she wondered if she could make both happen. When she had heard about the party, she envisaged taking Liz, getting her slightly tipsy, and then everyone laughing and chatting about it in the morning. If it all worked out well, she might even have got Liz to kiss a boy, and Suzanne would have brought her out of her shell. Never in a million years did she foresee what would happen, but she should have done. She knew that now. She should have kept a wary eye on Liz throughout the party. When she saw her dancing with the boy, she should have gone over and danced with them to assess the situation. She had a similar occasion at school when one of her friends had become drunk, and both Suzanne and another girl had gone over to dance with her just to check on her and to let the boy see that she had friends. But she hadn't done this, she had left Liz by herself, and she now wondered whether deep down inside her, some of the situation had been intentional on her part. She was young and had been jealous of Liz's looks and her athlete body. Thinking back now, as a more worldly-wise woman, she thought perhaps she had driven the situation in the direction it actually went.

After the party, things had gone well between them. Suzanne thought she was making things up with Liz by taking her to the police station and the hospital. And later when she met Graham, she thought it was a little bit of a laugh – Liz going with the gangly man interested in the geeky computers. But as the relationship developed and Liz and Graham clearly hit it off, running together, going to the gym, and then getting deeper into their relationship, Suzanne now saw that she had felt pushed away. She should have celebrated her friend's good fortune, but instead there it was again, that little devil deep inside. Her little devil voice saying, can I split them up. When the opportunity had arisen in those last few days, she had been stupid. She saw that now, all these years later. She had been a jealous, spiteful little girl who had let her friend down. No, it was more than that, she had deliberately deceived her for her own gain. She had wanted to go to Spain with Liz, and was afraid with Graham and Liz still together she would have had no one to go with. So, she had taken a wrecking ball to their relationship just so she had a companion on holiday; she had been totally pathetic. In the cold light of the day, she saw her twenty-year-old self as a malicious adolescent. She felt guilt, regret, and embarrassment. If she had a time machine, she would have gone back and corrected all of her mistakes, but she didn't. You can't go back, you can only move forwards was a favourite saying of her mother, and that was exactly what Suzanne was going to do, engineer a better future for Liz.

***

The first thing that Suzanne needed to do was to find Neil. For this, she had a couple of clues. Firstly, she had the timeline. She knew the date of the party because that was forever etched on her soul. It was the 21st of November 1981. Secondly, she knew there had been an article about Neil when he was arrested, because Mark's mother had seen it and told Mark when he was in Germany, according to Liz. She went to the university library at work and contacted somebody in the journalism department. Because she taught geography, she knew everyone close to her, but journalism was another course. She got chatting and explained she was a human geographer who wanted to find an article in a local Swindon newspaper which had occurred within a window of about three years. They searched online and found there was only a single evening paper which had existed in Swindon for some time; all the other papers were free-ad sheets. She breathed a sigh of relief when the journalism tutor phoned the evening paper and found it had digitised its articles since the 1990s. She knew Neil's full name because Mark had given it to Liz in a conversation. She searched using the terms Neil Carter-Brown and arrest, police, drugs. The article came up fairly quickly, to her surprise, and there it was on the screen in front of her. Neil Carter-Brown had been arrested and charged with theft and possession of drugs. The article explained a search of his lockup had found a whole selection of stolen items and he was given a five-year prison term. She then knew that she had to search using police records in the public domain to find his name linked to the approximate date of his release, which would have been in 1990, perhaps earlier if he got out early for good behaviour. She knew from an article she had read that those with a sentence of four years or more could apply for parole. It was relatively easy to find him. She had a few false starts as there was a Neil Jones who had also been released around that time, but he was in Scotland and had served a twenty-year term. She found her man. He was released in late 1988. She now had to find where he had gone from there and fill in the gaps of the last twenty years.

Over the next two hours, she ploughed through dozens of records with the assistance of her newfound friend Brindley from the journalism department. She learnt that he had done his PhD using records from newspapers and the police, and so was familiar with this type of work. They found Neil had been released in 1988 and, without having any direct family members, had gone to a hostel for ex-offenders, through a resettlement scheme. He had a period of eight months of unemployment when he received benefit, before working as a gardener with the local parks department. He stayed in the hostel, according to their own records, until 2008, and once he left, there was no trace of him. They had no forwarding address, but they did now know his National Insurance number. With that, they were able to find that he had a series of short-term jobs and moved to Bristol. Looking at the council records, census, and voting records, they were able to find three likely addresses for him. They then used a national people tracking website to find his location. This was something Suzanne was unfamiliar with. It could provide basic information for free but for a fee gave more in-depth details. It searched dozens of social media sites, websites, and online sources as well as public records. She sent in all the details they had found, paid her fee, and waited. A week later there he was, his current address and employment details. He lived in a rented flat on a housing estate in Bristol and worked in a tyre-fitting franchise. After all this work, she did not really know what to feel. On the one hand she felt success that the academic exercise had been successful, but on the other hand she had found the man who raped her close friend Liz twenty years ago. What now? she thought.

***

To protect herself from cross-infection, Liz should wear two pairs of surgical gloves. Double-gloving was a rule, but she, like many surgeons, chose to wear only a single pair. Gloves dulled the sensation of touch, and she found that two gloves impaired her dexterity and subtle feeling. It was a question of risk-benefit in her view, the slightly increased risk of infection being outweighed by the huge benefit in her technique. She was a top surgeon and had fought long and hard to get where she was, and she was not going to give anyone else an edge. And it worked. Her results were the best, and when things did go wrong, as chance always meant that they would, they were minor and easily corrected errors. Except this one. A mistimed movement when the registrar was stitching deep tissue layers had caused a small cut. That was all it had taken. A 2-millimetre break in the glove in the presence of bodily fluids carried the risk of transference of a blood-borne virus, be it hepatitis or HIV. She would need a course of antibiotics and a hepatitis test and possibly a booster. While all this was being done, her surgical list would be delayed, and she was at the mercy of this barely adolescent nurse sitting in front of her in the occupational health department. Her name, according to her badge, was Mezzie. Liz gave an inward sigh.

"I'll just need to inspect the wound, Dr McClennan, sorry, Ms McClennan."

Liz noticed the nurse gradually going pink and thought it nicely matched the heart-shaped NHS badge she was wearing on her tunic.

"The wound is fine."

"But it's for our records!" said with a flash of fear across her face.

"Fine, go ahead then, Mezzie."

Liz hated all this politically correct first-name stuff. She came from a generation who thought hierarchy was the foundation of society. Her parents were a war generation, and she had regularly had her Brownie uniform inspected by her father before she was allowed to leave the house.

The nurse looked closely at Liz's finger, and Liz wondered what she could possibly be looking at for a full twenty seconds in an area no bigger than a pinhole.

"The wound seems OK. It's clean and not jagged."

Liz put on her best friendly and tolerant smile, while she thought, Mezzie, you are an obsequious prepubescent prat.

"That's good, then!"

***

Suzanne had arranged to meet Liz for a coffee in Manchester. She had phoned Liz a couple of times but each time she suggested going out, Liz had been working. She had not told her of her plan to find Neil and wasn't sure now how she would break it to her or even if she should. Suzanne arrived at the coffee shop first, found a table, and ordered herself a coffee. She saw Liz coming down the street who, as she pushed the door to open it, gave her a wave. Liz looked tired and drawn and slightly haggard. Suzanne's heart bled a little for her friend. Liz went to the counter and ordered a cappuccino with no chocolate sprinkles, brought it over to the table, and slipped her coat off, popping it on the back of the chair. Suzanne thought, if you are on cappuccino rather than green tea, things are bad. Liz sat down heavily and looked at Suzanne with searching eyes. Suzanne smiled at her and said, "How's it going?"

"Not so good, if I'm honest. Work's been a bit rushed, with a couple of complex cases, and to be honest, I think I've lost a bit of my mojo."

"That's understandable after what you learnt, it must have brought everything back."

They sat in silence for a while, Suzanne slowly stirring her coffee.

"I did something, and I don't know how you feel about it."

"What was it?"

"I used my university contacts through the journalism department to find Neil."

The air around the table appeared to have been sucked out, and even within the bustle of the coffee shop, there seemed to be a microcosm of silence. Liz looked at Suzanne.

"What do you mean you found Neil, I don't understand."

"With the help of a journalism researcher, I traced the article in the local newspaper and over a two-hour period we were able to find where he went when he got out of prison and where he now lives."

"I can't believe you did that," said Liz.

"I know, I was conflicted, but I thought if I found him, at least it gave you the opportunity to confront him even if you never did. It helps to take away the unknowing, that little voice inside you that you said kept saying did it really ever happen. It sort of puts you back in control, do you see what I mean?"

Liz was silent for a while and then said, "I don't think there's any point in confronting him, it is water under the bridge now. It was hurtful at the time; many years have passed. I am no longer a hurt uni student."

"But you said Mark was shocked to think it was Neil who might have raped you. I don't know really, but I felt finding him would be helping, somehow. Saying it out loud now, it seems a bit odd, but my intentions were good, I assure you."

"I know, but if we just arrived at his door and said, remember me from over twenty years ago when you raped me? I think we might just get punched. I've heard of several cases where victim and offender meet, I think it's called restorative justice or something. But that is very well organised and done in stages with a trained facilitator. We are just two early-middle-aged women feeling a bit sad for themselves."

Suzanne laughed and said, "I might have a plan, hear me out. Brindley, the journalist guy who I was talking about, did his PhD looking at the reintegration of offenders into the community. What we could do is say that we're extending that project. Go in with some examples from his work and then say we're contacting people in the area to do a pilot study of offenders who've had a short-term sentence, say three to seven years. Perhaps say we're interested in where they're living, the jobs they're doing, the experience after being released from prison, to see if we can improve the system. That's not a complete lie because that was the nature of his work, and, as you know, often research is repeated to see if it maintains its validity. In addition, I am in that department, albeit the geography department and not journalism, but I have been working of sorts with Brindley on human geography. Just asking around; I don't think getting information of this type is in any way illegal and most research projects start by scratching around for details to try and size up the project, as it were."

Liz looked at Suzanne with a look of mild shock on her face. She sat for a while and Suzanne could almost see her brain working, electrical sparks flying around inside her head. Liz's expression gradually changed and then she said, "Actually, that sort of makes sense because in a number of studies I've done, we have started exactly like that. You get an idea and before putting anything down on paper, you test the water first."

"Exactly that," said Suzanne.

"We'd be testing the water and, if necessary, we could find several others who we could ask related questions to and come up with a bit of a questionnaire. If we pick a sample of ten people initially in the Bristol area, he is just one."

"Now that sounds more sensible, especially if we could get this Brindley guy on board. Any chance of that, do you think?"

"Absolutely, I think we could for two reasons. Firstly, because that's the nature of his work and he is looking to get some funding, and secondly, I think he quite fancies me."

They both laughed, it was a light moment they both needed.

"Oh, Suzanne, you have changed so little since uni. Still using your sexuality to get what you want."

"Definitely, it's a young man's fantasy to go with an older woman, isn't it? I'm just indulging him."

And so it was set up. Suzanne had several meetings with Brindley at the university and they used the questionnaire from his PhD and modified it. The general thrust was reintegration of ex-offenders into society. She made the case that they would be interested in employment, where the person was living, their experience getting back into the community, and their social interactions. In this latter category, she included sexuality, arguing that many ex-offenders found their relationships damaged by a prison term and found it difficult to interact socially upon release. She thought she could embellish her questions here to get the details she wanted. They had selected thirty potential subjects, and of these, ten had replied to their request for interview, after offering payment. Fourth on their list was one Neil Carter-Brown.

24

Meeting Neil

They travelled down to Bristol in the car together, chatting about what they were going to do but more widely about things in general. Suzanne learnt a bit more about Liz's life as a surgeon, and Liz in turn learnt about Suzanne's work at the university. It was casual, matter-of-fact conversation between two friends. Then they got on to the topic of how to get the information they wanted.

"We can't just ask him outright if he raped a girl at a party in Leeds twenty years ago," said Suzanne.

"No, we can try techniques I use when taking a history from a patient. Rather than just asking stuff, you casually chat and gradually guide the conversation. It's based on a counselling technique called motivational interviewing. You follow the conversation, showing that you understand and share their feelings, officially referred to as showing empathy. As the person speaks, you reflect what they are saying back to them, showing you are actively listening and understand the points they're making. You can summarise what they've said as well, this clarifies things and helps get them onside with you. Also, we can work along the timeline from when he was released. Finally, we can begin to go back in time, discussing where he was and what he did and then bring up the subject of Leeds indirectly. You typically find that people like to talk about themselves, so it's usually quite easy."

Suzanne was silent for a while, and then said, "I'm never going to talk to a doctor in the same way again."

Liz smiled. "It's all in the training. If you just ask a list of questions, people close up and are inhibited. As I say to my students, listen to the patient and they will often guide you to the answer."

"So, you're a good listener, then."

"I am."

"I'm a good listener when it comes to men. They tell me all their problems; it makes them feel secure. Not young men, of course, I tell them what to do. They like a bit of older woman dominatrix."

"You're incorrigible."

"I try."

***

They were staying in a chain hotel in Bristol overnight to get an early start and meeting Brindley in the morning. The interviews were to be conducted in a hotel meeting room which they had rented. The subjects only got paid if they turned up, as Liz said no shows were very common unless money was involved. It had been agreed that they would conduct the interviews in pairs so as not to intimidate the subjects. Suzanne began with Brindley with the first subject who was a man released from prison eight years ago. It had been agreed never to talk about an ex-offender's crime, and even if it came up, they would gloss over it as they were more interested in what was happening in their lives now rather than in the past. Liz had told them not to have a sheet of questions in front of themselves but to remember the themes they wanted to cover. She said they should just pretend they were having a conversation with the guy.

"I tell my students a good consultation should be like a conversation in a coffee shop, nudge the conversation along but listen more than you speak," she said.

When they came out, she asked, "How did it go?"

"Not bad," said Brindley.

"Although it was a bit sad, really," added Suzanne. "It turns out when he was released from prison, he discovered that his wife was now with another bloke and so he had nowhere to live. He started off in a hostel and then was diagnosed with depression, so he couldn't work. He was on benefits for two years with a couple of hospital visits and then he eventually took some work as a food-delivery rider using a moped with a topbox. This is just casually paid, and sometimes at weekends he could be working for twelve hours, and other times he'd have no work at all. He doesn't really know anyone other than people in the fast-food outlet, and he tried to commit suicide two years ago."

Suzanne and Liz took the next person. She was a thirty-three-year-old woman who had been released from prison five years ago. She had a two-year-old child and was living in a single-room bedsit on the fourth floor of a dilapidated building. There was mould growing on the tops of the walls, and apparently, she asked the council to come out and sort things out, but this had been going on for ten months and the child had started to cough. Her GP thought it was asthma brought on by the mould in the building. Social services had only just become involved because of the child's health.

Suzanne could see Liz gradually getting agitated and knew she was just about to explode with fury at what she was hearing, so she took over.

"Are you working at all?" she asked casually.

"Am I bollocks, on the social. Just scared he's gunna find me a' take me money. He's done it before, the bastard. Beat me up, took me money and then helped himself to stuff from me fridge."

"OK," said Suzanne. "I can see that must be terrifying."

"Bloody is, but nobody does nothin'."

Suzanne just looked at her, not knowing what to say.

"Are your parents still around?" said Liz.

"Me mum lives in Liverpool. Not seen her in a while. Never knew me dad. Left home and lived on the street for a bit when I was fourteen, didn't like school. Got done for thieving from a shop but I had to eat, you know? Lived with a bloke who put me on the game for a bit, but he gave me this."

She held up her left arm to show a jagged red scar.

"Bottle," she said. "Aimed at me 'ed but I put me 'and up."

Liz looked and nodded, saying nothing.

"Got banged up for dealing and they got me off the drugs. MacKenzie was born couple of years ago."

Neither Liz nor Suzanne asked anything about the father.

"OK, thanks," said Liz.

"Do I get me money?"

"Yes, when you leave, give this ticket to the hotel reception and they will give you payment."

"Not a cheque, is it?"

"No, it is a plain envelope with cash inside. You will need to sign to say you have received it."

As she closed the door, Suzanne said, "That was terrifying."

"All too common, I'm afraid."

"Yes, another world really, isn't it. We both come from sheltered backgrounds, so will have been insulated from the real world as we were growing up."

"My eyes were not really opened until I started medical training. Uni was insulated as well when we were there. Nowadays, I think students struggle a bit more, but even so, it is nothing like that girl."

They had a break for coffee and cake provided by the hotel, and all three compared notes to check they were getting the information they required. They had told Brindley it was an extension to his work but had not told him the real reason they set the interviews up.

The next person to arrive was Neil Carter-Brown.

***

Suzanne and Liz sat facing him. He was fat and shorter than Liz had thought. He appeared slightly sweaty with mottled skin, no hair on the top of his head, and the sides greasy. He wore dirty jogging bottoms, old trainers with the soles worn down, and a stained hoody which lifted up as he sat down, to reveal a hairy, flabby belly. His fingers were stained yellow on one hand and his nails were all dirty and bitten, and he had faded tattoos on his forearms. As Liz looked at him, he was unable to make eye contact.

"Can I just check your name and details?" she said in a bright friendly tone with a smile.

God, you're good, Suzanne thought.

"Neil, Neil Carter-Brown. That's me, always has been, always will."

"Tell me a little about what has been happening to you since you were released from prison," Liz said with a smile, followed by friendly eye contact. She rested her chin lightly on her hand to show she was paying close attention. Her practised posture said 'I am really interested in what you are saying, and I have all the time in the world to listen to you'. Suzanne knew internally Liz would have liked to jump up and punch him over and over again. This girl was a real pro, she was chillingly good. Cool, calm, and professional.

He talked for ten minutes about moving into the hostel, finding a job, living in his small flat. All the time Liz paid attention, summing up what he had said. Smiling, even laughing with him at his jokes. She empathised, sympathised, and understood what he had gone through.

"It must have been hard; I can only imagine."

"No, really? That sounds terrible. How did you cope?"

Suzanne said little, being in awe of Liz, the master interrogator.

After one light-hearted moment when Liz had laughed with Neil, she said, "Let me take you back to the period before your conviction. I'd be interested to know what your life was like and how you got into the situation you found yourself in before your arrest. Tell me about school and your first jobs."

Suzanne found herself getting slightly hot and prickly.

"Left school with nothing really. Had a few jobs and worked a bit as a chef in a department store. That was quite good, I started in the kitchen just loading the plate-washing machine. After a while one of the blokes left and they trained me on the hotplate. Burgers, sausages, fried eggs, and stuff."

"So, you obviously got into crime, and it would be useful to us to know how that happened. Would you be comfortable discussing that? Only if you want to, I don't want to press you."

Suzanne felt her mouth go dry. Oh, Liz, my friend, you are an expert manipulator. I'm glad you're on my side, she thought.

"No, no, glad to help."

"Well, if I'm honest, it all started in the department store. I thieved a bit of stuff and found I could take it out of the store through the kitchen entrance. That's where we went to the bins and took the food in, like raw meat and stuff. The main staff all had to go through a door near the security guard's lodge, see, but we kitchen staff didn't. I had a mate on men's clothing who could nick stuff from the storeroom. He passed it to me, and I flogged it, giving him half. Later on, I had the same thing going on with a bloke from electricals, cassette tapes and stuff. We did alright."

Liz was nodding as though this was all perfectly respectable business practice, and even took notes.

"That must have been quite exciting, though, almost leading a team of people, I suppose."

"Well, yeah, I guess. I've always been good with people, you know. Managing them and stuff."

Suzanne stayed frozen to her chair.

"And what happened?"

"One of the blokes got caught, silly bugger, so that put paid to that."

"Oh, dear. That must have been worrying."

"Well, yeah, but by that time I was sharing a house and making contacts with bigger people."

Suzanne was almost wetting herself and had to look down at her notes to stop herself from shouting out.

"Bigger people, really?"

"Yeah, there was a bloke we shared a house with – had good contacts with some major crime people."

"We – were there a couple of you?"

"Yeah, me and a guy from the department store and this other bloke with the contacts."

"So, the person from the department store, was that one who got you the clothing or the one with the cassette tapes?"

"Cassette tapes, Mark, his name was, I think. Bit of an odd bugger."

"In what way?"

"Thought he was as quiet as a mouse when I first met him. To be honest, that's why I chose him to share with. But it's like they say, it's always the quiet ones, isn't it."

Liz smiled, "Oh, I agree, it often is."

She left a silence, clearly hoping he would fill it, a look of eager expectancy on her face. She smiled and maintained friendly eye contact.

"So, this guy with the contacts – Ted, his name was – had some deals going in Leeds and cut me in. The house all split up then; I went to live with my girlfriend, and Mark went back to his parents. Ted was usually in Leeds and just stayed there."

"It's amazing how quickly things change sometimes, isn't it?" said Liz. "Did you ever see any of them again?"

"Saw Ted a few times in Leeds on business."

"And Mark?"

"Yeah, he ended up in Leeds as well, strangely. Working there for an engineering company or summat. He was brainy, not like me. Made a go of it."

Liz maintained eye contact and waited. Neil filled the silence.

"I stayed with him once, in his flat in Leeds."

Suzanne felt slightly faint, and a light sweat broke out on her forehead. Liz maintained eye contact with a fixed, friendly smile and open expression.

"Really, what happened?"

"I was doing some business with Ted, but in the evening, we had takeouts and stuff. Even went to a party that one of Ted's friends found out about."

"Just you and Ted's mate?"

"No, no. Mark and me went. Posh do, lots of students from Leeds uni. All hoity-toity like. Bloke in a nice car, girls in dresses, that sort of stuff. Flash booze as well. Vodka and mulled whatever. Never had that before, bit sweet, to be honest."

"Anyone you know at the party? Did anything happen?"

"Well, that's when I found out about Mark. As I said, quiet bloke. He got chatting to some students about work stuff and I went into the kitchen to pinch food and get a bit of drink. To be honest, I felt a bit out of it, what with all that posh lot. Next thing I knew he was dancing, never seen him do that, it was like he'd grown up since we shared a house. With his job and stuff, I suppose. I got stuck into the food in the kitchen, crisps and stuff, not talking to anyone, really. About twenty minutes later Mark comes in, bit sweaty, like, from dancing, I suppose. Takes the vodka bottle off me a' pours some in a can. 'Let's see if Ted's trick works,' he says. I looked at him a bit puzzled, and then I remembered back in the house Ted had talked about how he spiked girls' drinks. Didn't know Mark had heard, to be honest, but he must have."

Suzanne sensed an energy change in the room. Liz was no longer in charge. She was withdrawing into herself as though a monster had reared up in front of her. Suzanne took over the lead and said, "And what happened?"

"Not sure, to be honest. Around midnight I went to the bog, there was a big queue. Waited around and when I came downstairs, I saw Mark. Next thing I know there was a load of noise and stuff upstairs and some people come down holding a girl between them. I recognised her as one of the ones dancing because everyone said they could see through her skirt. The disco lights, like."

Liz was still silent, and Neil looked at her.

"She alright?" he said to Suzanne, "looks a bit peaky."

"Yes, we take it in turn to lead the interviews because it can be exhausting. We have to be quite focused."

"Right, yeah, I suppose. That it, then?"

"Yes, thank you. That's been really helpful. You can pick up your interview fee at reception."

"What, the money, like?"

"That's right."

"OK."

Suzanne closed the door and turned to Liz. She was sheet white and just looked through her.

"It can't be," she said. "It just can't be."

25

1981

Aftermath

As I walked back from the party with Neil, I just wanted to turn back time. I felt sick and dizzy. I was shivering and my heart was pounding. Sometimes I just lose control and do things on autopilot. Afterwards I suffer waves of regret and say I'll never do it again. Until the next time, and I do. I remember over the summer holidays at school going with Dad to see one of his workmates. It turned out his son was only bloody Duncan Hoodie who had kicked my camera and threatened me at school. By himself, though, he was OK. He had an air rifle which he showed me. He set some paper targets up on an outside wall and we spent about half an hour both taking turns to shoot at them. I did pretty well, actually. Then Duncan suggested going into the woods to shoot birds. I like birds because on one birthday I got a bird book, and Dad and I sometimes look at the garden birds through his binoculars. I should have said to Duncan that I didn't want to shoot birds, but

I didn't because I thought I would look like a sissy. Like a loser who wasn't up to it. Duncan started first, aiming at a bird in the trees, and shooting but missing each time. He gave the rifle to me, and I deliberately shot to the side. I don't think he noticed, just assumed I was a poor shot, I suppose. Duncan took the rifle again, aimed at a bird, and shot. He said, "I can't believe I missed him, he's just up there."

I looked up into the tree but couldn't see the bird he was aiming for. Duncan shot the rifle again and missed. He broke the rifle, loaded another pellet, and shot once more. A small bird, a bluetit, I think, fell from the tree.

"Now you can see the bugger," Duncan said, laughing.

I looked at the bird on the floor, and its beak was faintly moving, poor thing. I felt sick and couldn't bring myself to speak to Dad on the car journey back. I regretted it for weeks afterwards and couldn't sleep. That's when I started to hurt myself the first time. I just felt overwhelmed. Sometimes anger at my weakness, and other times, sadness and despair. I took a pair of dividers from maths and put deep scratches into my forearms. It seemed to shock me out of it, the pain. I kept my pullover pulled down over my forearms so nobody at school would notice.

But this was different. It hadn't been a small bird, and I wasn't just watching. When I went through the house door with Neil, there were a load of university students, and I felt intimidated at first. It brought all those feelings of failure back from my exam results, and I just stood at the wall holding my drink and chatting to a couple of people. A lad next to me said, "What are you studying?"

"Engineering," I said. Didn't say I wasn't at uni.

"No way, we are as well, this is Steve," and he introduced me to his mate.

"Are you over in the main block or at Chatham?"

"Neither, I work in industry," I said.

Not sure where Chatham was, an engineering building, I guess.

"Fantastic, that's what we want to do eventually."

We got chatting and it quickly became obvious that I knew much more about engineering than they did. To be honest, I was a bit buoyed up. It made me feel superior after failing my A levels and not being able to go to uni. It was as though I had fallen, got back up, and was now flying high. I had more to drink and the combination of alcohol, talking to the engineering students, and the party atmosphere was like a drug. I could feel myself getting out of control, I didn't care, I was on a high. I felt that this was my time at last.

There was a girl dancing in the middle of the room. She was gorgeous, not like the girls at school. She was a real woman. Tall, athletic, with great hair. She wore a summer dress, and the disco lights shone through it, showing the outline of her legs and even her knickers. All the lads were looking but she was oblivious to the attention, I think. I could tell she was a bit drunk because she was bumping into people. Neil came out of the kitchen and started dancing like a prat. Sort of walking with small steps and shuffling. Suppose he thought he looked cool or something. I thought everyone would see him as a prat, but nobody paid any attention, and he even started dancing with the long-haired girl for a bit. I couldn't believe it – why was Neil so confident and not me. Neil was a thief and a loser, I was the one who had got out of that dodgy house and made it through YTS and on to an engineering firm. He was nothing, cadging money and sleeping on the floor of my nice flat. I just felt annoyed by the hand that life had dealt me, I suppose.

Anyway, I left the living room and went through to the kitchen. I had a few crisps and nuts and stuff, and there was a guy kissing a girl in the corner. Things were getting a bit heavy, she had her hand on his crotch, and he had lifted her top and was feeling her tits. I'd never seen that at school parties and wanted some myself. New job, new flat, and big city, and all that. I realised I'd never really had a girlfriend except for Joanne at school, and that had been a brief childhood platonic relationship, if I'm honest. Don't even know what happened to her. I thought, here I am, done a bit of stealing and got away with it, been chosen from the YTS group to work at Moorfields, had my own smart flat, and knew more about engineering than those uni students put together. I had a flashback to the house and Ted the loser talking to Neil when I came in late one night. He'd been talking about spiking a drink with vodka, and I thought, why not. Just for a laugh. Before I knew it, I had a can of lager in my hand, and had reached for an open vodka bottle. I thought, she's drinking anyway, what difference would a bit more do? I went back into the room, and she was still dancing, so I started moving a bit, feeling more confident, and shuffled up to her pretending to drink from the can. I thought it would be a bit of a laugh, that's all. I thought she was out of my class. She was at uni and would have passed her exams when I failed mine. When she got her results envelope, she would have been all smiles with her mum and dad, and off to uni, while I went to a department store to sell men's clothing. It was a way of getting back at the system, I thought, that's all. Show them that they couldn't muck around with me.

Later on, I was feeling quite dizzy, so I went to find Neil, thought I would call it a day before I threw up. Couldn't find him downstairs or in the garden, so I went upstairs where everyone was queuing for the toilet. The girl with the summer dress was on the landing. She was sitting on the floor, and I spoke to her. I couldn't believe myself, I was actually speaking to her! She looked up with glazed eyes and tried to stand up, but couldn't, she was so drunk. She reached out for me and pulled herself up using my leg for leverage. She stood close and leant into me to steady herself. Then we started kissing, it just happened. Initially, I was shocked, but then turned on. I was a bit drunk and so high on everything that I just kept going. Sometimes I get like this, and I can't control myself, it's almost as though I'm watching someone else doing stuff, not me. I walked her into a bedroom, joking, like, and then started kissing her again. I knew she was drunk because, although she kissed me, she could hardly stand up. I just kept going, thinking of the couple in the kitchen. That girl had been wearing jeans but the one I was with wore a dress. I started feeling her bum and stuff, and she didn't seem to mind. It went too far, I pulled her knickers down, I didn't even think. I don't know why I did it, I really don't. She was so beautiful, and I just kept going. She was so drunk I don't think she even knew what was happening.

As I walked back with Neil, we got to the end of the street and the party music faded. Further on we got closer to my flat and he asked what happened to me. I told him I got chatting to the uni students and then went silent while we walked a bit further.

"Never guess what happened to me," I said.

"What?"

"That girl dancing, I shagged her!"

"You what?"

"She was upstairs and drunk, and she came on to me."

"No way!"

"Straight up. Started kissing me, so I thought my luck's in. Pushed her into a bedroom and pulled her knickers off."

"You old dog. Never thought you had it in you."

"Summer dress, mate, see. Easy access."

Neil laughed and said, "You know that's rape, right?"

"What is?"

"Shagging someone when they are out of it. Drunk, or drugs, or whatever."

"Can't be, she came on to me."

"Pretty sure it is. Mate of Ted's got done for spiking a girl's drink and shagging her afterwards. Cops said she couldn't give consent or something."

***

Next day I went to the college library and browsed through the law section, looking for the law on rape. It couldn't be rape because she came on to me. Anyway, I was drunk and didn't really mean anything. I wouldn't have done it had she been sober, or I saw her in college or something. It was the atmosphere of the party, inhibitions down and that. The law book said: *a man commits rape if he intentionally penetrates the vagina, anus, or mouth of another person with his penis, and that person does not consent to the penetration, and the man does not reasonably believe that person consents*. Not sure what it means by penetrate the anus, don't know how that is possible. Penetrate the mouth must be a blow job, I reckon. Never done that but wouldn't mind with the right girl. Tom Giddings said his girlfriend used to give him blow jobs at school. Don't think she did, as he was always exaggerating stuff. She couldn't say she gave consent, I suppose, as she was drunk, and anyway, I didn't ask her. But she kissed me first, so I thought she was giving consent in a way, I suppose. That must be what reasonably believe that the person consents means, surely.

***

I lie awake at night thinking about the party. Did I rape her or didn't I? Thinking over the events of that night, she was drunk and so was I. I think she was probably more drunk because she was knocking into people, and anyway I put some vodka in the can I gave her, and she must have drunk some, I think. She came on to me, as she pulled herself up on my leg when she was sitting on the ground. Did she kiss me, or did it just happen as our faces were close? I'm not sure, but it wasn't just a peck on the cheek, as Mum used to say, it was a full-blown kiss, so she didn't resist. I pushed her into the bedroom, I can remember that. We were leaning against the door, and I turned the door handle and pushed the door open and continued to kiss her. Can't remember whether her arms were around me or not, I don't think so, as I would have felt them. I pulled her dress up, I remember that. It was quite thin, and I saw her knickers and those long legs. I had been seeing them all night when she was dancing. I kept kissing her and feeling her underneath her dress, pressing myself against her. Next thing I knew, we were lying on the bed. We must have fallen onto it together. I was still pressing myself against her, and then I remember. I pulled her knickers down and undid my jeans.

A cold shiver went through me at the thought, the hairs on my back stood on end. She was pushing me away, and I held her hands. It was only for about half a minute. I was inside her, and I suddenly realised what I was doing. I sobered up quickly and stood up, pulling my pants and jeans back up. I left the room, leaving her there. I raped her, oh my God, I raped her. Why did I do it, why did I not just stop, why am I such a loser.

Over the next few weeks, I kept looking through the local newspaper. It's a free sheet they have in the canteen at work. I kept reading the articles to see if there was any mention of a girl being raped but there wasn't. I thought about going to the police. I could tell them what happened and say I was drunk, and it was just high spirits. I regretted it and wanted to come clean. They would understand, surely. I never went, however, didn't have the courage, and didn't want work to find out. Not sure who she was, I assume she was a student like the engineering guys. She came down the stairs with her mates and they all got into a bloke's car, so I think they were all students, or perhaps they just worked in the same office or something. I thought about going to the university and asking, but where would I start? I didn't know if she was there, and if she was, which year she was in or what she was studying. In the end I did nothing, I always do nothing. I just let things be.

***

I tried to commit suicide yesterday. I keep going back to the party, and I feel so guilty about what I did and even more guilty about not admitting it to anyone or trying to fix things. I never went to the police or the university or really tried to find the girl. I'm just so weak. I could never stand up for myself. I mucked up my schoolwork, failed my A levels, and just as things started to go well, I was a total pratt. I don't know why I did it. That poor girl. Someone's sister, someone's daughter.

I felt trapped by what I had done. It was unbearable. I just couldn't think of any other way to get out. I kept feeling on edge, agitated, and overwhelmed by feelings of failure. I just wanted it to end. I took half a bottle of paracetamol and washed it down with half a bottle of whiskey I bought from the off-licence and just went to sleep. When I woke up in the morning, I realised I had been sick, and it slowly dawned on me what I had done. My immediate feeling was one of failure once again, and I thought, I can't even do that right.

26

2010

Restorative justice

"But how can I face him?"

Liz and Suzanne were sitting in a coffee shop following the revelation that it was Mark and not Neil who had raped Liz at the freshers' party in Liz's first year at university.

"You can't just leave it, now you know. He has made you look a fool."

"I'm not sure he even knew, he seemed genuinely troubled and surprised in the café in Leeds."

"That's what he told you. How do you know that he didn't recognise you on the train and target you from the very start?"

"I think I'm a better character judge of that, I suppose. I've nothing factual to base it on, but he seemed like a really nice bloke."

"I bet there are some murder victims who would have said that."

Liz looked at Suzanne and knew she was right. She needed some facts. She was an evidence-based clinician, and what she needed now was hard evidence and not opinion.

"I'll have to meet him and ask. That's the only way forward."

"But he has lied to you, how do you know he won't simply do it again?"

"Because I'm going to tell him we've met Neil and get him to admit that he raped me."

"Well, if you are going to do that, I'm going to be there for support or if the bugger decides to go crazy."

Mark had phoned Liz on his return from Germany to tell her what had happened on his work visit and generally catch up. Liz was cautious about what she said but agreed to go for a coffee with him as he was passing through Manchester train station on his way back from the airport. Although she had seen Mark on several occasions and quite liked him, the new revelations put her on her guard, and she wasn't quite sure how to handle it. She agreed with Suzanne that it was probably not the best idea to spring something on him if she were alone, but equally did not want to blindside him by having another person there, having not previously told him. She decided that a public coffee shop was certainly better than meeting at her flat, and Suzanne agreed to be in the coffee shop by herself on another table to offer support or get help if it was needed.

"Liz, hi. That was a flight and a half. Turbulence midway and then a bumpy landing, reminding me why I hate flying."

"I'm with you there, a form of transport to be tolerated at best."

"So, what's new with you. Still busy in clinic?"

"Actually, Mark, there is something else I wanted to talk to you about."

"Fire away."

"Remember in Leeds when we passed that house and you remembered you had been at the same party with your friend Neil?"

"Yes, sorry about that. I never realised or I wouldn't have taken you past the house. He wasn't a friend, he was a former acquaintance, best forgotten."

"You mentioned Neil's full name and the fact that your mum had found a paper cutting about him going to prison."

"Yes, some time ago now."

"Well, with a friend, I was able to trace him."

Mark looked at Liz and his face dropped.

"OK," he said.

"Listen, Mark. I going to come straight to the point here. With a friend we were able to locate Neil, and we interviewed him as part of a social science project that she was involved with."

Mark was staring at her, and fear started to show on his face.

"Mark, he said it was you who raped me at that party, not him."

Liz looked straight into his eyes, a cold hard stare which said, I know the truth now. Mark stared in silence and then looked down at his coffee. He began breathing deeply and she noticed sweat forming on his brow. Thirty seconds, then a minute and he said nothing. No reaction, no movement. Liz thought, he is either going to explode – and she was prepared in case he threw his coffee – or he was going to crack.

"I knew one day this would catch up with me," he said with a tremble in his voice.

Liz was tempted to relax a little but instead remained on guard. She perched on the side of her chair with one leg back, ready to turn suddenly if she needed to.

"It was me; I did rape a girl at a party over twenty years ago. I was a stupid young twit who didn't really know what he was doing. I was drunk and high on the party atmosphere, and she kissed me. I just kept going. I've regretted it ever since and done my best to make up for it, I really have. But honestly Liz, up until that moment outside the house, I had no idea it was you. I would have never started seeing you if I had known."

"Listen, Mark, we need this all out. Would you agree to talk with another person there? It could be a type of restorative justice that I've heard about on the news with that rugby player, Gareth Thomas. I can see it has affected you and it has obviously affected me, so perhaps talking would help us both. What do you think?"

"I'd like that, I really would. I've not tried to mislead you, I just had a panic in the café in Leeds. To be honest, I was going to suggest something similar, as I've done a lot of thinking while I was away in Germany."

"Normally, I think there is a formal set-up with a councillor, or facilitator, or whatever, but we could just talk. We've been out several times and even slept together, for heaven's sake, so I think if you were going to murder me, you would have done it by now."

"I would never hurt you, Liz, and to be honest, I don't think my nineteen-year-old self would have done had he not been drunk, so whatever you want, I'll agree to. Bring a friend there if it helps."

"I would like that, but don't want it to intimidate you."

***

Liz arranged to meet Mark and decided that it should be on neutral ground, so rented a meeting room at a local hotel for half a day. She considered the cost a small price to pay for closure after all these years. Mark had agreed that it was OK for Suzanne to be there, as she had accompanied Liz when they had interviewed Neil.

Liz had set out a bit of a structure with headings to guide the process, thinking that a clear direction would help. Essentially, she thought it was about talking and recognised that although she and Mark had talked a lot when they had gone out, they had both kept the emotions of the event tightly bound up over the years. Suzanne had gone one stage further and spoken at length to a social science lecturer who had been involved in teaching restorative justice facilitators and also introducing restorative practice to schools. She had provided Suzanne with a basic template which began with understanding the impact of a crime and then getting the offender to take responsibility. The middle phase was about building empathy with the victim, and the final section about making amends, agreeing a way forward and concluding. Liz smiled as she saw Suzanne had even made a flow chart and a few slides, and they had joked about Suzanne channelling her inner teacher which had lightened the mood a little for both of them. Mark had read a couple of newspaper stories on restorative justice from links that Liz had sent him, so he knew roughly what might happen and wouldn't run away screaming, she hoped.

***

Liz introduced Suzanne and Mark, and she noted Suzanne's cool exchange and hoped she wouldn't be a problem.

"Shall we start with each of our memories of the party," suggested Liz, "it might help just to get us talking."

"Well, you know that I went with Neil, who had an invite from a friend of a friend. I really went as I was new in Leeds and wanted to meet people away from work. To be honest, I was a bit embarrassed by Neil as I thought my life had moved on from the time I shared a house with him. I remember the house was in an area of Leeds I hadn't been to and that's about it."

"I went with Suzanne who had heard about the party, and I had decided I needed to let my hair down a bit and stop being the Miss Goody Two-Shoes I was at school. I remember thinking it might be a good opportunity to sort of rebrand myself. I admired the fact that Suzanne was a bit of an 'it' girl and thought some of it might rub off."

Suzanne smiled and said nothing, looking down at her papers.

"I got chatting to a couple of engineering students and found that I knew more about engineering than they did," said Mark. "It was a bit of a revelation to me as I was still smarting from failing my A levels and not going to uni, losing all my school friends and what have you. I ended up working in a department store and then signing on, and eventually, a YTS scheme. I guess talking to the students made me feel OK about myself again. As a teenager, I had extremely low esteem and even had a couple of phases of self-harm."

"I was simply happy dancing and letting my hair down. I wouldn't normally dance, but a combination of glühwein and the music made me a bit crazy I suppose," said Liz. "I remember one of the girls telling me my knickers were showing through my summer dress because of the disco lights and I felt so wicked continuing to allow it to happen. Oh, the innocence, wouldn't we all like to be nineteen again."

Liz and Mark chatted about the party and the dancing and gradually getting drunk, while Suzanne looked on, saying nothing. She thought they looked like two old school friends recounting happy memories. Liz described feeling dizzy and going upstairs but then said she could remember virtually nothing concrete until the next morning. She had flashbacks to a bedroom and a memory of music and the car journey back to uni. When she woke, she had a sore throat and remembered she was nude, rather than wearing her normal shorts and T-shirt. It was not until she was in the shower that she knew something was wrong.

Mark said he had felt very drunk and went looking for Neil when he saw the girl sitting on the landing floor and asked if she was OK. He described her as the one dancing in a summer dress and being able to see her legs through the dress because of the position of the flashing disco lights. He and the boys he was talking to had all been making lewd comments like young men do.

"I thought the girl was gorgeous but did not realise it was you until you mentioned it in Leeds when we walked past the house. I never really saw your face, I suppose, you were just one of many new faces to me. Even now, if you showed me a picture of you when you were nineteen, I wouldn't recognise you."

Suzanne spoke for the first time. Liz had thought she would be angry and had welcomed the fact that she kept quiet, but she surprised her by saying gently, "Can you remember what happened in the bedroom, Mark?"

"If I'm honest, I'm not sure what is real and what is my made-up memory of the time through the fog of drink, guilt, and simply the passage of time. I'll give it a try.

"I remember the girl. I have to call you that, Liz. It was a different time, and I was a different person. The girl pulled herself up using my leg and kissed me. I don't know with hindsight if it was intentional, or our heads just came close and it happened, and I'm not even sure who initiated the kiss. Looking back now, if a drunk girl kissed me, I would pull back. But at nineteen, full of drink and high on the atmosphere, when a beautiful girl kissed me, I kept kissing her. We were pressed up against a bedroom door, so I turned the door handle, and we sort of fell in, I think. Next thing I knew, we were on the bed. I felt up inside her dress like a typical nineteen-year-old boy and just kept going, I'm ashamed to say. I pulled her knickers down and kept pressing myself against her, a combination of passion, drunkenness, and youthful foolhardiness, I suppose. Suddenly I was inside her and I began thrusting until about two minutes later when I came to my senses. I felt so ashamed, I just left her there. I found Neil and walked back to my flat. I've replayed that scene so many times in my mind over the years, and in dreams and nightmares, it still haunts me. Each time, it is slightly different. Did she start the kiss or did I, did she push me away or allow me to continue, were her eyes open or closed, was she even conscious of what was happening. I wish I had the answers, I really do, but I don't."

Liz listened in silence and tears slowly formed in her eyes and began to run down her face. Suzanne saw what was happening and put her arm around Liz's shoulders. The tears tumbled freely until she was crying silently, hardly able to breathe. Mark looked at her and said, "Oh, Liz, I'm so sorry. If I could undo what I did, I would have done so a thousand times."

Suzanne said, "Let's finish with the party and go on to the days following the rape."

Liz was amazed at how calm she seemed. At the word rape, Liz noticed Mark's face. It was a look of disappointment rather than fear or hate. Had he hoped to avoid this term and be forgiven? Had he hoped the meeting would somehow undo the past?

Eventually, Mark began speaking, "Over the next few weeks, I kept looking in the local free paper to see if there was any mention of what had happened. I looked through law books and learnt about consent and everything about it, together with alcohol and rape. I thought about going to the police and even going to the university to try to find you, but I didn't do either. The memory of the rape has eaten away at me ever since and has destroyed my life, I think. I attempted suicide and had counselling afterwards. I think it partially wrecked my marriage. I've always been so careful with female employees since, making sure I'm never alone with them, encouraging them to succeed. I've not really had a successful relationship since. When I met you, it was a breath of fresh air. Even then, I never recognised you and didn't connect the two events until we passed the house in Leeds."

Suzanne let him finish and left a short silence.

"What happened to you following the rape, Liz?"

Liz talked about the police station and being made to feel as though she were a silly student making things up. Then the SARC centre and the tests. Finding excessive alcohol in her bloodstream and the counselling sessions with Isabella. Mark listened, occasionally shifting in his seat or sighing. A couple of times he said, "Oh, Liz, I'm so sorry." Eventually, when she had finished, he looked up with moist eyes and said, "I spiked your drink, Liz."

Liz just looked on; she had no energy left.

"Put vodka in a can and thought it would make you more drunk. I had heard about spiking but never done it, so I thought, as you were drunk and making a bit of a fool of yourself, it would be a laugh. It was an immature, stupid thing to do. I realise that now, but at the time I was immature and stupid. That's not an excuse, unfortunately, it's just factual."

Liz thought Suzanne would erupt and was surprised when she simply said, "Thank you for saying that, Mark, it's hard to confess to something when it is so hurtful."

Liz began again. "I couldn't really form a relationship with a man – boy, I suppose – for the next two years.

"I kept blaming myself in some ways. I shouldn't have drunk so much, shouldn't have lost control. I didn't feel safe or confident around men. I kept in my room or in the library. If I was on a table and girls left, leaving me with just one boy, I would move. I had the running club and the toastie bar at the uni which gradually brought me round, and then I met a boy, Graham, in my final year who I grew up with, I suppose. It was hard."

They talked about life after the rape, and there were more tears from Liz and a few from Suzanne. At one stage, Liz thought Mark was going to pass out and stopped everything, making them all go out for a breath of fresh air. Eventually, they just ran out of energy. Liz had thought Suzanne would be aggressive towards Mark, but she wasn't. Suzanne thought Liz would be very upset, but on the whole, she thought she coped well and guessed time had healed some of the damage. They were both surprised at the effect the rape had had on Mark. He had been the perpetrator, the offender, and yet the rape had affected him more than they had imagined.

Eventually, Suzanne said they should try to go for closure; apparently that is what most of the guidance said.

"Mark, is there something final you want to say to Liz?"

"I can't undo what I did, and I understand the hurt I have caused you. I can't change what happened to you or how it affected your life. I have tried to make amends by supporting female staff throughout my career, so that when I meet my maker, I hope that may be taken into consideration."

"Your turn, Liz."

"Mark, your actions hurt me and spoiled much of my young life. It nearly defeated me and made me give up uni. Throughout my life, the memory has always been there. I can't forgive your nineteen-year-old self, but I realise that you are no longer that person anymore than I am a young uni student. The evil here is a crime which affected both of us."

There was a pause, a silence.

"OK, I think we are done," said Liz.

"Actually, I'd like to say something as well," said Suzanne.

Both Liz and Mark looked at Suzanne, one with a look of surprise, the other shock.

"Liz, I took you to that party with the intention of getting you a bit drunk and letting your hair down. I failed to protect you when I knew you were a bit green, and for that, I apologise. I'm so glad I met up with you after all this time as it has given me an opportunity for closure as well. Mark, I came here ready to hate you and even slap you. I can see now that the rape was a factor in your marriage breakdown and suicide attempt. I hope meeting Liz after all this time has gone some way towards closure for you as well."

Liz never saw Mark again and was never contacted by him or tried to reach out to him. She hoped that his life direction changed for the better, but she never knew. The hurt ran too deep to see him again, and she thought it best for both of them that she made no attempt. She had lanced and cleaned the festering wound, only time could heal it now. Suzanne had one more task.

27

A mindful life

The room where the yoga class was held was quite plain. A clean wooden floor, white walls, and a few posters of yoga practitioners. The lights were bright but not stark, and the yoga mats were lined up like soldiers on parade. The atmosphere was one of silent reverence. No music, no chatter. Liz rolled her yoga mat out. She always went to the same place in the room, near the middle of class, close to the wall. She placed her yoga blocks and bricks to one side and rolled up her yoga belt, placing it on top. She was ready to go. Yoga to her was like a little island of calm in the rough sea of life. She had begun at her first university before she was even twenty to help her running. Then, it had been all about flexibility and recovery. As she progressed, yoga became a sanctuary. Over the years, she had learnt mindfulness meditation, yoga breathing techniques, and a vast variety of postures to draw on. Whenever she was stressed, she would practise yoga, whether it be sitting quietly and breathing using mindfulness techniques that she first learnt at university all those years ago, or simply having a good workout blasting through the yoga poses to create a good sweat. But while yoga was her anchor in life, it was also something deeply personal which she alone enjoyed. She had been going to this particular yoga class for about fifteen years. She knew the people by their faces, but they never met outside the class, preferring to have a yoga identity in the class away from their daily lives. They were friendly to each other and would sometimes work in partner activities, but they rarely met outside other than for an occasional after-class coffee to maintain civility. She knew little of the others in the class. One was a GP, another a policeman, but other than that, they were her yoga buddies, and not knowing their full lives allowed her some sense of freedom. It gave them all permission to simply focus on their yoga practice away from the distractions of daily life. In this room, they weren't defined by their life activity, but by their yoga practice.

They had begun with a mountain pose, standing straight and tall, and then moved into triangle, stretching the side of the body and the backs of the legs. As she turned and held each pose, she fixed her eyes on a distant point. She was aware of others around her, muscles tightening, skin stretching, but it was not her main focus. Her focus was inside herself. She could feel each part of her body, powerful sensations, not painful but intense. Each pose was held as they all allowed their breath to flow freely, feeling the shape of the pose. Their faces were relaxed, showing no strain. With experience, each person seemed to float through the poses. The class progressed to floor movements, bending, twisting, pushing, and pulling. With each position, the breath flowed naturally, the muscles warm and pliable. They were a group of individuals, each focused on themselves, feeling the movements, the blood flowing, the heart beating.

Liz loved this mindful approach to movement and would often allow it to spill over into her daily life. When she was presenting at conferences, she would become aware of the weight of her body through her feet contacting the ground. Sometimes she would stand tall and draw her shoulder blades back, tightening her thigh muscles. She felt part of her soul was anchored to her yoga practice and it gave her a type of defensive shield against the external world. It was something deeply rooted within her, which traced back in time to her young student days. It seemed to connect her to the earth, to other human beings and to life itself. Over the years, she had attended many lectures and workshops with different yoga teachers, and each time, she took something away with her. Life force, or prana, which should flow freely though all body regions, body energy centres called chakras to focus on during meditation, energy locks to use with breathing techniques, all seemed strictly non-scientific and at odds with Liz's professional life. That's what she liked about it; it was an antidote to her career. Slightly wacky perhaps, spiritual certainly, and deeply personal to her.

Today she needed yoga more than ever. The revelations of her meeting with Mark had left her feeling hurt and vulnerable. She needed to recharge her batteries, centre herself, and move forwards. She had tried a relationship, and it had failed spectacularly. She felt it was a sign that she should be content being alone. Solitude was OK, she decided. She remembered a talk about solitude and loneliness she had attended with Denise, one of her fellow alternative types at the Community Hospital. Loneliness was something forced upon you and solitude something you chose. She decided she would choose solitude and be happy within herself. She thought back to the feeling of sharing a bed with Mark and dismissed it.

***

"An X-ray is just a snapshot in time, really, we use it to guide ourselves and it indicates only structural changes."

Liz was seeing a patient in her new clinic at a private hospital on the outskirts of Leeds. She had never taken private patients, being immensely proud to be an NHS surgeon alone. But one of her younger colleagues who worked at the hospital had said that another surgeon had to take three months' leave due to a health concern, and so the hospital was looking for an interim cover. Liz had decided to take this as a respite from what had been happening recently. With all the stuff going on following the meeting with Mark, she felt she needed a change. Suzanne had flown to America to catch up with a friend she made when teaching over there, and the two of them had agreed to get together when she came back in two weeks' time. Liz quite enjoyed the private hospital because she could spend longer with each patient, and things were less rushed. What she didn't like was the undercurrent of pressure to encourage patients to have surgery. She had always believed in rehabilitation prior to surgery. One of her closest working colleagues was Colin, a physiotherapist who was ten years older than herself. Her interest in running and yoga had often led her to believe in the magic of exercise. Many of her male colleagues didn't share this, tending to push people towards surgery. It wasn't that they operated unnecessarily, it was just that they had, in her opinion, a slightly blinkered approach. She stuck to escalation of care, preferring to explore rehabilitation and assess its merits first. In many cases it negated the need for surgery, particularly in those with minor changes on scans. She knew of one surgeon at the hospital who seemed to suggest that everyone with hip pain needed surgery. She had to acknowledge that she was slightly biased against him because their paths had crossed several times as they were both training. Although he was a good surgeon, she viewed him critically as a man in his late fifties who was slightly overweight, wore skinny trousers, and drove a Porsche. She had to constantly tell herself to keep her personal and professional feelings separate.

"What I mean is, it can't tell us about pain and how easy a movement is. So, for example, I could take one hundred people on the street and X-ray their hips, and they would all have tiny changes around the bone if they were over fifty. Just as we show signs of ageing outside, such as grey hair and wrinkles, those same signs of ageing occur inside. Our joints, which were once as smooth as a snooker ball in our youth, become slightly rougher, a bit like a tennis ball.

We can see that on X-rays because nowadays they are so accurate. But these changes don't necessarily relate to pain, so many of those with roughening on X-rays don't have pain, and equally some people have pain in their hip and when we X-ray there is no roughening. Your X-ray shows that you are fifty-eight, but looking at the movements of your hip, they're actually quite good.

"I'm looking at two movements particularly, bringing your knee towards your chest, which is called flexion, and pushing your knee across your body inwards, which is called adduction. On your good leg, the joint is normal and springy with full movement. On your painful side, the movement is actually quite good, but you've lost some of your springiness, and I think that is what's giving you pain. What I would like you to do is to have a course of physiotherapy to see what effect getting some of that springiness back in the joint has, and then to restrengthen the muscles around your hips. You've mentioned that you're conscious of being overweight, and, according to the charts, you are carrying an extra 2 to 2½ stone. I think if we could lose a little bit of that weight so that the joint was under less loading and couple this with restrengthening muscles, we could probably sort your hip out without the need for surgery. How does that sound?"

***

Suzanne had gone to America to see her friend Mia, who she had met while teaching. They had been friendly, but Mia had been a little surprised when she received

Suzanne's call to say could she come and visit. Suzanne had explained that she was passing through seeing several people and thought it would be good to catch up. She knew that this was a lie, as she and Mia had never been particularly close, but it was a convenient stop. Her real intention was to meet Graham again. She was gradually hatching a plan in her head. She had tried to make things up with Liz by finding Neil but had never anticipated the negative consequences of this. Although it had brought Liz and Suzanne closer, it resulted in Liz's ex-boyfriend turning out to be the person who raped her in the first year at university. Suzanne knew now that she had to go further. Liz had retracted into her shell and was immersing herself in work. She had seen this before, after the rape at university; she knew it was a character trait that Liz fell back on when things got tough. She anticipated if she didn't act quickly, they would gradually drift apart again, and it would be another twenty years before she saw Liz. They would both be retired by that time and opportunities would have flown past. Suzanne had one simple idea: to get Liz and Graham back together. They both had successful careers, were in separate countries, and hadn't spoken since university. That was a huge problem, but not an insurmountable one. In Suzanne's mind, it would just take a little bit of planning and an awful lot of luck.

***

"Hello, Graham? It's Suzanne from uni."
"I know, I know, twice in ten years is too much!"

"Listen, I'm in the US visiting a couple of friends. Just wondered if you fancied a coffee and catch up, or whatever."

"Yes, OK, I could do with a bit of a break as things are a bit crazy at work at the moment," he said.

"OK, when's good for you?"

"How about Wednesday evening in two days' time, does that work?"

"Yes, that's brilliant for me."

***

Graham booked a restaurant and ordered a taxi to pick Suzanne up from her hotel. He arrived at the restaurant first and was sitting down at the table with a glass of mineral water in his hand when she walked through the door. He was tanned, lean, and looked very much as he did when he was at university. Last time she had seen him he had really been the same gangly youth with an interest in computers. This time he looked similar, but he had a business edge about him. In addition, she could see that he had money. He had never dressed particularly well at university, and even now he was in jeans, trainers, and a sweatshirt. But they were all designer labels which made him look fantastic. Her first thought was that Liz would like him. Liz and Graham had both grown into successful forty somethings, and she knew this was going to work. Please let it work, she thought.

***

Liz was sitting in the physiotherapy department staffroom drinking green tea and eating a protein flapjack which one of the boys had made. His name was Zac, and he was a bodybuilder. She had seen him around a couple of times but did not know him as he had just joined the department. She judged he was early twenties. He sat beside her in a pair of shorts, and his thigh was about the size of her waist, she guessed, he smelt faintly of toasted skin from a sunbed and heavy body spray. He was waxing lyrical about his flapjacks.

"They are low sugar, high protein, and contain oats, nuts, and seeds to be high in omega-3 oils. I used date syrup as it is a slow sugar, and hemp protein to keep it vegan."

"Did you make the date syrup?" one of the girls asked.

"Yes, chopped a few dates and soaked them in boiling water, like you said. Cheaper than buying the bottled stuff from the organic store, certainly, so thanks for that."

Liz preferred the company of physios to surgeons if she was honest. Conversation often got round to training and diet, whereas surgeons nearly always talked shop. At a Christmas party once, one of the physio girls had presented her with a certificate saying 'adopted physio' with her full name on. She had thought it such a nice gesture and still had it in a desk drawer somewhere.

"Hey, Zac, you should have given her a good spanking, mate." Another unknown male face put its head around the door.

"Oh, shit," he said. "Didn't realise there were girls here."

"Clearly," said one of the girls as he came into the

room. "You are a misogynistic bastard, Pete, and no girl wants to be spanked. It's a male fantasy."

"Right, well, I don't really spank girls."

"Good to know," said two girls at the same time.

Liz always got on well with physio staff. Over the years she had various aches and pains which had been attended to by a variety of physios, but Colin had been a constant since he joined the Royal as a junior physio fifteen years ago. Although he was a junior physio, he was actually a lot older, being in his late thirties when he started. Prior to taking up physiotherapy he'd been in the military, and this period of his life had always been a little mysterious. He hadn't shared it with the young physio students at university, and when he got to the hospital, because he was slightly older he didn't really fit in with the young crowd. In fact, she knew little about him other than the fact that he had been married and had been through a separation which was not particularly amicable. Apparently, his wife had gone off with a mutual friend and left Colin with virtually nothing. He had to spend six weeks sleeping on a friend's sofa before he was able to release enough funds to get his own place. Over the years Liz's and Colin's careers had paralleled each other in many ways. She had grown from a junior doctor to an experienced surgeon, and he in turn had gone up through the ranks and now headed the physio department. In that time, she knew he'd got various qualifications, and she thought he was now finishing a PhD. But what she really liked about him was his old-school forces-type approach. She had once caught him using floor cleaner on his hands and asked why; he simply said, "I couldn't find any alcohol hand gel to clean my hands. We used this stuff often in Afghanistan."

She had accepted this but thought what a very practical solution to a relatively simple problem. Whenever she had minor strains or niggles, she would seek Colin out and he would normally take a hands-on approach. He would then give her some mysterious exercise which would sort the problem out. This had come to a head about seven years ago when she had severe sudden onset hip pain. She'd been practising an exercise in the gym and had jumped down suddenly feeling something in her hip go. Next day it was so painful that she couldn't walk on it. She took time off work and rested. Although it had changed, it really wasn't improving. The runner in her said it will just take time, rest, and a gradual return to activity, but the surgeon in her had told her to get a scan. The scan had shown arthritic changes, and an orthopaedic colleague had intimated that she would probably need a hip replacement in ten years' time. She had gone to Colin, who said he thought it was simply hip impingement, and the scan findings were probably incidental. He had given her a series of exercises building up to a full rehabilitation programme, and here she was, seven years later, able to do everything normally with her hip. She had never looked back. This incident was always in the back of her mind when she lectured to students; "treat the patient not the scan" was one of her favourite sayings. She would use herself as a case history, showing her X-ray and stating a thirty-eight-year-old female runner had sudden onset hip pain. She would put up the history and findings, and then ask, what treatment would you choose? She would not say who the patient was, but sometimes a bright student in the class would make knowing eye contact with her and she would give a gentle smile.

During treatment sessions over the years, a few things about Colin had trickled out. She knew he had joined the forces from school where he had struggled with exams, and came from a broken family background. He often said the forces had straightened him out, although she didn't really know what had happened previously in his life to judge this. She presumed Colin would be about the same age as Mark, and wondered if things would have been different for Mark if someone had straightened him out as a youth.

When Colin had left the forces, he had become a personal trainer. After some years working in gyms, he gradually accumulated qualifications and went to physiotherapy school. At that stage, the training had been in a hospital rather than university, but he had eventually got his physiotherapy degree. She always suspected he felt slightly inferior to the present crop of students who were the classic university set, having come straight from sixth form to train. However, she knew that although he wasn't especially academic, he was highly practical and certainly got results. Over the years she had seen evidence of this herself and with the dozens of patients she had referred to him. She would ask him what he had done with the patient, and he would often answer quite self-effacingly, "I'm not sure really, I just twiddled about a bit and got them doing exercises and stuff."

She often found men reserved at first with her, and when she first met Colin, he seemed to communicate using a series of grunts and smiles.

Colin poked his head around the staffroom door. "Are they treating you well, Ms McClennan?"

"Yes, green tea and healthy flapjack."

"Brilliant, pop through and I'll have a look."

As she left the staffroom with Colin, she heard Zac speaking. "You are joking me?"

"She's Ms McClennan, the orthopaedic surgeon."

"Oh God, I thought she was a physio sitting there in running kit."

"You are such a good judge of people, Zac," said one of the younger girls.

"At least he didn't say he spanked girls," added Pete.

"There is that," replied the girl.

***

"So," said Suzanne. "What has happened since we last met? Business good, new computer stuff, married with eight children"

"Business is good, some new stuff and not married. No children I'm aware of, what about you?"

"A few men have passed under the bridge."

"Poor choice of words," said Graham.

"I know, but you know me. All conversation is an opportunity for innuendo. No children and don't want any. Lots of nephews and nieces, that's enough."

They chatted about what had happened in their

respective lives. Suzanne showed an interest in Graham's job, understanding little about anything technical. She was biding her time and waiting for an opportune moment to change the direction of the conversation. Graham mentioned that they had a couple of interns working who were studying at the local university.

"Do you ever wish you could be back in uni. Not a care in the world apart from what you were eating tonight and what lectures you were missing?"

"Sometimes, life was certainly simpler, or it seemed that way when we were in our late teens."

"I know what you mean. I look at the students coming through the department at Huddersfield and listen to them talking about clubs, parties, and stuff, and I think I would love to come! But you just know they see you as an old person who has never lived life like they are doing now. I sometimes ask myself, when did we change. At what point did we as students become responsible adults and a bit boring?"

"Gradual process, I suppose. You evolve through uni, leave, and get out into the real world and bits are knocked off you like a sculptor chipping away at a block of stone."

"I guess you're right, but deep down inside we are the same people, just a bit grey and wrinkled."

"And with less hair in my case!"

"Tell you who I met up with recently," (said in as casual a manner as she could muster).

"Who?"

"Liz McClennan."

Suzanne stared into his eyes, searching his soul, and

there it was. A flicker, a longing, a deep love which never left. Gotcha!

***

Liz was pleased to be back running. She had developed pain in the sole of her foot, diagnosed as plantar fasciitis. One of her colleagues had offered to give her a steroid injection but she had gone to see her faithful physio department at the Royal and had a chat with Colin, the physio in charge.

"It's all a bit tight," he had said. "Try this self-massage technique, moving your bare foot over a golf ball. Bit of pressure into the sole of your foot will help. Also, your big toe joint is a bit stiff. I've done some mobilisation techniques on it but use this wall stretch to target the area below the big toe right through into the sole of your foot. Be gentle with it, though, and hold the stretch for about twenty to thirty seconds. Just once a day as feet are delicate things."

After two days the pain had started to subside, and a week later, she was back running. As instructed, she was building up slowly and had begun on a soft surface, rather than hammering away on roads to begin with. As she relaxed into her stride, she thought about recent events and started to take stock. She was a late-forties professional woman with no man in her life and several failed attempts. Was this a problem? Only if she made it so. As a student she had loved and lost, then embarked on some serious studying and ended up top of her career ladder, but a bit lonely. She had seen tragedy, but she was still here, and life was not all fresh-smelling roses. She could cope. She would cope. A rape, and then a sad man over twenty years later. Someone was perhaps trying to tell her something, she felt. Life often tries to tell you things, and she had been to a talk once where the teacher had said, if you keep resisting you will end up smashed on the rocks, but if you go with the flow, the river will carry you to a better place. So, there she had it. Don't sweat the small stuff (like rape and failed relationships), just go with the flow. As she finished her run, she thought, do I feel better? No, not really.

Her phone buzzed, telling her she had a message. It was Suzanne texting from the States. *Catch up?* it said. *OK, give me thirty mins, just back from a run*, she replied.

"How's it going, kid?" said Suzanne.

"OK, things are a bit raw still, but I'm getting there. How is the US of A?"

"Big and bold, as always. I've been doing the rounds and seeing a few people and taking in the sights. Guess who I bumped into?"

"Don't tell me, the president."

"Now that would be good. Actually, it was somebody better known to us both."

"Who's that?"

"Graham Edwards. Mr computer geek and former boyfriend of yourself."

Suzanne detected a brief pause, a hesitation, even over the phone. It would not have been heard by anyone listening in to the conversation, but it was there. She knew she wasn't imagining it, it was there.

"Goodness, now there's a name from the past. How is he?"

"He has excelled in his geekiness, and is now a very rich boy, as I may have mentioned before."

"Well, he certainly deserves that, because he always was a bit of a computer genius."

"Do you miss him, Liz?"

"I haven't really thought about him over all these years."

"Liar."

"What? No, really, I haven't."

"Liar, liar, pants on fire!"

"Well, we all go back to uni days in our minds at some point, don't we, but he moved on and so did I."

"But that's just the point, I don't think he has. He was with someone, but they split up years ago and I could tell from how he was talking he still misses you."

"Never return to a firework once lit is what they say, don't they?"

"Yes, but you two were quite a firework at uni, and it's worth a go. At least phone him and catch up."

"I don't have his number and don't know where he is."

"I may be able to help there."

***

"Well, that was a delicious meal, Mr Edwards."

"Why, thank you, Ms Davis."

"Do you ever come back to the UK?"

"Meetings and stuff. My parents died, and I have a

sister in Edinburgh, but she tends to come over here to visit."

"When's your next visit? I could bring friends."

"I'm there next month actually, in London."

"I have a particularly good friend I'd like you to meet."

"Please tell me you're not playing Cupid."

"Would I ever?"

28

Get them together

Suzanne had arranged to go to London with Liz. The excuse was it would be good for Liz to get away for a weekend and get a change of surroundings. They could stay in a hotel taking in a show, have a couple of meals out, and just generally have a girls' weekend. This quite appealed to Liz because she had been working intensely the last three weeks and recognised she needed a break. She was able to take a couple of extra days off and make it into a long weekend. Suzanne stayed the night in Liz's flat as it was convenient for the train. That night, it flashed through Liz's mind that the last person who stayed in her flat was Mark, and she wobbled a bit at the thought. They took the train down to London next morning. Unbeknown to Liz, Suzanne knew Graham's itinerary and had suggested to him that he and Suzanne met for a meal next time he was in London. She hadn't exactly said that she would bring a friend, but she would cross that bridge when she came to it.

On the evening of the meal, Suzanne was quite nervous, wondering whether she had done the right thing. Liz didn't know Graham would be there, and Graham thought Suzanne would be alone. Suzanne feared they might look at each other and then run screaming from the restaurant. It had, after all, been over twenty years, and they both thought the other person had blanked them at the end of the final university term. She didn't really know how to approach this. Should she just admit everything and say that it was the result of her own selfishness? If she did, she risked losing her best friend. Should she try and work around it somehow? As time went on, she was getting increasingly nervous and thinking that perhaps this was an unbelievably bad idea. She sighed to herself and decided to just play it by ear.

The restaurant she picked was quite nice, without being too flashy, as she knew she couldn't outdo Graham on that front. It was a small Italian she had found a couple of years ago in a side street off the Tottenham Court Road. She had eaten there a couple of times, and the food had always been good. It had a relaxed atmosphere with low lighting and for this area of central London it had quite a lot of space between tables. Exactly what she wanted in case voices were raised. She remembered from university that both Graham and Liz had liked Italian, and she thought you can't really go wrong with pasta, pizza, and salad. She had booked one of the round tables so there wouldn't be a two against one situation and knew from eating previously that they had nice white tablecloths and modern funky cutlery. The music was normally quite low, and the restaurant wouldn't be busy, as she had decided on an earlier meal at 7.00pm.

Suzanne arrived at the restaurant with Liz, and they were shown to their table; Suzanne noting the corner position as requested. They took menus and ordered drinks, chatting as they did so. In the back of Suzanne's mind, she wondered whether Graham would actually turn up, and she quickly glanced at her phone, checking for messages just in case. All OK, so far. If Liz suspected anything, she didn't make it known, assuming that the table for three was all the restaurant had. Suzanne saw a taxi pull up outside the restaurant and a gangly form get out. She could feel her heart pounding against her rib cage, and a light cold sweat was evaporating from her forehead. The gangly form was chatting to the taxi driver while paying. She hoped he wasn't telling him to wait just in case he needed to make a speedy getaway. Liz had not noticed the taxi and so was oblivious to what was happening, chatting away about a new pair of running trainers she had bought that day.

The taxi door closed with a thump, and the gangly form straightened and turned, revealing the man himself. Suzanne had now progressed from rapid heartbeat and light sweat to the light-headed and dry-throat stage. As the door opened, Graham scanned the restaurant looking for a familiar face. He saw Suzanne and smiled. Liz looked up and saw him. Time stood still, and Suzanne held her breath, wondering what was going to happen. Please make it be OK, she said to herself, not daring to breathe. Liz met Graham's eyes and time reversed by thirty years. Her face lit up and the weight of the world seemed to fall from her. Graham hurried forwards, and as Liz stood up from the table, he leant forwards kissing her on the cheek.

"Well, you are a sight for sore eyes," he said, smiling like a little boy.

Liz's eyes were slightly moist, Suzanne noticed.

***

The conversation got more heated from the moment Suzanne said, "Do you remember when…" They were reliving their university years blow by blow and month by month. Liz reminded Suzanne of Manni, an ex-boyfriend who Suzanne had referred to as athletic in the bedroom and had been with for six months.

"I remember him," said Suzanne, laughing and spluttering her wine. "A hunk with a chunk!"

"A what!!" said Graham.

"She's a brazen hussy, always has been, always will be," said Liz.

"Anyway, what about you two dark horses meeting in the student union?"

"I have to confess I saw you both coming in and noticed Liz's hair, that's why I came over."

"Everyone noticed Liz's hair at uni."

"It's still very nice."

"Well, thank you, kind sir, but it has silver bits now."

"At least you still have all of yours," said Graham. "I'm a bit thin on top."

"Buzz cuts are all the fashion," said Suzanne.

"Suntanned all-American male. You need a Porsche with over-the-top red leather. Do you have a Porsche?"

"No, Tesla with fabric seats." He took a sip of wine.

"And then the running club," said Graham.

"Oh, you guys and the running club!"

"I remember the first run and you were striding out at the front with another girl, and I was struggling to keep up with the rest of the runners without looking too out of breath."

"That was Martha, my running partner. I recently reconnected with her on social media. We post each other messages and links about the best kit offers on sports websites and stuff."

"You never change," said Suzanne.

"A girl can never have too much sports kit," replied Liz.

"What about Dawn or Ellie, have you seen them since uni?" Liz asked Suzanne, remembering tales of drunkenness and a cone placed on someone's head in a fountain.

"Not really, kept up with them for about two years and then lost contact. I heard Dawn was working in Poland for a chemical company or something, not sure what happened to Ellie."

"And what about big Dave? Anyone see or hear anything about him," said Suzanne.

"He who was afraid of fireworks and things that go bump in the night," said Liz.

"The very same."

"I had Mike and Pete across in the States three years

out of uni and they were still in contact with Dave. Not sure what he is doing now."

"Didn't Pete become a solicitor?"

"He did, and he was across with his law firm doing something with a British guy who was being prosecuted in America for supplying steel tubes to Iraq. They said they could be used to make rockets, and he said he was just fulfilling an order which came from another department. Not sure what happened eventually."

"Do you remember Tenbury Road and the saggy sofa with a board underneath?" said Liz.

"That was a fine sofa," answered Graham. "It tested a person's mettle. If you could not survive sitting down quickly on the Tenbury Road sofa, you were not worthy."

"Worthy of what?" asked Suzanne.

"Just worthy," replied Graham.

"And it now features in your company," said Suzanne.

"Why?" said Liz.

"It's called Hard Sofa," replied Graham.

"Priceless!"

"Anyway. Didn't you have a girlfriend before Liz?" asked Suzanne.

"You had a life before me?" asked Liz. "This is news!"

"It was the dreaded Paula; she was six months older than me, and she made me into a man. Sadly, I heard she died in a car crash about five years after uni."

"Oh, bloody hell, I didn't know that," said Suzanne.

"Drunk driving, apparently."

The energy of the group dropped noticeably, and they were all silent for a while.

"So, has your sister been over to the States?" Liz asked Graham.

"Yes, quite a few times now," he said, cutting a piece of his pizza and dropping a slice of mushroom as he lifted it. "They come over for about five weeks in the summer and the kids go to a summer camp sometimes."

"How old are they?" said Suzanne.

"Seven and nine, so a good age to play stuff with. It was baseball back in the summer, and I got them a couple of shirts signed. They love to take loads of American stuff back to school to impress all their mates."

They ordered dessert and some more wine, and conversation gradually moved to the present.

"So, you're still running, what about the yoga?"

"Yep. Still doing yoga and meditation and stuff," said Liz, placing her flat hand over her wine glass as the waiter offered to top it up.

"I actually started yoga. A bit, at the gym. You must have been a good influence on me."

"You were a bit useless doing yoga at uni, though," said Suzanne, spooning cheesecake into her mouth.

Graham and Liz both looked at her.

"What? You told me that, Liz, don't deny it," she said, covering her mouth with the back of her hand as she ate the piece of cheesecake.

"I did not."

"Did."

"Did not."

"Now, girls, play nicely."

As the coffees were being served, Suzanne said, "So,

Graham, tell all about your considerable success and enviable lifestyle."

"Well, you saw me a couple of times in the States, so you know it all started with my master's degree work."

"Hang on," said Liz abruptly, stopping stirring her coffee. "You two met up in the States?"

"Yes, when I was teaching in New York," said Suzanne. "I looked up a few ex-uni people. Had a big tick list to go through."

"Was I high up on the list?"

"No, you were on the reserve list, in case some of the others dropped out."

Suzanne took a chocolate mint and quickly steered the conversation away from the fact that she had met up with Graham twice with the underlying plan of getting him back together with Liz.

"Gaming is where we're at now, but it all started with a computer game with a few unique features. Liz, you remember the time-scribble programme I worked on at uni."

"Certainly do."

"Well, the idea sort of came from that and grew."

"Into a multimillion-dollar company," said Suzanne.

"Yes, but that was not the intention. I just enjoy programming. It's fun, you can lose yourself for hours in computer stuff. It's your own world, a bit like meditation, I guess."

He looked at Liz, who smiled and looked into his eyes. Graham would know those eyes anywhere.

***

Suzanne and Liz were going to walk back to their hotel which was just around the corner and Graham intended ordering a taxi to his hotel as he had an early meeting next morning.

"I can walk with you guys back to your hotel and get a taxi from there."

"OK, that sounds good," said Liz, "we'll have a chaperone."

They started to walk as a group, with Graham in the middle and the two girls either side. The conversation on university years continued with much laughing and denial of accusations.

"Yes, I heard Mike's girlfriend broke someone's jaw in a pub fight," Liz was laughing at the mention of Graham's ex-housemate.

"I don't think she broke it, but she certainly hit the guy. Mike always liked to exaggerate stuff to get a reaction."

"He of the boxers and strange hat combined with a straw," said Liz.

"He had that for years and never washed it out. It must have been a serious source of infection," replied Graham.

Suzanne noticed in his energetic talking, Graham had touched Liz's shoulder affectionately. This is going well so far, she thought.

When they got to their hotel, Graham phoned for his taxi.

"I'm just going to nip to my room," said Suzanne. "I'll be back in a few minutes." She left Liz and Graham chatting in the hotel foyer, and heard Liz say, "No, really?"

"He did, he really did!"

They both laughed, and as Suzanne closed the lift doors, she noticed Liz gently punch Graham's shoulder. As the lift ascended, Suzanne took a deep breath and exhaled slowly. Well, girl, that went very well she said out loud to the empty lift, very well indeed.

***

Next morning Liz and Suzanne had breakfast together, Suzanne coming down slightly later and joining Liz at her table. As she sat down the waitress appeared at her shoulder, and she ordered a coffee.

"So, girlie, what happened with you and Graham after I left?"

"You are a scheming, conniving girl," said Liz, smiling at Suzanne.

"Harsh but true," she replied.

"How long has this been planned?"

"I didn't really plan it that well, but I had met Graham in America when I was there two weeks ago. With everything you've been going through, I thought, why not? He obviously still likes you. How do you feel about him?"

"Suzanne, it's been more than twenty years and we're very different people now."

"You're only different from the outside; from the inside, you're still the same two young lovers from uni."

Liz looked at Suzanne for a good ten seconds.

"I'm not sure that's true. We've both been through a lot career-wise. He had a relationship which folded, I had all the Mark stuff. Relationships are built on shared experiences, and we haven't shared the last twenty odd years."

"Relationships are also built on each person bringing different stuff to the table. It would be very boring if both parties knew absolutely everything about each other and lived and breathed the same stuff day-to-day. What have you to lose?"

"I'm not sure I am as courageous as my nineteen-year-old self."

"Said the leading orthopaedic surgeon exposed to life-or-death situations every day of her life."

Suzanne cut up her sausage and put a piece in her mouth, looking down at her plate.

"God, I've missed your blunt, honest approach to life. Even if it is very annoying at times."

Suzanne swallowed the piece of sausage she was chewing, smiled, and looked up at Liz. "I aim to serve."

29

Preparation

The night before a presentation, Liz's sleep was often disturbed. From back in her schooldays, she would get nervous. Her mind would churn over and over, often meaning she would get up in the middle of the night to read through her work. Her parents would sometimes see the bedroom light spilling under her door and in the morning ask if anything was wrong. "I was just checking on something," she would say.

At university after her first term, things got worse and at night the demons came. She had to practise relaxation techniques before going to bed in the months after the rape. Her sleep improved, and she found using a few yoga poses before getting into bed helpful as well. Graham once caught her practising the triangle pose when she thought he had dropped off to sleep.

"What are you doing?"

"A couple of yoga poses, it helps me sleep."

"Thought you would be knackered, I certainly am."

"That's because you're such an energetic lover."

"Yeah, I'm a real stud. Come back to bed."

She would, but sometimes she lay there with her eyes closed and mind whirling for ten minutes until sleep finally came.

At medical school, she began to suffer chronic imposter syndrome which made her work even harder. She never felt good enough and was often anxious for days before presenting. When the day eventually came, she always over prepared, and her presentations were generally the best of her peers. Sometimes when it was really bad and she lay in bed tossing and turning, she would dig her fingernails into the top of her thigh, willing her mind to stop. In the morning she would wake at 5am exhausted.

As Liz was presenting to a conference in the morning, she had expected things to feel much the same. Lying in bed, thoughts had flitted through her mind, her lecture material, the conference. But then she thought of Graham and remembered the feeling as he had touched her arm when they got back to his hotel. It was just a simple playful action, but it had felt so good. Almost like an electric shock, a spark connecting her to her twenty-year-old self. In the morning she woke refreshed, a first for her before a conference. She realised now what had been in the back of her mind just out of reach for over twenty years; he simply completed her.

She was well prepared for her lecture, having chosen a subject she had presented before, but the precise content was slightly different to suit the conference requirements. As usual, she found it difficult to cut her material down to the time given, having forty-five minutes of material to trim into a thirty-minute slot.

As she always did, she would rehearse her lecture firstly sitting in front of her computer so she could change slides if she found any mistakes, then she would take a break. Later she would come back to give the presentation again, standing up with the slide changer in her hand as though she were addressing an actual audience. This allowed her to predict the slides, practise the timing, and get used to her own voice. Everything done, she knew when she stood on the stage she was giving a well-rehearsed act. She was her father's daughter in this respect as he had schooled her in the 5Ps, perfect preparation prevents poor performance, and got her to dress in her best school uniform to rehearse if she gave a talk at school. That training as a twelve-year-old placed her in good stead for her professional life.

Liz would never stay on the stage while people were arriving in a lecture room; instead, she would walk up the steps when the lecture theatre was full. Someone had once told her that this was the best way to make a sudden impact, and it certainly felt better. Now, she stood in the wings as the lecture theatre began to fill. Courageous individuals came to the front, the timid at the back. People shook hands and made small talk, meeting up with friends they may not have seen since last year. The noise level ramped up and then, as the time approached, the lights were dimmed and a spontaneous hush settled on the audience. As it descended to its lowest peak, she would wait for two seconds to build up tension as people thought, is she here? She would then slowly walk onto the stage and the applause would steadily build to a respectful crescendo and the lecture chair would introduce her.

"And now it is my immense pleasure to introduce our keynote speaker. A world-famous orthopaedic surgeon known to many. Her work straddles several areas in both surgery and patient examination, with an underlying focus on rehabilitation. Ladies and gentlemen, Liz McClennan."

As she walked towards the lectern, there were a few shouts and friendly catcalls and then the volume dipped.

"Thank you. Today I want to ask a simple question. Do we always do what is best for our patients?"

She scanned the faces with eyebrows raised. She clicked the first slide. On the left it showed a healthy mid-forties female runner from the back, and on the right the X-ray of a hip. She turned away from the audience to look up at the slide and used a red dot pointer to draw attention to a portion of the slide.

"This X-ray shows stage 3 osteoarthritis of the hip. There's significant cartilage erosion with loss of joint space. The patient should be in pain, have limited movement, and probably be awaiting a hip replacement if we rely solely on a hip X-ray to plan our treatment."

She clicked the next slide, which showed the same X-ray to the right, with the runner to the left turned around and facing the camera. It was herself. She turned back to the audience and smiled.

"This runner did not choose surgery but saw her friendly physiotherapist. She is now fully functional and pain-free. What will the future hold? We can never tell, but I would predict more of the same. Tempus fugit, ladies and gentlemen, we can't stop it, but we can try to make it work for us."

She clicked the next slide. It was a quote from the English poet John Dryden in 1670 saying, "The wise for cure on exercise depend".

"The body is adaptable, ladies and gentlemen, use it or lose it."

She was educating now, using her knowledgeable face, and emphasising each point. She was willing the audience to be with her.

"Training creates positive adaptation, conditioning."

She emphasised the last word as she had practised at home.

"We get stronger, joints lubricate, tissues stay healthy."

Each phrase punched out and delivered with a staccato hand gesture.

"Inactivity creates negative adaptation, deconditioning." Again, that emphasis.

"With inactivity and poor diet, we become weaker, joints stiffen, and we pile on the pounds."

She waited for the inevitable guilty murmur and nods of agreement.

"As an orthopaedic surgeon, I deal in structure. I replace joints. But that does not mean I choose to ignore good function and the ability of the body to heal itself. I want to operate well, but less often."

As she stood on the stage giving her well-rehearsed lecture, she felt as though she had stepped onto another plane of consciousness. She often felt this when meditating or practising yoga, but when she taught at a big conference it could be the same. She didn't feel godlike, far from it, she felt at one with the audience. She had once been talking to Graham about computers and he had used the expression "information dump". That was what she felt, as though she were giving and receiving information other than through the filter of speech. Some different form of communication was going on between herself and the audience, a bridge of consciousness.

***

Liz was in America presenting a keynote lecture at a conference. She had agreed with Graham that they would meet up afterwards for a meal. She was conflicted. She had enjoyed meeting Graham again last month and catching up, and it had been great fun reliving all the old university memories. But, looking back, was it not just a pleasant experience between a group of old friends? Suzanne thought she was being matchmaker, and she meant well, but in the back of Liz's mind there were voices whispering. It had been more than twenty years, and they were both quite different people. It was almost as long again as their entire lives when they first met at uni. They were not the same, and if they met today, having never known each other, would they get together or would they just nod politely and move on? They had drifted apart at uni and Graham had not tried to find her in those last days. Did that not tell her something? Would trying to rekindle a relationship simply end in the same way. Better, she thought, to remain casual friends than to risk splitting apart again. She had been hurt at university and again with Mark. She was feeling fragile and did not know if she could cope with more loss.

Another memory was nudging her. She still remembered cutting her hand in the toastie bar and being taken to the hospital by Suzanne and Tracey. When she had looked back at Graham, all she had wanted was to be held by him. Had she seen ambivalence or dismissal in his face, she would have known, but she didn't. She saw hurt and longing. Their eyes had met like magnets and in that moment, she had known that they were still connected, and she felt it now more than twenty years later. All logic told her to hold back and not make the same mistakes again, but she was not running on logic, she was running on gut feeling.

***

They were sitting in a vegetarian café which Graham had recommended.

"Thought you might like the place. I come here when I want to get away from fancy restaurants and the high life. Recharges my batteries and keeps me grounded."

The café was called All the Greens and was full of students and alternative types. Tattoos, coloured hair, and piercings were in abundance and in one corner someone was juggling to entertain her mates. Graham had told Liz to wear something casual and not too flash, so she had chosen jeans, trainers, and a long-sleeve T-shirt. She remembered wearing pretty much the same at uni, and it was still her best choice for comfort.

"I love it. Reminds me of Beano's at uni."

"You still remember it!"

"Oh yes, if I remember correctly, I introduced you to hot apple juice and cinnamon."

"You did, you bad girl, and you enticed me by sharing your date slice."

"The fastest way to a man's heart is through his stomach."

The juggling girl was now trying to encourage her friend to learn, and small beanbags were flying everywhere, much to the amusement of the surrounding fellow diners. There were pans hanging from the ceiling, an overflowing noticeboard, and all the chairs were different. Liz could have just curled up in a ball and purred.

They ate an enjoyable and entertaining meal, both bathing in each other's company but there was an underlying current, Liz felt. Things avoided, stuff not said. She felt that Graham wanted to talk about something and couldn't. He had always been reticent when talking, and it used to take her some time to get him to open up. At uni she had learnt most about him when lying in a slightly sweaty bed in a post-coital haze. She felt like jumping up and screaming, "Just tell me, what is it. Talk, man!"

As the juggling stopped, the noise hit a lull and she looked at him.

"What?" he said.

"I feel there's something you want to talk about, but you're holding back."

"No, not really."

"OK."

She looked at him and fell silent, waiting. It was her patient-history-taking technique and it didn't seem fair somehow using it on Graham, but she could think of no other way.

"It's just."

Silence and maintain eye contact. Allow the patient to fill the vacuum, she would tell students.

"I know it's more than twenty years ago, but meeting again brings stuff back."

"I know, that's bound to happen." Classic empathy statement, students would be proud.

"When we left uni in that last term, I told Suzanne to tell you I was looking for you and she said she did, but you didn't contact me. Was it because of the way I treated you or because things had ended? I just wanted to know, and I've always wondered since."

"Hang on, you asked Suzanne to tell me you were looking for me?"

"Yes."

"She never told me that."

"Perhaps you'd left by then."

"But we went to Spain together, and she never mentioned it."

"I didn't realise, I thought she had, and you just didn't want to see me again."

"Seeing you again was precisely what I did want. I assumed you didn't want to see me."

They looked at each other over the table. There was a long silence, as two world-leading brains simply ticked over, cogs grinding almost audibly.

"Oh, shit," said Graham.

"Bugger," said Liz.

30

Confessions

It had all happened very quickly. Liz had assumed after the vegetarian meal that they would perhaps go out a couple of times, get to know each other again and either drift apart or back together as fate would determine. But no, love which had been silently smouldering for over twenty years was suddenly given air. It flared and then rapidly burst into flames. Liz invited Graham back to her hotel for a coffee to end their meal and continue their conversation. It never got that far. As they entered the hotel lobby, Liz went to reception to ask if she had any messages and picked up her key while she was there. As she turned around, Graham said, "I don't suppose you have green tea in your room, do you?"

She smiled gently and said, "You know what happens when you come to my room, and I make green tea."

"I remember, God, do I remember."

"My green tea-making may be a bit out of practice."

"Mine too, shall we try to relearn together? Tea is always better when you let it brew."

"I would love that, slow but steady."

They took the lift up to the eighth floor and walked along the corridor to room 817. She still wasn't sure what she was doing was right, but really didn't care. She touched the magnetic key to her door which gave a reassuring click and showed a green light, the only signal she needed. Opening the door, she turned to face him.

"Last time I saw that look, you were leaving the toastie bar and heading for the hospital."

"Yes, and I so wanted you to hold me."

"Better late than never."

Graham wrapped his arms around Liz and held her tight. He smelt of fresh skin, clean clothes, and the barest hint of suntan lotion. She closed her eyes.

***

Liz was lying in bed with Graham, in a post-coital haze. Her mind went back over twenty years to a room in a shared house at uni. Graham had been a good holder but not a good talker, she had once told Suzanne. She had simply said, in her experience, that was men in general. Getting them to talk about their feelings was a hopeless pursuit, so she had given up years ago. Liz had always thought of Suzanne as being experienced and worldly-wise, but with hindsight, she realised that she was only six months older and had probably been just muddling her way through adolescent life as Liz had been. Liz was reliving a conversation she had had with Graham on the night when they had first gone back to her room. She had told him she had been a bit innocent when she came to uni, and that she had been to a party and had too much glühwein. She said she had been taken advantage of and had no memory of what really happened later on at the party. She had wanted to tell him about the rape but had held back and said it was just morning-after stuff because she hadn't wanted to kill the moment. Withholding the true facts had been an underlying current within their uni relationship, she now realised, perhaps preventing her from committing. In the back of her mind, she wondered whether there was a section in her mind, a file somewhere which said, you stymied the relationship. Had it been silently eating away at her for over twenty years, preventing her from moving on? She couldn't undo what was done, but she could avoid making the same mistake again.

"I can still remember the first time you came back to my room at uni."

"So can I, God, I was so nervous."

She looked into Graham's eyes and flicked her focus across his face. More lines now and a few grey bits of stubble, but his eyes were still the same eyes she had first looked into. They had lost a little of their youthful brightness, but this had been replaced by the wisdom of age. He was an extremely attractive older man, in many ways better looking now than he had ever been. The gangly sci-fi nerd had morphed into an athletic silver fox.

"On that first night I started trying to tell you something, but I lost my courage and bottled it up instead."

"What was it?"

"Do you remember me saying I was at a party and drank too much and couldn't really remember what happened?"

"I think I can, you know. It was a long time ago, but that night is etched into my memories like a bit of source code."

"Well, access that source code, Mr Geeky, and buckle up because I'm about to tweak it."

"God, I love it when you talk dirty."

"I'm being serious."

"Sorry. OK, I'm listening."

Liz studied his face. At nineteen he would have said he was listening, but his mind would have been elsewhere, playing with his computer or still enjoying his last snack, and she would have been able to tell. One of the advantages of age, she guessed, was that he had learnt to listen, and she liked it.

"In the morning when I woke up, I felt awful, and I went for a shower."

He stayed silent, giving her time, another advantage of age, she guessed.

"You have to remember that I was a virgin and had never seen a man totally nude until you, never mind had sex."

"So, I was your first?"

"That's just it. The answer to that question is yes and no. I gradually realised that I had had sex at the party and had no memory of it. Later, I realised that I had been raped."

"Shit, that's terrible."

"So you were my first by choice, but the memory of the rape, which gradually began to surface over the following months, really affected me."

"I bet. I wish you had told me but can see why you didn't. Nineteen-year-old men are not the best listeners and keepers of secrets, but I like to think I would have understood and not told anyone. So, what happened afterwards, then?"

"All very involved, I'm afraid, and quite a story, the précised version is I went with Suzanne to the police, and they were hopeless. Her mum was a nurse and knew of sexual assault referral centres, or SARCs for short, which are commonplace now but at the time were just starting up. Tests, and more tests and then counselling over a few months, but I was pretty broken in my first year. By the time I met you in the third year, I was getting better, and you brought me out of myself, I think."

"So, I was your knight in shining armour, then."

"Well, I wouldn't say that, but you were a useful item at the time."

"Useful for what?"

"Come here and I'll show you."

***

The next day, Liz was due to fly back to England and they had arranged to meet for a quick pre-flight coffee.

"I'm really glad you told me all that stuff yesterday," said Graham. "It made me feel like you trust me somehow."

"I do, and I think I always have. You're not just my lover, but my friend and soulmate as well, I think."

"I feel the same. I'm just comfortable with you somehow. I know that seems boring and terrible probably, and I really enjoyed sleeping with you, but there was more to it than that for me. Does that make sense?"

"It does, you are a nice man."

Liz gave Graham's forearm a friendly poke, and he smiled.

"The rape story became more involved actually," said Liz.

"Why?"

"Well, you are not going to believe this, but I met my rapist fairly recently."

"You did what?" said Graham, looking aghast.

"I met a guy on a train who sat by me. Long story short, we went for a coffee and a hill walk. Platonic stuff, really, and he had a flat in Leeds. While there, we nipped into a coffee shop and walked past the house where the party had taken place."

"Oh, no."

"Incredibly, it turned out that he had been working in Leeds at the time, went to the party with a mate and he said he thought this mate was the one who raped me."

"Did you go to the police?"

"It was a bit more involved and long-winded. It turned out that it was not the mate, but the guy from the train who raped me. He was drunk and deeply regretted what had happened, he said, and only found out when we walked past that house."

"So he said."

"Well, he tried to commit suicide afterwards, so I think he was genuine."

"Shit."

"We agreed to set up a restorative justice session to talk it all through, with Suzanne acting a facilitator, friend, witness, or whatever."

"How long ago was this?"

"Last year."

"Have you seen him since?"

"No, and I never will. I think it would be too painful for both of us, really."

"Did the talking help, or did it bring everything back?"

"Well, the effect was different than I imagined. I thought it would be one of two extremes. Either it would bring stuff back or allow me to put it behind me, and I guess it has, but in a strange way. I just felt exhausted afterwards, as though I had given the whole experience so much energy over the years that I had nothing left. It was almost as though I was finally looking at what had happened, and it was so small and meaningless I wondered why I had given it so much power over me."

"It's funny, isn't it, how some things just fester away."

"Yes, I saw it finally through my surgeon's eyes, as though it was an infected wound which I had opened, allowed the infected stuff out and now it would heal. I thought it would stop me from reliving the experience, and it has, to a large degree. I can still think of what happened, but now it's like, so what? It has no power over me. I remember the councillor at the time telling me that

I was still raping myself and I thought she was mad, but now I realise what she was saying. The rape ended at the party, and everything subsequent to that was my own doing. I wasn't guilty of making things happen, but I was responsible, as she said. That feeling gave me power and control over the memory, and now, finally, after over twenty years, I'm able to move on."

"And back to me."

"And back to you."

"Because I am so incredibly good-looking, and a real stud."

"Nah, but you'll do."

31

Be with me

"I'm so sorry, I should have told you both. I was a selfish prat who just wanted Liz to herself to go to Spain, and over the years layer upon layer of guilt has built up. I feel that I have destroyed your lives when you could have been together from uni."

"Yeah, but I wouldn't have become a millionaire and Liz wouldn't have become surgeon extraordinaire."

"That's true, and I am bloody good. Does anyone want a hip replacement, by the way?"

They were sitting around Graham's pool in California drinking margaritas and trying to avoid getting sunburnt. After Liz's conference, she spent time with Graham. She told him everything about the rape, the aftermath at university and about Mark and talking to him with Suzanne acting as facilitator. Suzanne had said at the meeting how she felt guilty about letting Liz down at uni and not looking out for her and had now told Liz and Graham about what she did on the last day of term.

"I knew Liz had gone to the library and when you asked, Graham, I should have told you so you could find her. I didn't because I suppose deep down, I thought you two might choose to spend the summer together and I wouldn't be able to go to Spain with Liz."

"You don't know that, Suzanne. He might not have found me, or dozens of other things might have played out. Don't beat yourself up about it."

"I know, but over the years I have felt guilty and was so glad when I met up with you at the rail station."

"Fate, meaningful coincidence, as I always say," said Liz.

"You always used to say that at uni," said Graham, "and at the time it just went over my head, but in my old age I'm thinking there might be something in it. Law of attraction, quantum entanglement, and all that."

"Geek," said Suzanne.

"You're just jealous of my superior intellect and laser-like understanding of all things sci-fi."

"Bugger off."

***

Graham was staying in Liz's flat in Manchester. Recently, she had it redecorated. The previous décor had been fine, but she just felt she needed something new. It was as if she was saying, I'm drawing a line under the past and moving on, and she was. People noticed the difference. At work her staff were saying, "Liz is a bit chipper this morning", and some of her girlfriends noticed a brighter colour in her face. She chose her clothes with more care in the mornings, adding a colourful scarf here or a long-forgotten brooch there. She bought new trainers (always a good thing, she thought) but they were not for running, they were bright colours with large logos just to wear. And she found herself singing which she never did. In the kitchen while waiting for the kettle to boil, in the shower, while entering lists of numbers into a spreadsheet on her computer. It was all very strange, she thought, but definitely pleasant.

"Are you getting up, you sloth?"

Graham was still in bed.

"It's cold and rainy outside."

"It's England, and worse than that, it's Manchester. It always rains. We're surrounded by hills, it's a thing."

Graham loved England. It was his home. It had nurtured him and given him so much. He remembered a snippet of a poem by Rupert Brooke from school, "A dust whom England bore, shaped, made aware, gave once her flowers to love, her ways to roam."

He felt more English when he was away than when he was home. At home it was always raining, and queues formed everywhere. Outside shops, at bus stops, even at tills in shops. What was it about the English and queuing? In California a group of people would just huddle, but not in England. A group of more than three would form a queue.

He threw the quilt back and got up, heading for the bathroom. When he had showered and dressed, he came into the kitchen and sat down for breakfast with Liz.

"I think there will be about five of them today," Liz said.

"OK. We'll just go through the anatomy programme

first with each of them using a VR headset to get used to it, and then I'll pass to you for the surgical bit."

Graham had been working with Liz on a programme to train doctors and allied health professionals on anatomy using virtual reality or 'VR' headsets. There were others on the market, but Hard Sofa's lead in graphics quality meant they could extend it to help train surgeons. They had filmed several dozen hip replacement operations, digitised the images, and used AI to produce infinite variables of situations that surgeons may come across. The result was the ability to operate on a patient, going through the entire process, from choosing the right instruments, performing each stage, and overcoming unknown problems when they were introduced. Today they were showing it to surgeons from one of the royal colleges as part of the process of getting it approved for surgical training within the NHS. Graham knew that if he got approval, every other country would follow the UK, and he could progress to other operations, as the principles were essentially the same. The potential was massive, especially for training surgeons in the developing world where facilities were often limited.

The meeting was in one of the large Manchester hospitals and Graham let Liz take the lead, as this was her world. She introduced him to various colleagues and noticed several of them becoming flustered. What was it about people that made them uncomfortable around money? He might be rich, she thought, but he was in my bed this morning, and he had very cold feet.

***

Graham put his margarita down and picked up a bowl of cherries, which he had slowly been working his way through all morning. He placed one delicately in Liz's tummy button.

"That's very annoying," she said.

"I know, it's a man thing."

"Which is obviously why men are the inferior sex."

"I wish you two would stop it, you're like two teenagers on heat," said Suzanne.

"It's her. She's tempting me with her long limbs."

Graham got up and sat on the edge of the pool, dangling his legs in the water. California definitely had better weather than Manchester, he thought. Was it home to him now? It felt like it when he was here, but when he was in England, that also felt like home, but more so in some ways. He guessed where you were brought up and lived your formative years would always feel more like home.

"What are you thinking, young man?"

Liz sat beside him at the pool edge.

"Just pondering, nothing much, really."

"Should we start working on the new code? Suzanne's going to meet someone about that teaching post."

"Yeah, the sun's getting a bit hot anyway."

"I'll shower and we can go to your office."

"It's a deal."

***

Liz had the new VR headset on, which was lighter and less restrictive. It enabled her to move her head more freely, and because it wasn't as heavy, she didn't have neck ache at the end of her virtual operation. Today she was performing a revision arthroplasty on a hip. She had explained to Graham that replacement joints were either metal, ceramic, or plastic, and they generally lasted for ten to twenty years. If the patient was younger when they had the replacement, it may not last for their remaining life and would need to be replaced. Sometimes a replacement joint would have worn loose over time, and if so, would come out fairly easily, but if not, the replacement would be bonded to the hip bones and removing the components of the old replacement was more demanding. The VR programme was designed to throw up things which might go wrong, and just like a standard computer game, it could do this at various levels. At a basic level, the operation went smoothly, but at the next level a few things would be introduced to tax the user. Perhaps the blood vessels wouldn't seal correctly, or the joint would not fit as it should. At higher levels, more challenges were introduced to see how the trainee surgeon would react under stress.

When Liz was not engrossed in the surgery part of the programme, she loved to walk around Graham's offices looking on with amazement at all the things going on. She was amused that they all referred to his offices as a campus which she thought was very grand. He had explained that the term was used by tech companies to try to create a community feeling and to imply innovation rather than trying to be an upstart university. She thought it was a case of boys and their toys, although she had to admit that Hard Sofa had as many women tech people as men.

As Liz worked, Graham, who was in another room entirely, looked at how the programme was performing and liaised with the designers and programmers to tweak aspects of code. He loved this, working with Liz and his team. It seemed that everything important to him was in one place.

The meetings in the UK had gone well, and they were well on their way to putting the first group of students through the training. Graham was working with a local university in the States to get some students to act as a pilot study. Although not surgeons, Liz had decided to divide them into two groups and teach them both the same series of surgical steps to see what they retained in terms of both knowledge and skills. She would assess what they knew and what they could do after the training, with one group trained traditionally with demonstration and copying what had been demonstrated, and the other group using the VR programme and watching, learning, and practising on their virtual patient. So far, the results had exceeded expectations, with the VR group easily outstripping the traditional group.

***

Graham, Liz, and Suzanne were sitting in a coffee shop chatting. Suzanne had been offered a teaching post at a local university after Liz persuaded her that she should apply. At first, Suzanne had said that she didn't want to move to America again because they might lose touch, but Liz had argued that as she and Graham were basically spending an equal amount of time in both countries, that wouldn't happen.

"But you're still an NHS consultant, so you will be in the UK."

"I'm thinking of giving that up, actually. The private hospital where I was covering have offered me some surgical hours and that would allow me to select what I do and when, so it will be better with all the stuff going on with the VR programme. Also, the amount of teaching and lecturing in the States is building up just through networking. One of the local medical schools wants me to come in as a visiting professor so I can teach and use the VR with students."

"You could stay here, Suzanne, until you get your own place set up if you like," said Graham.

Graham thought that Liz might be more settled when she was in the States if she had her friend around. In the UK, at least she knew a few people through work, but in the States, they were all his contacts, and he didn't want to suffocate her.

"It's a lot more money than I am getting now, with better teaching facilities and a great climate, so I guess I'm sold. I'll go and phone them to accept the job."

After Suzanne got up to go outside for her call, Graham said, "You know what she needs, don't you?"

"What's that?"

"A man."

Laughing, Liz said, "She has plenty of men!"

"Yes, but those are sex partners and shallow relationships. She needs a soulmate."

Liz looked at Graham for a while.

"You know, you may be right."

Acknowledgements

The characters and situations in this novel are entirely fictitious, however ideas have been generated from personal experience and research material initially accessed while completing a writing course with Faber Academy.

Thanks to Judith Bryan tutor at Faber Academy for guiding my early writing and encouraging ideas.

Thanks to the staff at Jericho writers for endless advice, and to Kate Rizzo for assessing the manuscript and suggesting useful changes.

The following web pages were accessed when researching the effects of rape:

BBC report on date rape https://www.bbc.co.uk/news/uk-51006504

The police rape interview that shocked 1980s Britain
https://www.bbc.co.uk/news/av/stories-57485617 accessed 09/10/2023

Forensic evidence in rape and sexual assault https://www.btp.police.uk/ro/report/rsa/alpha-v1/advice/rape-sexual-assault-and-other-sexual-offences/forensic-evidence-rape-sexual-assault/

Rape reactions https://rapecrisis.org.uk/get-help/tools-for-victims-and-survivors/difficult-feelings/

SARC video with patient views https://www.youtube.com/watch?v=Et6Ja2eCW6E

Grange park SARC centre https://grangepark.org.uk/

Manchester St Marys SARC https://www.stmaryscentre.org/

Report on sexual assault of female surgeons when training Female surgeons sexually assaulted while operating - BBC News

YTS schemes in Blackpool https://www.blackpoolgazette.co.uk/heritage-and-retro/retro/how-the-training-schemes-of-the-1980s-helped-young-people-to-get-a-foot-on-the-career-ladder-1890573

Experience of government work schemes 1980's https://www.sheffieldforum.co.uk/topic/33873-anyone-work-on-a-government-work-scheme-in-the-80s/page/3/

Legal aspects of rape in the UK

https://www.legislation.gov.uk/ukpga/2003/42/part/1/crossheading/rape accessed 18/11/2023

Details of the gaming industry

https://www.gameindustrycareerguide.com/typical-day-of-a-video-game-developer/ accessed 27/11/2023

Quotes from:

The Soldier, Rupert Brooke. 1914, and other poems. Internet Archive.

This book is printed on paper from sustainable sources managed under the Forest Stewardship Council (FSC) scheme.

It has been printed in the UK to reduce transportation miles and their impact upon the environment.

For every new title that Troubador publishes, we plant a tree to offset CO_2, partnering with the More Trees scheme.

For more about how Troubador offsets its environmental impact, see www.troubador.co.uk/sustainability-and-community